Theophilus Waldmeier

The Autobiography of Theophilus Waldmeier, Missionary

being an account of ten years' life in Abyssinia - and sixteen years in Syria

Theophilus Waldmeier

The Autobiography of Theophilus Waldmeier, Missionary
being an account of ten years' life in Abyssinia - and sixteen years in Syria

ISBN/EAN: 9783337248055

Printed in Europe, USA, Canada, Australia, Japan

Cover: Foto ©Raphael Reischuk / pixelio.de

More available books at **www.hansebooks.com**

THE
AUTOBIOGRAPHY

OF

THEOPHILUS WALDMEIER,

MISSIONARY:

BEING AN ACCOUNT OF

Ten Years' Life in Abyssinia;

AND

Sixteen Years in Syria.

LONDON :
S. W. PARTRIDGE & Co., 9, PATERNOSTER ROW, E.C.
LEOMINSTER :
THE ORPHANS' PRINTING PRESS, 10 & 12, BROAD STREET.

PREFACE.

——

MANY friends have repeatedly asked me to write down my experiences in Abyssinia and Syria. I have hesitated for many reasons, but finally I have thought it good to comply with their wishes. Some years ago I wrote a book in German about my ten years' residence in Abyssinia which was translated into French, Swedish, and Arabic, but not into English. As I have the privilege of knowing so many dear friends in England and America I have therefore written this Autobiography in the English language. My great aim in doing so is to show forth to the reader how wonderfully our heavenly Father has led me from my early childhood until the present time. Not only in the beautiful highlands of Abyssinia, where the greatest and most wonderful events of my life have taken place, but in Beirut and Mount Lebanon also I have experienced the overshadowing power of the Almighty. I therefore say with the Psalmist, "Blessed be the Lord, the God of Israel, who only doeth wondrous things" (Psalm lxix. 18).

The description of the different religious sects in the East, especially that of the Druses, as well as much other information connected with my journeys will, I trust be acceptable and useful to many. That this humble and simple book may now go forth in the name of the Lord, and become a blessing to its readers is the earnest desire of the author.

TH. WALDMEIER.

Brummana, Mount Lebanon,
October, 1886.

CONTENTS.

CHAPTER VII.

THE BEGINNING OF TROUBLES.

CHAPTER VIII.

RASSAM'S EXPEDITION TO ABYSSINIA.

CHAPTER IX.

DEPARTURE FROM DEBRA TABOR—ARRIVAL AT MAGDALA.

CHAPTER X.

THE FIVE LAST DAYS IN MAGDALA.

CHAPTER XI.

DEPARTURE FROM MAGDALA.

CHAPTER XII.

PRESENT CONDITION OF ABYSSINIA.

CHAPTER XIII.

TRANSITION.

PAGE

CHAPTER XXI.

THE ISMAILIYEHS AND NUSARIEHS.

CHAPTER XXII.

OUR REMOVAL TO BRUMMANA.

CHAPTER XXIII.

SECOND VISIT TO ENGLAND.

CHAPTER XXIV.

THE PURCHASE OF AIN SALAAM.

CHAPTER XXV.

PRIESTLY OPPOSITION.

CHAPTER XXVI.

WELCOME VISITORS.

CHAPTER XXVII.

THE BOYS' TRAINING HOME.

CHAPTER XXVIII.

PROGRESS OF THE MISSION.

LIST OF ILLUSTRATIONS.

List of Illustrations.

AUTOBIOGRAPHY OF THEOPHILUS WALDMEIER.

CHAPTER I.

EARLY HISTORY, MISSION TO EGYPT, SOUDAN, AND ABYSSINIA.

I WAS born a Roman Catholic in Canton Ar-
gau, Switzerland, and brought up under severe
religious instruction by my dear mother and
grandmother, who were very anxious for the salvation of my soul, and strict with me on matters of
religion. My grandmother forced me to kneel
down on the ground for three hours daily praying
with rosaries and Psalter. Once when I refused to
do so she was very much displeased and punished
me severely, and when I told her that God would
not listen to prayers that were forced out by the
stick, she beat me even more, but this cruel treatment only hardened my heart and made me feel
sure that such prayers could not be acceptable to
the Lord. I used to go to a quarry near our house
where I could be alone and pray out of my heart,
which gave me much comfort. But my troubles
did not end here, for when the time of Confession
came, it was impossible for me to believe that the
priest could give me absolution for my sins, as I
had often seen him indulging in intoxicating drink
and playing cards ; so I said, " The Priest himself

is a greater sinner than other people:" and for this I
was severely punished.   I then became very miserable, not knowing what was really right to do; so
at last in despair I ran away from home to my uncle
at Lörrach, who received me very kindly and adop
ted me as his son.   Here I was sent to a Roman
Catholic school, and began to feel much happier,
for I was well treated.

In Lörrach, near Bâle, there was a young man
named Deimler, who often came to my uncle and
aunt, and spoke much about the Gospel, which
made my uncle angry with him, so that he wished
to send him out of the house; but the young man
patiently endured all unkindness, and explained
the way of salvation more fully.   He did not speak
in vain, for my aunt began to be enlightened, and
not long after both she and my uncle were converted.

J. G. Deimler entered as missionary student into
the Bâle Mission College, where he studied for six
years.   During this time he often came to Lörrach
and had Gospel meetings, which were held in our
house by the students from Bâle and St. Chrischona
in turn.   J. G. Deimler was ultimately sent to India,
where he has been working since 1855 amongst the
Mohammedans.

I was so much influenced by the dear missionary
brethren, and the blessed meetings, that I was convinced that the Evangelical Christians were on the
right basis. Soon after my mind was enlightened, my
heart also became changed, and I resigned all mere
worldly joy and pleasure, to join with the Lord's
people wherever I went.   Through them I became
acquainted with the great need of the world for missionaries.   This made me long to be a missionary
also, and often in the night I went out into the
fields and asked the Lord that He would take me into

His service, after which I felt assured that He was indeed ready to take me up, if I, on my part, was willing to give myself entirely to Him. After this I resolved to write a letter to the Committee of the St. Chrischona Mission and ask to be admitted as a missionary student, but I was too young, and had to wait three years before I was accepted. During this time I went to Geneva to study French, where I met with Dr. Malan, J. H. Merle D'Aubigné, Pastor Gossain, and others. Their acquaintance, and the meetings at the Oratoire and the Pelliserie, helped me on my way.

I was very glad when I was at last accepted as a student of the St. Chrischona College, but it was no easy life that we students led there. We had to work hard for our living, and to study much, so that if there were any not in earnest they would hardly stay there long; but the belief that we were called of the Lord made it no hardship to bear all for His sake.

Bishop Gobat came one day to St. Chrischona and wanted a missionary for Abyssinia. I was selected, and was asked if I would like to go to that distant mission field, and, after making it a subject of earnest prayer, I agreed to go. In September, 1858, a large congregation assembled at St. Chrischona College, when I was consecrated, with other students, by Dean Ledderhose, to go out into the Lord's harvest field. When I left Europe I travelled with Bishop Gobat as far as Alexandria, from thence he went on to Jerusalem, and I was joined by Mr. and Mrs. Flad, Mr. Saalmüller, and Mr. Schroth and his son. The two latter were sent as workmen to King Theodore, but both died subsequently on our road to Abyssinia.

I was interested in seeing the land of the Pharaohs, the land which is as old as history itself.

Its monoliths, like Cleopatra's Needle, seventy feet high, of syenite granite, covered with hieroglyphics, lead us back to the time of the Exodus of the children of Israel from Egypt. From Alexandria we went by rail to Cairo, a distance of 130 miles. In the neighbourhood of Cairo we visited the large pyramids of Gizeh, Cheops, and Mycrenes, of which it is said, "that all things dread Time, but Time itself dreads the pyramids." From Cairo onwards towards the south there was no railroad, we therefore had to travel in a boat on the old Yaro (Nile), the life-giving river. The journey was slow, and as we needed strong wind to force the vessel against the current of the stream, sometimes we were stopped for whole days; this gave us leisure to study the past and present condition of the land of the Pharaohs. We passed the territory of the three old gods of Egypt: Phtha in Lower, Ammon in Middle, and Ra in Upper Egypt, whose temples we saw.

We arrived after much patience at Luxor and Karnak, which are situated on the right bank of the Nile, and at Medinet Abu, where we saw the palace of Ramses III. and IV. At Karnak we entered the great hall, with its one hundred gigantic pillars, and saw sphinxes and obelisks in monoliths ninety feet in height, often with poor mud huts, contrasting strangely, at the bottom. Then we visited the hundred-gated city of Thebes. In a tomb there, a drawing of brickmaking is still distinctly to be seen, and many think that it refers to the children of Israel, who might easily have come so far south, and under circumstances of war have run away to Abyssinia (Ethiopia). From Thebes we sailed to Korosko, and from thence travelled through the desert of Nubia with thirty-two camels, which were mostly loaded

HIPPOPOTAMUSES ON THE NILE.

with Amharic Bibles and Testaments for Abyssinia. Crossing the desert was no easy task, as water is scarce. We loaded some of the camels with leathern sacks filled with water, but after ten days it became very bad, and we suffered much in the day from thirst and the great heat, and in the night from cold. After sixteen days' journey we reached Abu-Hamed, a poor village on the bank of the Nile, and we rejoiced and thanked our Father in heaven who had led us safely through the dangers of the desert where so often men and animals are buried in the sand. The whole plain looks like a past world burnt by the wrath of God. From Abu-Hamed we went to Berber along the Nile, and thence by boat to Khartoum, the great city of Soudan. Whilst we were travelling on the Nile we saw hundreds of crocodiles, like fallen trunks of large trees lying on the sandy islands in the river, opening their immense mouths towards the sun, and little birds feeding in their open jaws, fearlessly eating up the worms, till the least movement of the crocodile caused the bird to fly away. We saw also many hippopotamuses often in the middle and often on the banks of the river. Khartoum, the capital of Soudan, with its 30,000 inhabitants, was the residence of the Governor General. It was founded by Mohammed Ali in 1823, but its climate is deadly, owing to its situation between the junction of the Blue and White Nile, the water line of which is not much below the level of the plain.

From Khartoum we travelled on the Blue Nile, which comes from the tropical Alps of Abyssinia, to Abu-Harres, and from thence we journeyed south-east on camels through desert and wilderness, by Assar and Dokah, south of the stagnant river Rahat, a tributary to the Blue Nile. The heat was very great in the day, and in the night we were in danger from wild beasts,—lions, leopards, rhinoceroses, hyenas, and serpents,—but we were still more afraid of the wild Nubians.

The heat was so great that the ground was much cracked, the earth often gaping before us; but the camels learned to pass these deep crevices in the ground very cleverly. After much trouble and danger we finally arrived at Methemmeh, a place notorious on account of its deadly climate and the large slave market which exists here. From Methemmeh (pronounced Mothamma and meaning "Abode of Death") the slaves are carried to Kassala, Khartoum, Suakim, Massowah, and Hodeidah. From this place we went to Wachnee, which stands at the base of the Abyssinian mountains. Between Methemmeh and Wachnee, we suffered intensely from the heat, which was so great that the sperm candles melted in the boxes on the camels' backs. In Wachnee we all fell ill except Mrs. Flad, who nursed us all as well as she could. Here Mr. Schroth died, and we had hardly strength to bury him, as we lay on the sand and scooped out a hollow with our hands as best we could, whilst the plaintive cooing of a turtle-dove, on a sycamore tree near by, added to the melancholy feelings that possessed us, and we made up our minds that we should soon follow him. But the Lord spared our lives, and we left Wachnee and soon began to ascend the Abyssinian mountains through large bamboo forests.

After five months' travelling we reached the tropical Alps of Abyssinia; but the journey through Soudan to Abyssinia was really a journey of sickness and death. Now we found ourselves 6,000 feet above the sea level, with beautiful flowers, wild roses, fresh water, and a pure salubrious atmosphere to strengthen our weak bodies and faint-

BAMBOOS.

ing hearts. We began to breathe easier, and thankfulness flowed from our hearts to Him who had guided us safely through desert and wilderness, and brought us to the land of our destination. At that time we did not know that we had just entered into the land of our sufferings ; for we were not aware that on entering this country we had lost our liberty, as the sequel proved.

Soon after our arrival we were presented to King Theodore by John Bell, an English gentleman who was Prime Minister. His Majesty received us very kindly, and expressed his sorrow at the loss of our two companions, who had been appointed as workmen for him, saying, "It is on account of my sins that God took these two men away from me."

King Theodore ordered us to reside at the natural fortification of Magdala, where we lived with our missionary brethren, who had already been working three years in Abyssinia. The elder brethren who knew the language were occupied with missionary and literary work, whilst we, the younger ones, were studying the language and teaching mechanical work to some Abyssinians, for which the King was very glad and thankful. We were seven missionaries with Mrs. Flad ; she and her husband occupied one house, and the other five, of whom I was one, occupied a second house. Each house in Abyssinia consists of one room, so that we felt very crowded ; but Christian love was exercised, which wonderfully enlarged the small accommodation.

The royal Secretary, Debtera Sanneb, came daily to us, with whom our elder brethren had long religious conversations, and they read the Bible through with him. Ere long he was converted to evangelical truth, and is still witnessing for Jesus

in that distant land.   He is now engaged by King
Menelek, the son of Sahela Salassa, who was
conquered by King Theodore.   Prince Menelek
was at Magdala when we were ;   he was a very
nice young gentleman, and we were on intimate
terms with him.   He is now King of Shoa, and
has been very helpful to the Anti-slavery Society
in stopping the slave trade.

Magdala was the safe place for King Theodore's
enemies, and also for his friends ; the former in
prison and in chains, the latter at liberty as far as
the boundary of the fortifications goes.   The treasury of the King was there, with an accumulation
of presents from India, Egypt and Europe.   The
Abuna Salama, the head of the Abyssinian Church,
and the Queen, were also with us at Magdala as
semi-prisoners ;   and one thousand soldiers had
charge of us during the long absences of the King
when at war with distant rebels.

It was in Magdala, on the 4th of December, 1859,
that I was married to Susan Bell, the daughter of
the Prime Minister John Bell before-mentioned.
He was indeed the guardian angel of the King, and
the protector and good counsellor of the Europeans.   He was formerly a Lieutenant of the British
Navy, and accompanied Lord Chesney on his expedition to the Euphrates in the year 1850 ; after
which he became English Consul at Aleppo, and
finally entered into the service of Ras Ali, and
King Theodore of Abyssinia.

CHAPTER II.

ABYSSINIA is a country of great natural interest. The Sandy Desert of Samhara is intensely hot between the Red Sea and the mountains of Tigré; but though so near the equator, the different elevations formed by volcanic eruption produce an agreeable climate. The average height of the country is 9,000 feet above the sea; the thermometer shows at this height 45° during the night, and 59° in the day (Fahrenheit). In the low country, which is called Kolla, at the height of 3,000 to 4,000 feet, the thermometer stands at 122° in the day, and half as much during the night; whilst on elevations of 14,000 feet the thermometer goes down to zero. Kolla in the Wollo Galla country looks in summer like Mount Hermon, and in winter like Sanneen in the Lebanon. There is a great similarity in form between the mountains round Magdala and the mountains of Lebanon at Ain-Zahalta in Syria; the only difference is those are of trachyte, and the others of grey fossiliferous limestone, intersected with ferruginous soft sandy soil. It is said that from Hauran to Bab-el-Mandeb there were once twenty-eight powerful volcanos, but they are not now in action.

On the west side of the Red Sea, on the plains bounding Abyssinia, the large volcano Edd was in full action in 1860, and the ashes of its eruptions were carried by the wind into the interior of the country to a distance of from sixty to one hundred miles.   Half-way down the Red Sea, between Hodeidah and Massowah, is a volcano which is called by the natives the Fire Mountain—Terr. So that we can imagine that there might have been a volcanic connection from Abyssinia under the Red Sea through Arabia to Hauran.

On account of the variations of climate caused by the different elevations of the country, the vegetation is abundant.   The winter of the tropical Alps begins with June and lasts till the beginning of September.   It is not a cold season, and consists only of heavy and short rains, accompanied by fearful thunder and lightning ; in the morning, for instance, there may be a nice shower of rain, while the afternoon is as sunny and pleasant as possible.   Streams and rivulets abound, forming here and there waterfalls from fifty to five hundred feet in depth.   In the month of September, Abyssinia is like a beautiful flower garden, even the stony and poor soil being clothed with grass and flowers.   Lilies, aloes, orchids, wild roses, ferns, brambles, honeysuckles, tulips, and prickly broom, grow under the rich foliage of beautiful trees, such as the Wansa tree (Cordia Abyssinica), the sycamore, the mimosa, and the kosso tree.   The flowers of the latter are used in medicine.   The wild olive, the juniper, and euphorbia are also abundant.   Monkeys delight to climb amongst the branches of the Wansa tree, whilst various birds of brilliant plumage but unmusical voices, flit from bough to bough.   The farmers cultivate their land with a very poor primitive kind of plough, and obtain a rich harvest with but little trouble, growing barley, wheat, maize, lentils, cotton, oil plants, and different vegetables.

The farmers might easily be rich so far as the fertility of the soil is concerned, but they are very poor, for they get quite disheartened in their work. They sow the seed but are not sure of gathering the harvest, for the Abyssinian soldiers, when passing through the land, put their horses, mules, and donkeys, into a prosperous harvest-field until they have ruined the crop ; and often have I seen the owners imploring the intruders, with tears, to remove their animals, but they would neither hear nor pity them.

If Abyssinia could only have good government, and its own old sea-port at Massowah, it might soon become one of the most prosperous countries in the world. King Theodore once said to me, " My country is like a paradise, only I am sorry to say it is inhabited by donkeys." Many people in Europe and America are of opinion that the Abyssinians belong to the slave race of Africa, but it is not so. They are of thorough Caucasian type, and generally tall, nice-looking people ; their colour is not black, but chestnut brown ; ladies who are always in the house are not so dark, and some of them are white. The Abyssinians are an intelligent race, clever in everything when taught, kind hearted, full of sympathy, loving, and obliging ; but when harshly or unjustly treated, nothing can appease their excitement but revenge. I had some boys in my school who were taught reading, writing, arithmetic, geography, and history, and was astonished to see how quickly they understood everything.

Time is apparently of no value in Abyssinia ; the people do not work hard, as the soil being so rich and productive, easily supplies their small wants. Having little to do, they are fond of sitting together, telling story after story to each other, and thus spend much time in useless and worthless conversation. They are also very fond of litigation, and embroil themselves in long processes, in which the King is their tribunal of final appeal. The people do not know how to read or write; this is an art known only to the priest and debteras (the learned). Nevertheless, they are wonderfully eloquent and clever in demonstration. During my ten years' stay in Abyssinia, I had a good opportunity of seeing and learning the ways and manners of the people. I was often surprised at their eloquence, quick-wittedness, and ability, in judicial cases especially. Each village has its Shum (Governor), who is the judge; but if he has not settled the case well, it can be brought before the Governor of the district, and if he has failed in his judgment, it can be brought to the King, who will punish both officers if they have been wrong.

The Abyssinians have a law book, which is called Fetana Negest, and in difficult cases it is consulted, and a decision is made accordingly. This code is regarded as a translation of the Justinian law book of the fifth century; others say it comes from Constantine the Great. The general way of bringing a process before the King is as follows. The King's camp consists of about 10,000 tents, in the midst of which stand his tent and the church, the latter being of red and purple, and around the King's tent is an empty space of some 200 yards. Early in the morning we could hear daily the melancholy cry, beginning at four o'clock, " Ishan Hoy, Ishan Hoy " (your Majesty), for twenty times and more. This is the cry of those who are bringing their lawsuits before the Sovereign, and as the people are not allowed to approach near the royal court, the King has a man appointed to stand between him and the people, who is named Afa Negus (the mouth of the King). This man has to hear the accusations and processes of the people, and to bring them before the King, who pronounces his judgment in low tones, and the Afa Negus then proclaims it in a loud voice to the people. Woe be to him if he misunderstands a case, and brings it wrongly before the King; for he must then be very sharp if he does not wish to have his hands and feet cut off. When daylight spreads itself over the camp, we see how judgment is executed; on one side a murderer is being hung; on the other, a guilty thief is flogged; whilst others are chained and put in prison.

Once I was riding along with the King through the country. A man stood afar off and cried, "Ishan Hoy! Ishan Hoy!" until the King said, "Speak, my son." The man said, "I have found twenty dollars on the way, and as I do not know to whom this money belongs, I have brought it to your Majesty." The King said, "That is good of you, keep the money with you until the man is found who has lost it, and for your uprightness I give you another twenty dollars." The man went his way rejoicing. But he was envied by one of his friends, who thought, "If money can be got so easily, I shall take my forty dollars, which I saved from many years' service, and bring it to the King, telling him that I found them." The man brought the money to the King, and said that he found it and did not know to whom it belonged. The King, perceiving the trick, said to the man, "Go and give it to my treasurer." The man went with great sorrow, and handed over his forty dollars to the royal treasury.

If some European travellers and soldiers speak against the demoralization of the social condition of the Abyssinian people, they might modify their judgment when they remember that the English expedition, and some other Europeans did not set them a very good example.   Then if these critics find themselves without sin, let them throw the first stone at the Abyssinians.

The women in that land work hard; they spin the cotton and wool, and prepare it for the weaver, who makes the stuff so universally worn by men and women for clothing.   They carry water and wood on their backs, grind corn, bake bread, cook for their husbands, help them in the fields, and often follow them to war.   The men wear white trousers with a *shamma* (or Roman toga), and the women wear a *shamma* with only one long shirt underneath; these are quite white when new, but become almost black with uncleanliness, and from anointing their heads with butter, which the sun causes to melt and run down.

The dress of the better class of people, however, is always neat, and as white as snow.   Shoes and stockings are not used in the country.   Everyone goes barefooted both in summer and winter.   As Abyssinia is so far off and difficult of approach, we were soon left without shoes or stockings, and had to go with bare feet like other people.   At first we suffered very much, especially from the stony and thorny roads, but finally we became accustomed to this privation; only when our feet got cut by flint stones, or stung by thorns, we were reminded of the comfort of stockings and shoes.

Living in Abyssinia is simple, with no plate, spoon, fork, or table.   A basket containing bread, over which some kind of red pepper curry is poured, forms the principal dish.   The people sit round about on the ground or on skins, and each one helps himself with his fingers.   Raw beef is not always eaten, but it is liked by the people; and honey wine

ABYSSINIAN WOMAN CLEANING CORN.

(mead) is much appreciated, but all cannot afford to obtain it, which is no loss to them, as it is intoxicating. The descriptions of some travellers, saying that the Abyssinians cut pieces of flesh from living animals to eat, are quite untrue : indeed I have read numbers of books about the customs of the country, which are much exaggerated, and in many cases erroneous.

The houses in the villages are round huts, with one room, plastered with a kind of mortar made of earth and straw, or cow-dung, which is considered still better : in cities like Gondar, there are massive stone houses, the roofs of which, however, are made with slender pieces of wood, reeds, or bamboo, covered with straw.

The Abyssinians are clever in different handicrafts ; they are saddlers, blacksmiths, carpenters, silver and goldsmiths, weavers of silk and cotton, builders, stonemasons, painters, and potters.

Money is not made in Abyssinia, and the current coin is the Austrian Maria Theresa silver dollar. There exists no smaller money. and if anyone wants to change a dollar, he gets thirty crystalized pieces of salt seven inches long, two inches broad, and one inch thick. Besides being used for small money, this is also the only salt for cooking.

CHAPTER III.

WE are told in Scripture that Ham, the son of
Noah, was the father of Cush, and from the
people of Cush are descended the Ethiopian
Habesh or Abyssinians ; his brother Mizraim was
the father of the Egyptians, and Canaan the father
of the Phœnicians or Canaanites ; between these
people and the Abyssinians there is a real relationship (Gen. x. 6, 7, 15).   We do not hear any more
of Abyssinia until the time of the Queen of Sheba,
who may have had her residence at Axum, on the
high land of Ethiopia, where there are still old
ruins, pillars, and obelisks, remaining, some standing, others lying broken on the ground.

According to Abyssinian legend the Queen of
Sheba became one of the wives of Solomon, and
gave birth to a son called Menelek, who subsequently became King of Abyssinia, and from that
time the Abyssinian Kings claim their descent from
Solomon.   Another legend says that a large number of Jews came to Abyssinia, who escaped from
Palestine at the time of the Assyrian and Babylonian captivity, first to Egypt (Jer. xliii.), and then
up the Nile to the south, until they came to the
district of Guara, in Abyssinia, where there are still
many Jews to this day.   The Abyssinians call the
Jews Falashas, which means Wanderers.   These
Falashas only acknowledge the five books of Moses,

AXUM AND ITS ANCIENT MONUMENTS.

Joshua, Judges, Samuel, and Ruth, calling them
Orit, or the Law; the Prophets are unknown to them.
There must, in any case, have been Jews in Abyssinia
before the Babylonian captivity, because it says in
Zeph. iii. 10, " From beyond the rivers of Ethiopia
my suppliants, even the daughter of my dispersed,
shall bring mine offering."   Mr. Martin Flad, a missionary among the Falashas, says, in his very interesting information of the Abyssinian Jews, that he
rebuked the Falashas for their idolatry in worshipping the goddess Sanbathoo, and thus transgressing
the second commandment.   One of the Falashas
answered, " We shall do as our forefathers did, we
shall burn incense unto the Queen of Heaven, and
pour out drink offerings unto her, as our fathers,
our kings, and our princes did in the cities of
Judah and in the streets of Jerusalem; for then
had we plenty of victuals, and were well, and saw
no evil.   But since we left off to burn incense to
the Queen of Heaven, and to pour out drink offerings unto her, we have wanted all things and have
been consumed by the sword and by the famine."
(See Jer. xliv. 17, 18).

The goddess Sanbathoo is certainly Ashtoreth,
Queen of Heaven (Jer. vii. 18).   She was worshipped mostly in Tyre and Sidon, Byblos and
Beirut, Babylon and Askelon ; and her worship extended to Jerusalem under Solomon (1
Kings xi. 5).   The Jews of Abyssinia offer her
drink offerings, make her cakes, and burn incense,
believing that she controls the heavens, and thus
they implore her blessing.   They have their syna-
gogues, priests, monks, nuns, and prophets.   They
circumcise, observe the Sabbath and feast days, and
make offerings according to the law of Moses,
which distinguishes them from all other Jews of
the present time.

With regard to the spread of the Christian religion in Abyssinia, we have a very interesting article translated by Mr. John Mayer, missionary in Abyssinia, from an old Ethiopian book, and also mentioned in Mr. Flad's " Falashas of Abyssinia." It says, " In the time when Herod was King of Judæa, and Basiru King in Ethiopia, when Akin was the High Priest of the Jews in Abyssinia, Jesus, according to His human nature, was born of the Virgin Mary in Bethlehem." Two hundred and fifty-seven years after the ascension of Jesus Christ, when part of the Abyssinian nation called themselves Christians, part were Jews and part were Ophites or worshippers of serpents, there came a Christian merchant with his two sons from Tyre. The Abyssinians say they came from Jerusalem, for they think that city includes all the places of the world. The names of these two sons were Frumentius and Ædesius. They were sent to the priest Anlaram in Axum, and they remained in his house with their father. Frumentius said to the priest, " You have a very curious religion, for though you believe in Jesus Christ and have circumcision, you have no baptism or communion." The priest answered, " The circumcision we get from our fathers, the children of Levi, and the belief in Christ we have from the eunuch of Queen Candace; but that we have no baptism or communion is due to the fact that no apostle was sent to us." Frumentius was sent to Athanasius in Alexandria, who ordained him Bishop of the Abyssinian Church, and sent him back under the name of Abuna Salama. He arrived in the year 315 A.D., when King Aberha was ruling over Ethiopia. Anlaram the priest was baptized and ordained to the office of bishop under the name of Hesba Kedoos. During the reign of the two good Kings Aberha and his son

Asbeha, who succeeded him, the Christian religion
was propagated by Hesba Kedoos, and from one
to two hundred thousand people are said to have
been baptized daily in Abyssinia.   Nubians, Sou-
danese, and Guderu (Gallas) were also baptized.
We can imagine what kind of Christianity must
have been propagated where no one could read, and
none were taught but simply baptized.   It is therefore no wonder that the Abyssinian Church is
notoriously the most corrupt Church in the world.

The Abyssinian King Aberha conquered Yemen,
and caused the heathen and the Jews there to embrace the Christian religion by force.   He and
Asbeha ruled about seventy years in Yemen.   The
Abyssinian occupation of Yemen became of sad
importance to the whole world through the small
pox which was brought by the Abyssinians for the
first time from their tropical mountains across the
Red Sea to the plains of Arabia and hills of Yemen.
There the dangerous epidemic took hold of the
people and soon spread over the whole world.
Here we have the origin of the small pox. *

The small number of Falashas and the mass
of nominal Christians have both gone astray
from the true principles of their religion ; yet,
geographically secluded as Abyssinia is, it is wonderful that in such a country in the midst of
Mohammedans and Heathen, Christianity and Juda-
ism should exist even in the most corrupted forms.
The Abyssinians are Monophysites, that is they believe that Jesus Christ had only one nature, which
is Divine.   In this they followed the teaching of
Dioscoros, Patriarch of Alexandria, 444 A.D., which
was condemned by Marcian and the Papal legates
at the Council of Chalcedon, in 451 A.D.   They

---

* See Ch. Knight, Cyclopædia Geograph., vol. 1, p. 419.

also say that Christ was born three times, the first
from the Father, the second by the Virgin Mary,
and the third by His baptism in the Jordan. The
Abyssinians put tradition on the same level with
Scripture. They believe that not only Jesus Christ,
but the Virgin Mary died for the salvation of the
world, and they also believe in the intercession of
the saints, and trust much in fastings. They have
192 fasting days in the year. The whole church
service is performed in the ancient Ethiopian language, of which the people understand nothing. St.
Mark is considered the Apostle of Egypt, and the
Abyssinians also regard him through Athanasius
and Frumentius as their own. In copying some
pictures from a church I found the winged lion
which is characteristic of Venice, where the Apostle
Mark is likewise adored. They have to get their
Abuna Salama, the head of their church, from
Egypt, for whom they have to pay to the Metro-
politan of the Coptic Church 10,000 dollars. He
ordains the priests, by conveying his breath into
the mouth of the theological candidate. I was told
that the Abuna Salama was not able to go to the distant kingdom of Shoa to ordain priests, on account
of rebellious tribes, who made the road dangerous.
After considering how he could surmount the difficulty, he got a leather sack and filled it with his
breath, so that it was regarded as a sack full of the
Holy Spirit. This sack was carried into the Shoa
country by delegates, where through a little tube
the holy air was transmitted into the mouths of
those who wanted to become priests.

The Abyssinians have only two sacraments, baptism and the communion. Boys are baptized forty
days after birth, but girls have to wait until eighty
days old ; because Adam entered into paradise
forty days after his creation, and Eve followed him

after another forty days. When the children are baptized they receive a blue silk cord to put round their necks. This distinguishes the Christians from the Mohammedans. The cord is considered holy, and hangs on the neck of every Christian until death, and is then even buried with them.

The churches are large round buildings, in the centre of which is a square room called the Holiest, where are kept the *tabot*, or ark of the covenant, the cup, bread, wine, and holy vestments. The four walls of this room are decorated with pictures from the Old and New Testaments and their mythology. No one but the priests is allowed to enter into the holiest place. All the common people have to stand outside. The only preaching in the year is on Easter Day, when the priests give a short address of which this is the translation : " My dear brethren, hear my words. The priest has fasted forty days. It is therefore proper for you to give to the priest fifty jars of good wine, fifty jars of good beer, fifty large good loaves of bread, fifty well-roasted hens without bones, fifty fat cows whose horns touch heaven and whose tails sweep the earth. Besides this, you are not to make fire in your houses, or cook anything, unless you have invited the priest. Follow these precepts, and you will be blessed." All the churches are built on the summits of the finest hills, and are surrounded by beautiful little groves of trees. When I looked at these churches, I was always reminded of 1 Kings xiv. 23, " They also built them high places, and images, and groves, on every high hill, and under every green tree." This way of building their places of worship probably had its origin in Judæa and Phœnicia.

The Abyssinian era does not begin with Christ's birth, but from the creation of the world. The year 1886 they call 7381, and the 10th of September is their New Year's Day. The greatest feast is on the 26th of September, and is held in remembrance of St. Helena finding the holy cross and using fire signals to let the news be known quickly in Constantinople. The people therefore come together and accumulate large heaps of wood, and burn them at night in memory of the discovery of the cross. We find this custom on Mount Lebanon in all the Eastern churches.

At the beginning of the 16th century the Pope of Rome and the King of Portugal sent a Jesuit Mission to try to bring the Abyssinian Church under the Church of Rome. The Abyssinians were divided by the Jesuits into two parties; the first held faithfully to the old faith, and the second with the King Sosneos and the Prince Facilidas, adhered to the newly-introduced religion of the Jesuits. The hatred between these two parties culminated in a bloody battle, in which 8,000 men of the old faith were slain in one day, over whom the Jesuits rejoiced. But as Prince Facilidas rode through the blood-stained field, he began to think, " A religion which causes so much bloodshed cannot be good. We had better, though victorious, return to the faith of the conquered, and remain faithful as they were." Facilidas became King, and expelled the Jesuits from his dominions in the year 1632, and the Abyssinian Church returned to its former head, the Coptic Patriarch of Alexandria. The remains of the Jesuit Mission in Abyssinia are the King's castle, bridges, and other buildings, mostly in ruins, which were erected by Portuguese workmen in connection with them.

The Mohammedans often tried to bring the Abyssinians under their dominion, but could not succeed until their seaport of Massowah, on the Red Sea, was taken by them in the year 1527, under Gerang

A BRIDGE OVER THE RIVER KAHAA IN ABYSSINIA.

(the left-handed), who entered Abyssinia, destroyed all the churches, and massacred numbers of the people. The Abyssinians had never seen firearms before, and made sure that resistance was vain, having up to that time only fought with shield and spear. In the time of King Claudius, Christopher da Gama was sent with an army by the King of Portugal to assist the Abyssinians against the Mohammedans. Christopher da Gama was killed by Gerang, but his army proved victorious. Just as the Jewish and Christian religions have not been truly taught and propagated in Abyssinia, so it is with the religion of the Koran. Its principles have never been known there by the Mohammedans themselves, and only the fear of the sword compelled them to embrace it in the time of Gerang.

There are now only a small number of Mohammedans in Abyssinia, but in the surrounding countries there are many. The main difference between the Christian and the Mohammedan is in their greeting of each other when they meet. The Christian says " Good morning," and the other answers in Arabic, though he does not understand the language, " *Hamdallah* " (God be praised). The Mohammedans acknowledge one God, and are a little cleaner than the Christians. These are the only differences between the two denominations. The Wollo Gallas are partly Mohammedans. They know very little of Mohammed, but adore one God. They abhor the Abyssinian Christians on account of their idolatry, and are always in a state of hostility with each other.

Three years ago King John, the reigning King of Abyssinia, who is much more cruel than King Theodore, tried to force the poor Wollo Galla people to embrace the distorted Abyssinian religion, and on their refusal he had them put to death.

Those who yielded to his unjust claims were merely baptized without any instruction.

The heathen Gallas consist of many tribes, the Kunnama, the Shangalla, the Danakeel, the Shoho, the Limoo, the Enaria, the Kaffa, the Tchensheroo, the Guarague, and other large heathen tribes numbering several millions of people with different languages. These Gallas are waiting for Christianity, not for the Abyssinian Christianity, but for the true Gospel of Christ. Some of them, sad to say, have embraced a nominal Mohammedanism. They believed originally in one supreme Being, whom they call Wack or Dossa, a name meaning the blue sky, which they say is the garment of God. We find the association of blue with the gods among the Hindus, and in other forms of ancient mythology, and in Exodus xxiv. 10 we read, "They saw the God of Israel, and there was under His feet as it were a paved work of a sapphire stone, and as it were the body of heaven in His clearness." The Gallas also worship certain trees, as the Wansa tree (Cordia Abyssinica, known in Syria as *Maksas*) and the *Shola* or Sycamore tree. When there is a very dry year the people think that Dossa is displeased with them on account of their sinfulness, and then they try to reconcile him with offerings of sheep and goats, and in times of danger, famine, or plague with human sacrifices. They sprinkle themselves with the blood of these sacrifices, and feel sure that in this way they will regain his love towards them.

The slave markets at Basso in Godjam, at Methemmeh, Khartoum, Kedarif, Suakim, and Kassala in Soudan, and the large slave market at Hodeidah in Yemen, on the other side of the Red Sea, are all supplied by the Galla slaves; for though so much is being done to put down the slave trade, it is still

SHOHO GALLA.

carried on, because Arabia and Egypt will not live without slaves. The Abyssinians also keep slaves, but they are very kindly treated and regarded as members of the families.

The Galla languages are different from the Ethiopian or Amharic language. This has a literature, but the others are not yet written languages. The Waitos and the Agau people in Abyssinia are neither Jews, Christians, Mohammedans, nor heathens, but a mixture of all these religions, composed according to their convenience. They have a curious unknown language, somewhat similar to the Falasha. I tried to compose the first vocabulary and a small grammar of their language, which have been printed by a friend of Oriental languages at Halle. These different tribes of Abyssinians are waiting for the preaching of the Gospel. If King John would tolerate religious liberty I am sure that a Mission exclusively for these tribes would prove a great success and blessing.

CHAPTER IV.

PROTESTANT MISSION TO ABYSSINIA.

EVERY feeling Christian must sympathize with the people of Abyssinia, who were brought into such a confusion of religious error; and it is no wonder that the Protestant churches felt it their duty to send missionaries there. It was in the year 1830, that Dr. Gobat and Mr. Kugler were sent by the Church Missionary Society to Abyssinia. They went by way of the Red Sea, and entered from the east into the district of Tigré in Abyssinia, where the Governor-General received them very kindly. Dr. Gobat travelled a good deal, learned the language of the country, and had a very good influence on the people, who respected and loved him; but he became ill, and had to return to Europe: and Mr. Kugler died. After Dr. Gobat left, Mr. Isenberg and Dr. Krapf took up the work. As soon as the Jesuit Propaganda in Rome saw that the Protestants had begun a Mission in Abyssinia, they sent the priest Sapeto to that country, and his intrigues were sufficient to influence the Governor to stop the Protestant Mission. This took place in 1838.

Dr. Krapf and Mr. Isenberg then went to the Abyssinian kingdom of Shoa, where they were kindly received by the King, Sahela Salassa. Their mission work there was hopeful and satisfactory; but, as there were no books or school

DR. GOBAT.

materials, Mr. Isenberg left Shoa, and went to Europe, in order to carry the Amharic Dictionary, Geography, and Prayer Book, through the press, while Dr. Krapf remained four years longer, working in Shoa and travelling in the service of the Gospel. As Dr. Krapf was returning to Europe, he fell into the hands of Adra Bille, the chief of the robbers in the Wollo Galla country. He there lost all his things ; but was himself liberated, and continued his journey like a beggar, amid great trouble and danger, by Edjoo, Lasta, Enderta, Massowah, and the Red Sea to Europe.* The above-mentioned Adra Bille was prisoner in Magdala when I was there in 1859.

Shortly after Dr. Gobat left the country, the military commander of three towns in Abyssinia, who had shown kindness to him, was driven into exile with his two sons during one of the revolutions frequent in that land. The fugitives fell in with the eccentric traveller, Joseph Wolff, who took them with him to Bombay, where they became the guests of Dr. John Wilson. The boys, then seventeen and twelve years of age, read Amharic and its Tigré dialect with great fluency. Up to this time Dr. Wilson's polyglot accomplishments had not extended to the tongue of Ethiopia, but Joseph Wolff left with him an Amharic and English vocabulary, through which the boys and their teacher at first learned from each other. Dr. Wilson wrote : " I trust they are not the only Christians connected with the eastern churches exterior to India who will be placed under our care."

For five years these two boys, Gabru and Maricha Warka, lived in Dr. Wilson's house, and were educated in the Mission college. When Dr. Wilson came

* See Dr. Gobat's "Abyssinia," published both in German and English.

home, in the year of the Disruption, he brought
them with him as far as Aden ; from there he sent
them back to Abyssinia, with the prayer "that to
their benighted countrymen they might be the instruments of great spiritual good, even as Frumentius and Ædesius, the tender Syrian youths, through
whom the Gospel was first introduced into Abyssinia."

Gabru and Maricha frequently sent gifts to the
Mission and letters to Dr. Wilson on his return to
Bombay.   Among the former were two young
lionesses, which they had received from the king.
Of these Dr. Wilson wrote in 1850 :—

" I lately heard from my two young Abyssinian
friends ; indeed, I may say my sons in the Gospel.
They have given me the two African lionesses presented to them by the king of their country.   These
are objects of great curiosity to the natives of
Bombay, hundreds of whom come to see them in
my compound.   I find it, however, very expensive
to maintain them, as they devour a goat at a meal.
I have been offered a thousand rupees for them, and
shall soon part with them, and devote the proceeds
to the enlightenment of Abyssinia.   .   .   They
followed Gabru and Maricha for several days' journey like dogs.   If they were tired, when they came
to a bush, they used to get into it and rest till they
were thumped up with clubs to proceed on the
march.   Their growl is terrible."

Gabru died soon after their return.   In 1864,
Maricha Warka, then about forty years of age, became of vast importance to the British Government.   He had risen to be the chief minister of
Prince Kasai, of Tigré, and proved the friend and
help of the British army, then invading Abyssinia.
In frequent telegrams and dispatches Lord Napier
of Magdala warmly acknowledged his services.

The special correspondents with the expedition were even more emphatic, the most experienced of them writing thus :—" The belief is entertained by not a few that in connection with the campaign in Abyssinia, England owes more to the Free Church of Scotland's Mission Institution in Bombay, than it does to any institution in the Presidency, the Government itself and the commissariat department not excepted."

When the British army left Abyssinia, Prince Kasai became sovereign of the whole country, and Maricha his Prime Minister. Lord Napier urged Her Majesty's Government to send Prince Alamayu, the son of the deceased King Theodore, to the Free Church College at Bombay; but, unhappily for the Prince, he was kept at Sandhurst, and did not long survive the climate and the exile. Two boys and two girls were rescued from slavery and sent to Dr. Wilson, to be trained as intelligent Christians in the college which now bears his name.

During the past twenty years Maricha Warka has made Abyssinia both stronger and more peaceful than it ever was before. On the outbreak of the war in Egypt and despatch of General Gordon to the Soudan, Admiral Hewitt went to the capital of Abyssinia, and succeeded, through Maricha's influence, in making a treaty with King John to put down the slave trade, and help General Gordon. To ratify this treaty, Maricha was sent as ambassador to the Queen. He was accompanied by his two nephews, and brought with him, among other royal gifts, a young African elephant, Gwola, and its keeper.*

What Maricha thought of Great Britain, and how he has clung to his early faith and love for the

---

* From " Maricha Warka," a tract published by the Free Church of Scotland.

Bible was thus told by *The Pall Mall Gazette*, which interviewed the now venerable man :—" 'All work, all work !' said Maricha. 'England is a great country. No one seems to be idle. . . . Your Queen, how great, how kind, how good, and how *humble* she is ! We all of us felt her goodness in receiving us at Osborne in your White Island. We walked in the beautiful gardens there, having with us our elephant and our presents ; and the Queen came and spoke kind words to us, and admired Gwola and the presents which we bore from King John. You are happy with such a mistress.' . . Maricha once accompanied General Gordon on a journey, and spoke with unfeigned zeal of his great qualities. 'I like him. He is a gentlemen, kind and gentle to everyone, seldom angry, and how fond he is of the Bible! Some people laugh at him for it. Why ?' He thought that General Gordon could escape easily enough, and that King John would lead an expedition against the Mahdi, whom he called 'an inspired carpenter,' and hated. . . . . Maricha is fond of reading history and any works about his own country, while geography is his favourite study. But he adds, 'There is only one book. That contains everything. Who will ever write another like it ?—I mean the Bible.' Although this is his first visit to England, and he is now an old man, his Excellency evidently knows something of us. 'It grieves me,' he remarked, with a sigh, as he played with the gold cross which hung from his neck, ' to think of the differences that exist as to religious matters in your country. You have I cannot say how many religions.' 'Do you like the missionary,' I asked. 'The Protestant, yes ; he tries but to teach : the Roman Catholic, no ; he thinks his religion much better than any other.' " . .

His Excellency Maricha Warka was often in my house at Gaffat, and we spent many happy hours together conversing about the progress and religious liberty of Abyssinia under King Theodore.

Dr. Krapf left Europe a second time, with Mr. Isenberg, in 1848, and arrived at the boundary of Shoa. During their absence, however, French influence had been strongly exerted upon King Sahela Salassa by the traveller Rochet, to prevent Protestant Missions from entering his dominion, and they had to return. Mr. Isenberg went to Tigré where he was before, and there he was able to work for some years with success. The somewhat incautious way in which he afterwards spoke against their worship of the Virgin Mary so exasperated the Abyssinians against him that it was easy for the Jesuit Sapeto, in connection with a Frenchman named Michel Abbadie, to induce King Ubie again to expel the Protestant missionaries from his country. This enabled the Jesuit Mission to be carried on with great success, especially in the eastern part of Abyssinia. The people were baptized, congregations organized, churches built, schools opened, and all remained in favour of the Jesuit Mission, until King Theodore appeared, who conquered King Ubie and sent him prisoner to Magdala. He afterwards, however, became father-in-law to King Theodore. We were in Magdala at that time, and often saw the imprisoned king. In 1859, King Theodore, who knew the history of the Jesuits in Abyssinia in former times, gave orders that they should leave his kingdom.

After Dr. Gobat returned from Abyssinia, he was ordained Bishop of Jerusalem. Having always been much interested in the welfare of Abyssinia, he sent Dr. Krapf and Mr. Flad to King Theodore, asking permission to start an

Apostolic Mission in his land, consisting of missionaries who would not only teach the people religion, but also European civilization and arts. To this latter part he readily agreed; but with respect to religious teaching, he said, "You must ask the Abuna Salama, who is the head of the Abyssinian Church." This prelate was consulted, and said that he had nothing against good Christian lay missionaries, but could not allow priests to come and organize new churches in the country, so as to subject their church to the supremacy of Rome. Dr. Krapf and Mr. Flad returned rejoicing to Bishop Gobat in Jerusalem, and reported the result of the mission to King Theodore. In the year 1855, Bishop Gobat sent Mr. Flad, Mr. Bender, Mr. John Mayer, and Mr. Gottlieb Kienzlen as lay missionaries to Abyssinia. They were most cordially received by the monarch, and also by the Abuna Salama. Mr. Flad became very ill and returned to Jerusalem. After his recovery he was married to Sister Paulina, a Deaconess in Jerusalem, and again resolved to go back to Abyssinia, and thither Mr. Charles Saalmüller, Mr. Shroth and his son, and I accompanied him, in 1858.

It may be interesting to insert here a translation of the true Apostolic instruction and Christian rules, which Bishop Gobat gave his missionaries before starting for Abyssinia, at the farewell meeting of the Protestant congregation on Mount Zion at Jerusalem, in December, 1855. Although I did not go till three years later, we all received the same instruction.

"Beloved Brethren,—The hour has come for which you have for some years been preparing yourselves, the hour for parting with the Christian friends in whose circle your spiritual life has been developed. Now you will have to lean on the

Lord in your weakness, in a land that is covered with darkness, and among a people that are still in the shadow of death. If you have ever felt and understood your infinite weakness and helplessness, as every one must into whose soul a ray from the Sun of Righteousness has penetrated, you must increasingly feel it in this solemn hour, as you see before you the difficulties of the journey, the deep degradation of the people to whom you are going, and the temptations of every kind to which you will be exposed from the might of the enemy against whom you are fighting. More especially as you look on the holiness of the Lord whom you wish to serve, and whose cause you have espoused before a stiff-necked nation, must you feel still more deeply your own unfitness, and your helplessness in yourselves, and be ready to exclaim with that pious king, ' O our God, we have no might against this great company that cometh against us, neither know we what to do, but our eyes are upon Thee.' Yes, to the Lord your eyes must be continually lifted that you neither stumble nor fall, and that the Sun of His mercy may open your hearts, that according to your aim, you may be a light in the midst of the darkness of the Ethiopian nation. If to-day, above all, I remind you of your unfitness and weakness in facing the difficulties and self-denial, and the dangers from within and from without, against which you will have to fight, it is not my aim to discourage you. But if your refuge, trust, or courage, be in your own strength, prudence, insight, wisdom, or judgment, I could wish you and the mission work nothing better, than that before you go a step further that courage may sink and that trust forsake you, so that you and we may not be put to shame. But I have a good faith that it stands better with you, that you really acknowledge you are weak and miserable in yourselves, unfitted for any good, inclined to all evil, and that if you were left alone, you could not but sin, fall, and be put to shame. Do you feel assured of this, are you painfully sensible of it? Do you pray to become strong in the Lord and in the power of His might, and thus fight the good fight? So shall the Lord be your strength, His mercy will be might in your weakness, His Spirit will become your light and wisdom, your courage and help will grow in the fight, and you will joyfully exclaim with the Apostle, 'I can do all things through Christ which strengtheneth me.'

"To be able to rely truly and under all circumstances on the the Lord, you must quite entirely give yourselves to Him, being ready to follow Him through honour and dishonour, through good and evil report, and for this especially you must be upright and virtuous in your whole conduct towards Him, towards each other, and towards everybody; for the righteous and upright, whether their talents be many or few, the Lord makes to prosper. The calling for which you have been chosen is an important one,—to lead souls from darkness to light, and from the power of Satan unto God. For this, you must first yourselves walk in the light, in truth and virtue, that you may have communion with the Father and with His Son Jesus Christ, and be able to take of His fulness, grace, mercy, wisdom, light, strength, and comfort. Never forget that you are sent like sheep among wolves, therefore be prudent without falsehood. Let your prudence consist chiefly in remaining immovably near the Good Shepherd, so shall you be safe, and you shall not want.

"The field that lies desert before you, and must

be worked and turned into a garden of God, is a wide, almost immeasurable field. It not only includes all Abyssinia, but the neighbouring heathenish Galla tribes, and the whole centre of Africa, of which Abyssinia is to be regarded only as the entrance. There the devil has his kingdom, and for thousands of years it has been allowed to go on quietly and undisturbed beneath his government. There his principles, hypocrisy, falsehood, superstition, sorcery, misrule, and cruelty flourish. It is a kingdom of darkness, where, till now, no Gospel ray has penetrated. This kingdom is to be attacked in the name of the Lord Jesus Christ, and to win the victory must be the aim of your lives, the aim of all your labour. Never forget this, for it is a thought to open your hearts to the needed sympathy, pity, and prayer; and it will also keep you humble in your own eyes. Your work will be at first in a small circle, and it is necessary that you be faithful to that which is entrusted to you.

"I wish to give you some advice before you start on your journey. Your duty at present is a double one: firstly, that as you go to Abyssinia with a good number of Bibles and New Testaments you should distribute them as widely as possible; and secondly, that you inform yourselves whether you may go and settle in different parts of the country, not yet as open preachers, but as quiet disciples of Jesus Christ who let their light shine before men through word and deed. According to the ideas of the present King, who himself reads the Bible in his own language, and according to the practice of the Abyssinian Abuna Salama, I do not think that you will have any obstacle in spreading the Word of God. Judging by my own experience, I believe that many an Abyssinian will receive the Bible with thankfulness, but you will nevertheless find oppo-

sition and obstacles. The Prince of darkness will
not easily give way to the light of the Word of
God being spread in that darkened region. You
will, perhaps, find most of the people at the beginning more inclined to follow their own ways, pre-
ferring them to the Bread of Life. Light-minded
scorners you will meet, especially amongst the
priesthood, sorcerers who hate the pure truth and
and are self-righteous hypocrites. Therefore in the
business of Bible distribution be wise as serpents
and harmless as doves. Watch, also, over your
own hearts and look continually to the Lord that
He shield you from pride and discouragement, and
especially against impatience and anger. Show
through your whole conduct that the word of God
which you praise dwells richly in your hearts, not
only as ruler but as leader of all your thoughts and
desires, as it is also the spring of your comfort and
hope. We must believe, as the dear brothers
Krapf and Flad have found, that there are here
and there solitary souls yearning for something
better than their church offers to them ; but we
cannot say that there is a general desire in the
Abyssinian nation for the pure word of God. This
desire must be awakened, and we know that the
only real remedy for awaking it is by spreading the
knowledge of God far and wide. Therefore it is
needful that on the road to Cairo, and on the Nile,
you practice the reading of the Amharic language,
that when you praise the Word of God to the people you may clearly, comprehensively, and pene-
tratingly read it to them, with some remarks, but
not more than is necessary to explain what has
been read. Trust more to the Word of God than
your own explanation of it. I do not mean to say that
you are not to witness, according to your experience, for words of life founded on the Holy Scrip-

tures, flowing from a faithful and loving heart, also lead to salvation. What I mean is this, that you lead the people to read the Word of God with understanding by themselves. This, however, you will understand better when you are there among the people. If you thus succeed in circulating some hundreds of Bibles and New Testaments as widely as possible, with the hope and knowledge that the people will read them, and if you are able to teach some to read for themselves, and thus receive profit for the salvation of their souls, then I can say you have accomplished the first and most important thing which is the aim of your mission. And should you be obliged to leave the country, which is quite possible in the present state of Abyssinia, you can leave the Word of God which you have begun to distribute, with comfort in the hand of God and His Holy Spirit. The seed which you sow will undoubtedly begin to show signs of life in many, and bear fruit, and the longing for the Word of Life will not be wanting, so that, perhaps, it will be said in a few years the Abyssinian field is white for the harvest, and the Lord will send other workers, with whom you will be able to rejoice before Him in eternity. God grant that it may be so, through the riches of His grace.

" But one or another may be asking anxiously, ' If this does not succeed, if we may not enter the land with our books, or if we are allowed to distribute them and then have to leave and go back, what shall we do then ?' To this question I feel the reply of the English drummer boy is applicable. He was asked in a foreign country to strike the different marches which he played so skilfully, and when asked to play a retreat he said, ' I can never do that ; such a thing as going back we do not learn.' I find it no where written in the Scriptures that God told His servants to do this or that, in case anything happened to them. He did not tell the children of Israel what they were to do if they did not enter the land of Canaan. Only this has the Lord said, 'If they persecute you in one city, flee ye to another;' and let this be enough for you and us. If this undertaking is of God, He will surely make a way for its accomplishment; but if it is only from man, it cannot succeed. So I can only tell you not to look to man for advice, but go direct and ask it of the Lord.

" Besides the Bible distribution your present journey has another aim in view, which to me was of the first importance, but is now a secondary matter; and this is that you should inform yourselves well and conscientiously whether it be possible or advisable to have an Evangelical Mission station in the country, and, if so, which would be the best spot for it. In case you find it possible, it would be best to go to the place yourselves. First ascertain, however, the present political and civil condition of the whole country. But do not put to the King direct questions, so as to get decisive answers, as to whether you may settle in his country as messengers of salvation. The better plan will be not to bring the matter forward, nor seem anxious about it, but try first to persuade and convince the King, through your behaviour, that you are true Christians who are led by the Spirit and the Word of God, so that if possible you may incline his heart towards you, and he may be convinced that you are servants of Jesus Christ, really seeking the good of his people. At the same time, even before you speak to the King, you must examine some parts of the country in regard to its fertility, see whether the place is healthy, choose a spot rich in wood and water, so as to be able to say what place you think fitting for your destination, when you eventually find it well to go decisively to the King. You must also pay attention to the character of the people in the neighbourhood of the situation you choose, and see if they will be inclined to receive you, for you will find a great variety of character in the different districts. Although it is the Lord's will that all men, both bad and good, should be helped, much depends upon where you first begin, and whether you are surrounded by those of more or less impressible character. It therefore becomes one of your chief duties from the day you enter Abyssinia, to study the character of the nation, and make yourselves friendly in every way amongst the people. You will meet with every description of bad men, for these always come to strangers, and if you give up too much time to them you will have no opportunity to know those who are better and inclined to good; for these latter do not generally come forward, but wait to be found.

"To return, however, to the subject of the mission station itself. The missionary must not at first show himself as a priest, as for instance in some parts of India and West Africa, where he declares himself directly as a public teacher of religion, and tries at once to open regular schools and meetings. This has been partly tried in Abyssinia, but was not successful, on account of the suspicions of the people, and particularly of the priesthood. To these I would like you to show love and charity, for I can say from experience that in addition to many bad priests, there are still numbers of faithful and conscientious men in their ranks, who only need enlightening and the best kind of knowledge to make them good examples.

The first mission station in Abyssinia should, according to my views, resemble the English and Irish Missions of the middle ages in Alsace, Germany, and Switzerland, founded with Christian liberty to draw back in some things as opportunity offers. That is, you must choose a place, not too far from the people, but good for farming, and at first give your attention mostly to this, with the help of some promising youths, whom you can instruct from time to time more particularly in the Word of God. You must teach these youths by your example how to work steadily, increasing their number until you have a good choice of the most promising to continue teaching, to employ as colporteurs, or to visit with you in the neighbouring villages when you carry the message of salvation. This you are to do, at least for a time, not as public preachers, but as good Christian neighbours, always speaking in humility and love. And do not forget that you must win the character of Christians in the eyes of the people before you will be able to declare yourselves preachers with success. You may feel it strange and disagreeable to hear that instead of preaching and baptizing you are asked to work with your hands, and partly to earn your own living. The devil will whisper to you, and your own hearts will answer him loudly enough: 'Work and earn our bread, live and die, we could have done in Germany, without the long preparation, and without going to wild Abyssinia.' But, dear brothers, remember to work the land and eat bread with the sweat of the brow is the work God Himself out of love gave to mankind. It is not below the dignity of the best and noblest man. Moreover, the apostle Paul has given us the example to work with the hands, and according to my view it is the most likely if not the only way, to win the Abyssinian nation and eventually to evangelize the whole country. However, I shall be true to my word which I gave to your first superintendent, that I will send you £100 per annum, if it be the Lord's will, as long as I live. This sum would perhaps be enough, considering the cheapness of food, to support you all, even if you did not work; but this would be good, neither for you nor the Mission, and thus it could not prosper. If, however, you succeed by the way in which you have been told to begin, give praise to the Lord when the doors are opened for the free preaching of the Gospel. It may be so in a few years time. Then your position will change, and your work be more entirely for the spiritual welfare of the people. Until this comes to pass you must bear all with patience, and I know you will do so gladly for the Lord's sake. I will readily do more for you if the Lord makes it possible for me, but I cannot promise further. Let us also give into His care even this outward matter.

"Your settling in different parts of the land is your second aim. On the coming journey your first aim must be the spreading of the word of God in Abyssinia. About these two things I shall be thankful if you send me clear and decisive answers. We do not expect long reports, but desire to know how it fares with you, what projects you have in view, what you hope, and what you fear; and at the same time, what you believe ought to be done, within the limits of reason and possibility. To enable such tidings to have full weight, they must be signed by all of you. Each one has full freedom to express his own views in private letters, and I will give every attention to them; but only the general information signed by all will be regarded as weighty. As our Lord

Jesus Christ put no one among His disciples as head or master, but told them to love each other, and be obliging to each other, saying to them, 'All ye are brethren,' therefore I must not put any of you above the others. Nevertheless it seems natural that in your own circle, where you are as brothers and make one family, you should look to Brother Bender as your House Father. He will advise you in cases of difficulty, and you will show him love and respect before the people. But as Brother Flad has already been in Abyssinia, and has had the most experience of travelling, he must take the arrangement of your journeyings under his care, until your arrival. But as you are all brothers, who have the same aim in view, it is desirable that you consult together before taking any decisive step, until you are all of one mind and heart. As already said, you cannot do anything well in Abyssinia as missionaries until you have proved yourselves true disciples of Christ, and this you can only do by loving one another in the Lord, and for His sake. He said Himself, 'By this shall all men know that ye are My disciples, if ye have love one toward another.' Walk in love, as Christ also hath loved us, remembering that He gave Himself an offering for us. Small disagreements will come from time to time, but do not let such differences destroy your work, or your inner peace and rest. Have much patience one with another. 'Bear one another's burdens, and so fulfil the law of Christ.' Forgive each other, as God also has forgiven you, and as you would be yourselves forgiven.

"Until now I have said nothing of the Abyssinian Falashas or Jews, although they have been in my thoughts. It will be desirable that you inform yourselves accurately about them, and all

their concerns. You should also give them the
Bible if they like to accept it. See particularly if
you can open a Mission among them. I shall be
glad if you can go amongst them as evangelists,
and seek to lead them to the Messiah, the Saviour
of Israel.

"Now, dear brothers, I have gone into many details which may seem now of little consequence,
but I am convinced that later on you will see their
benefit and profit by them. I have now only one
more remark before closing, and it is this: You go
now to Abyssinia where there is a Church, which,
I am sorry to say, is a dead one. Seek, by the
Lord's help, to put life into it, and with the seed of
the Word of God to make it bear fruit. You
go as messengers of salvation and as servants of
Christ. That you are not ordained of man makes
no difference, the conditions on which you go require this omission. And if only Jesus Christ our
great High Priest lay His hands upon you and
bless you, you will need nothing more, for He
alone is the one who gives the true authority. You
go to Abyssinia, I hope, with the simple aim and
earnest desire to spread the knowledge and the
kingdom of Jesus Christ, with the longing desire
to lead lost sheep to the Good Shepherd, to bring
lost sinners to the Saviour, to free them from the
slavery of Satan and sin, and to make them par-
takers of everlasting happiness. You know, however, that in you is neither light nor strength, and
of yourselves you are not able to lead one soul
to repentance. It all depends on how your own
hearts stand with the Lord, without whom you can
do nothing. The success of your important undertaking depends entirely on this, that each one
should have continual communion with the Lord,
living so near to Him that your personal piety con-

sists in daily, hourly connection of soul with the Lord.   This alone will fit you for your calling, and make blessing from above to flow into your work. Therefore, dear brethren, watch and pray at all times.   Let no day pass without your having had some time in private prayer with the Lord, and in reading and in studying His Holy Word.   Daily read and pray with one another.   It will strengthen and unite you more closely in love.   But if you become careless of yourselves, if you leave off watching and prayer, you must fall and be spoiled, so that even if you preached the truth the whole day long to others, your work would be lost, and all in vain.   Therefore go in the name of the Lord, and pray without ceasing for us also, and we, with God's help, will pray for you, that the Lord will send His angel before you to open a wide door for blessing on your work.   Oh! that He may use you as instruments to open the eyes of the blind Abyssinians, to lead them from darkness unto light, and from the power of Satan unto God : that they may, with you and us, have a portion in the kingdom and eternal life of our God.   Amen.

"SAMUEL GOBAT, Angl. Hierosol.

"Jerusalem, 7th Dec., 1855."

CHAPTER V.

THE LANGUAGE OF ABYSSINIA.

THE Ethiopic language, the ancient language of Abyssinia, now counts among the dead languages of that country, with the exception of the Tigreniya, which is a corrupted Ethiopic dialect spoken at Tigré in the eastern part of Abyssinia. The Bible was translated into the Ethiopic language from the Greek Septuagint in the 6th century; but as the Amharic language took the place of the Ethiopic, the Word of God became a hidden treasure to the common people, whilst the priests had to study the Ethiopic just as we have to study Latin or Greek. As the Gospel truth under such circumstances could not be the guide of the Abyssinians it is no wonder that the Church became distorted and corrupted. Abu Rumi, an Abyssinian monk, translated the Ethiopic Bible into the Amharic language in the year 1808, with the help of Asscline, the French consul at Cairo. The manuscript was bought, revised, and printed by the British and Foreign Bible Society in the year 1840, and by these means Abyssinia was supplied with the Word of God in the language of the people. The letters of the Ethiopic and Amharic languages are the same, and the adjoining alphabet illustrates the characters in which the Amharic Bible is printed. There are thirty-three original letters, and six vowels, oo, ay, āh, ee, ö, o, which are joined to the

THE ETHIOPIC OR AMHARIC ALPHABET OF THE ABYSSINIAN LANGUAGE.

Names of the letters.	Original.		Vowel oo		Vowel ay		Vowel āh		Vowel ee		Vowel ö		Vowel o	
Hoi	U	ha	U·	hoo	ሂ	hay	ህ	āh	ሄ	hee	ቢ	hö	U	ho
Lawi	ለ	la	ሉ	loo	ለ	lay	ለ	lāh	ለ	lee	ል	lö	ሎ	lo
Haut	ሐ	ha	ሑ	hoo	ሒ	hay	ሓ	hāh	ሔ	hee	ሕ	hö	ሖ	ho
Mai	መ	ma	መ·	moo	ሚ	may	ማ	māh	ሜ	mee	ም	mö	ሞ	mo
Saut	ሠ	sa	ሡ	soo	ሢ	say	ሣ	sāh	ሤ	see	ሥ	sö	ሦ	so
Rees	ረ	ra	ሩ	roo	ሪ	ray	ራ	rāh	ሬ	ree	ር	rö	ሮ	ro
Sat	ሰ	sa	ሱ	soo	ሲ	say	ሳ	sāh	ሴ	see	ስ	sö	ሶ	so
Shat	ሸ	sha	ሹ	shoo	ሺ	shay	ሻ	shāh	ሼ	shee	ሽ	shö	ሾ	sho
Kaaf	ቀ	ka	ቁ	koo	ቂ	kay	ቃ	kāh	ቄ	kee	ቅ	kö	ቆ	ko
Bet	በ	ba	ቡ	boo	ቢ	bay	ባ	bāh	ቤ	bee	·በ	bö	ቦ	bo
Tawi	ተ	ta	ቱ	too	ቲ	tay	ታ	tāh	ቴ	tee	ት	tö	ቶ	to
Tshawi	ጨ	tsha	ጩ	tshoo	ጪ	tshay	ጫ	tshāh	ጬ	tshee	ጭ	tshö	ጮ	tsho
Harm	ነ	ha	ኑ	hoo	ኒ	hay	ና	hāh	ኔ	hee	ን	hö	ኖ	ho
Nahas	ነ	na	ኑ	noo	ኒ	nay	ና	nāh	ኔ	nee	ን	nö	ኖ	no
Gnahas	ኘ	gna	ኙ	gnoo	ኚ	gnay	ኛ	gnāh	ኜ	gnee	ኝ	gnö	ኞ	gno
Alf	አ	a	አ·	oo	ኢ	ay	አ	āh	ኤ	ee	እ	ö	ኦ	o

Chaf	cha	choo	chay	chāh	chee	chö	cho
Wawi	wa	woo	way	wāh	wee	wö	wo
Ain	a	oo	ay	āh	ee	ö	o
Zai	za	zoo	zay	zāh	zee	zö	zo
Zshai	ja	joo	jay	jāh	jee	jö	jo
Yaman	ja	joo	jay	jāh	jee	jö	jo
Deut	da	doo	day	dāh	dee	dö	do
Jeut	ja	joo	jay	jāh	jee	jö	jo
Geml	ga	goo	gay	gāh	gee	gö	go
Tait	ta	too	tay	tāh	tee	tö	to
Tshait	tsha	tshoo	tshay	tshāh	tshee	tshö	tsho
Pait	pa	poo	pay	pāh	pee	pö	po
Tsadai	tsa	tsoo	tsay	tsāh	tsee	tsö	tso
Tsappa	tsa	tsoo	tsay	tsāh	tsee	tsö	tso
Af	fa	foo	fay	fāh	fee	fö	fo
Pa	pa	poo	pay	pāh	pee	pö	po

Dipthongs— kŭă   hhŭă   kŭă   găă

original characters and thus cause more or less change in the original forms of the letters; for instance—

ሀ ha ሁ hoo ሂ hay ሃ āh ሄ hee ህ hö ሆ ho

Each original letter has seven forms as shown in the accompanying alphabet; and besides these are four diphthongs, and each of these has four changes by taking up the vowels, thus making altogether 251 forms of letters in the Ethiopic and Amharic alphabet. The Amharic language belongs to the Semitic tongues. It is, however, written from left to right, and the same letters are used both for printing and writing. It sounds euphonious and looks pretty when well written. Each word is separated from the other by two dots, thus : and at the end of each sentence are four dots, thus :: as

ሐበሽ ፡ እጅዋን ፡ ለእግዚአብሐር ፡ ታደርሳለች ፡፡

"Ethiopia shall stretch out her hands unto God."—Ps. lxviii. 31.

Hiob Ludolf, a traveller in Abyssinia, produced the first history of the country and people, and compiled the first dictionary, called the Amharic Lexicon Latinum. Besides these he brought out an excellent Ethiopic Lexicon and Grammar. His interesting works on Abyssinia were published at Frankfort on the Maine, in the year 1698. These publications have formed the basis of all the writings of subsequent travellers and missionaries, respecting the habits and the language of the Abyssinians.

CHAPTER VI.

AS Magdala was not suitable for a mission station, I went to the camp of King Theodore and explained to my father-in-law, John Bell, that we required another place for our mission work. He brought the matter before the King, and obtained permission for us to go back and bring all our brethren and luggage, and settle at Gaffat, an eminence 8000 feet high, in the midst of fertile plains and hills, one hour east of Debra Tabor, the capital of the district of Begimder. Our party consisted of Mr. and Mrs. Flad, Mr. and Mrs. Mayer, Mr. Bender, Mr. Saalmüller, Mr. Kienzlen, Mrs. Waldmeier, and myself. We left Magdala in June, 1860, and after seven days' journey, arrived at Gaffat. Here we built twelve small houses or huts, each in five days, from small pieces of wood, covered with straw outside, and well plastered within. Each one of us had two huts, one for dwelling and sleeping, the other for a kitchen. The Gaffat hill was thus converted into quite a colony of Europeans. This attracted the Abyssinians, who soon came in large numbers to visit us, and opportunity presented for real apostolic mission work according to our instructions. Charles Saalmüller and I taught some of the Abyssinian young men mechanical work, which brought us into great favour with the King and people. Thousands and thousands of times all the people said to us, " You Europeans are a wonderful people, and God has revealed to you everything except a medicine against death, for you die just as we do." The King often kissed my hands, saying, " Poor hands, for these also must be laid in the grave." This outward work was the best means of procuring a solid basis for our mission amongst the ignorant Christians, and also among the Falashas, even as Paul said to the elders of Ephesus, " Ye yourselves know that these hands have ministered unto my necessities, and to them that were with me " (Acts xx. 34.   It is a great mistake for young missionaries to think it beneath their dignity to work with their own hands when commencing in a foreign mission field.

The more we understood of the Amharic language, the deeper we found was the ignorance and superstition of the people.

It often happens in Abyssinia that people seem possessed by an evil spirit. This the Abyssinians call *Boudah*. I witnessed these wonderful and dark occurrences many times, but will relate one only— and even in this case I must not describe the most horrible and disgusting details. One evening when I was in my house at Gaffat, a woman began to cry fearfully, and run up and down the road on her hands and feet like a wild beast, quite unconscious of what she was doing. The people said to me, " This is the *Boudah*; and if it is not driven out of her, she will die." A large number of people gathered round her, and many means were tried, but all in vain. She was always howling and roaring in an unnatural and most powerful voice. At length a man was called, a blacksmith by profession, of whom it was said that he was in secret connection with the evil spirit. He called the woman, who obeyed him at once. He took her hand in his and dropped the juice of the white onion or garlic into her nose, and said to her—or rather to the evil spirit which possessed her—"Why didst thou possess this poor woman ?"

"Because I was allowed to do so."

"What is thy name ?"

"My name is Gebroo."

"Where is thy country ?"

"My country is Godjam."

"How many people didst thou take possession of ?"

"I took possession of forty people, men and women."

"Now I command thee to leave this woman."

"I will leave her on one condition."

"What is that condition ?"

"I want to eat the flesh of a donkey."

"Very well," said the man, "thou mayst have that."

So a donkey was brought which had a wounded back from carrying heavy loads, and its back was quite sore and full of matter. The woman then ran upon the donkey and bit the flesh out of the poor creature's back ; and though the donkey kicked and ran off, she did not fall down, but clung to it just as if she was nailed on the animal's back. The man called the woman back to him, and said to the evil spirit, "Now art thou satisfied ?"

"Not yet," was the reply, and a disgusting mixture was asked for, which was prepared for the woman and put down in a secret place which she could not see ; but when the man said to her, "Go and look for your drink," she ran on all fours like an animal to that very place and drank the whole potful to the very last drop. Then she came back to the man, who said again, "Now take up this

F

stone." It was a very large stone which she would not have been able to move in her natural condition, but she took it up with ease upon her head, and turned round like a wheel until the stone flew off on one side and she on the other on the ground. The man then said, "Take her now away to bed, for the *Boudah* has left her." The poor woman slept for about ten hours, and awoke and went to her work, and did not know anything of that which had passed over her, nor what she did and said.

Much can be said about these Psychological phenomena. I only state the facts, which I often have witnessed, and leave the rest to the reader. Whether scientific and medical men are able to explain it or not, I cannot say; but in a country of darkness the power of darkness is fearful, and beyond human explanation.

I began my Mission work at Gaffat by opening a boarding school for poor children, who were instructed in reading and writing, while the older ones learned some useful handicrafts. Every Sunday we had divine service in our own language for ourselves, and another service in the Amharic language for the Abyssinians. On feast days we went to the Abyssinian churches, where hundreds, and sometimes thousands of people were gathered together, in and around the groves which surround the churches, dancing, playing, and occupied in other unprofitable amusements; to these we could preach and read the Gospel publicly, under the shade of the rich foliage of the sacred groves. The Abyssinian churches are not built for large gatherings of people, because the square building in the centre is the consecrated place for the priests only, in which is kept the ark of the covenant *(Tabot)*. This *Tabot* (Arabic and Heb. *Tabot*) is most reverently honoured in the Abyssinian churches, though it is nothing but a block of solid wood, eighteen inches square, and two inches thick, with a cross carved in the middle, and surrounded by ornamental engravings. This block of wood is considered by all the Abyssinians as a symbol of the Israelites' ark of the covenant, which they think the Queen of Sheba brought to Ethiopia after her visit to King Solomon, and are very angry if anyone supposes it is not still to be found in the old temple at Axum. Without this *Tabot* no church in Abyssinia can be regarded as a holy place by the natives, who are under the idea that God will not hear any prayer nor help anyone in a church where there is no *Tabot*.

The holy place is rather small, being usually not more than fourteen feet square, and the outer court also being inconvenient, the people prefer being in the groves of the church, and only go inside in rainy weather. The church itself is not at all well adapted for preaching the Gospel to the people. At first the Christian churches were built according to the plan of the temple at Jerusalem, the three divisions being arranged on the old Jewish plan.*

On great feast days every Abyssinian is expected to come to church, that is to say, he must come and kiss the church door, after which he joins the dancing, playing, and singing parties, in the so-called holy groves. As soon as I could use the boys of my school as Scripture readers and catechists, we often took them on such occasions, and placed them with their Bibles among the people, while some of the missionaries explained what had been read to the multitude. Priests and monks often interrupted, saying, " You do wrong by ex-

---

* See Neander's Church History, vol. 2, p. 408.

posing the holy Christian religion and the Word of
God to the public. Religious books and the ladies
of our country must be kept secret behind the
curtains, for as soon as they get revealed to the
public they will grow profane. You degrade our
most holy religion by reading and preaching the
Gospel in the common language of the people."
The Druses on Mount Lebanon likewise say that a
good religion, as well as women, must be kept
strictly secret.

For a number of years all went on very satisfactorily, and our prospects were hopeful for the future
of our Mission. In John Bell, the Prime Minister,
we had a most influential and faithful friend, who
always defended the cause of the Mission at the
court of the king against the Abyssinian priests
and other enemies; but he lost his life in a battle
against the rebel Garet at Waldiba in November,
1860. This loss was great beyond expression to
the king, the Mission, and all the Europeans. In
the same year, Dr. Stern, a proselyte of the London Society for Promoting Christianity among the
Jews, came to Abyssinia for the purpose of organizing a Mission to the Falashas. He came a
few months before the death of John Bell, and so
had the advantage of his friendly influence with
King Theodore, and was helped by him in many
ways. One of our brethren, Martin Flad, accompanied him on his journey among the Falashas, and
was subsequently engaged by him as a missionary
among those at Tchenta. We were all sorry to lose
Mrs. Flad from amongst us, for she was like a
mother to our mission station; to the missionaries
as well as the Abyssinians, among whom her medical
knowledge opened the door to the hearts of many
thousands.

Dr. Stern, after organizing his Mission among

the Jews, left the country in peace, in the same month that John Bell was killed in the battle of Waldiba. The great drawback in connection with the Falasha Mission was that its converts were obliged to be baptized by priest of the corrupt Abyssinian church, who are decided enemies to spiritual life. When Dr. Stern arrived in England he wrote a book called "Wanderings among the Falashas in Abyssinia," in which he mentioned many things against the King and the people, which afterwards turned out badly for him in his second visit to Abyssinia in the year 1863.

The Mission station at Gaffat became a powerful agency for the propagation of Gospel truth, as well as for the progress of civilization by the circulation of the Holy Scriptures in the Amharic language, by the free preaching of sound Christian doctrine, and by teaching the young. The Word of God, which was distributed among the people, often manifested its blessed power; and I could relate many interesting anecdotes in connection with it. For instance, a soldier came to me begging for an Amharic Bible. After a long conversation with him I found that he was a true inquirer, and gave him a Bible, for which he was very thankful. He went away on his road to Magdala, carrying on the one shoulder the Word of Life (Amharic Bibles are always very heavy on account of the largeness of the type) and on the other his deadly weapons. After his arrival at Magdala he began to read and study his Bible well without the help of any teacher or missionary; and through the influence of the Holy Spirit it became the means of his unmistakable conversion. He was not satisfied with having found the truth for himself, he soon began to teach and preach the Gospel to his fellow soldiers and other people. He also had regular meetings for worship, and wherever he went he took his Bible with him. Dr. Stern was at that time a prisoner at Magdala, and hearing of him, he wrote to one of his fellow missionaries, that the soldier to whom Theophilus Waldmeier gave a Bible at Gaffat, had become truly converted and was preaching the Gospel publicly at every opportunity, and if allowed to go on in this way would become a great power for God to his people.

Mr. Flad once gave some Bibles to a monk, who carried them into his convent at Godjam, the western province of Abyssinia, where some of the monks read the Bibles through with attention. One day one of the monks said to his fellow hermits, " Dear brethren, we have all been, or are still in error. We do not find in the Bible that God has ordered men to go and sit in solitude in convents and spend their life in idleness, but we read that Jesus Christ ordered His followers to go into all the world and preach the Gospel to every creature. So we must not remain in this convent, but go out into our neighbourhood and preach the Gospel of Jesus according to His order." And so some of them went forth to read and preach the Gospel to their poor ignorant fellow-countrymen."

As the King was a friend to both civilization and our Mission, he loved and supported us, and gave us many hundreds of Abyssinian workmen—Christians, heathen, Jews, and Mohammedans—whom we instructed in arts, and in true religious principles. Once the King wrote me a letter saying he had liberated some hundreds of slaves from a slave dealer whom he caught in the neighbourhood of Gondar. He sent me some of them, and said, " Teach these young boys arts and religion, and I shall send thee more of such unfortunate creatures to make them happy, and I will pay all

A SLAVE GANG.

their expenses." These poor slaves were brought from the interior of the Galla country. They had first to learn the Amharic language; but one of them, I remember in particular, was very diligent, and when he learned the Gospel and became converted to Christ. I employed him often as Bible reader. He afterwards left Abyssinia to preach the Gospel among his heathen brethren in the Galla country.

As King Theodore wanted to civilize his country he began to make good roads, asking us to superintend the work. By this means we were brought in connection with thousands of people, to whom we spoke of salvation through Christ Jesus. European workmen from France and Germany, who were not missionaries, came to Gaffat, and the first carriage for transport was constructed there. One of these workmen was a gunmaker, and another an ironfounder. Many houses were built, and a foundry constructed, where guns were cast and bored. A powerful water wheel for moving different kinds of machinery was built at Gaffat, and all the clever men of Abyssinia were brought thither by order of the King. Thousands and tens of thousands of Abyssinians and Gallas thus came in contact with us. Religion, civilization, arts, and trade, were the subjects of private and public conversation. I often sat for hours with the King, engaged in religious conversation, and speaking about the welfare of his country and its people. He was peacefully disposed towards all the Europeans, especially towards us as lay missionaries and instructors of arts.

One day when I was travelling with King Theodore over the country, we met a poor woman who had scarcely any clothing upon her half-starved body. The King got down from his mule and gave her his own *shamma*, and then, as he wanted also to give her some money and had none with him, he asked me whether I could lend him a few dollars. I answered, "Yes, your Majesty, I have about five dollars here, and you can have them." He took them and gave them to the poor woman, who went away rejoicing, for they would buy her as many sheep. In the evening the King gave me one hundred dollars. I said to him, "I gave your Majesty only five dollars; why have you given me ninety-five dollars too much?" He replied, "I return and give like a king." I thanked him, and went home rejoicing. So does the heavenly King do unto us for all that we give unto Him.

In Abyssinia nobody is allowed to keep a lion, except the King and those who have permission from him. One day King Theodore sent a young lion to me by a soldier who had the little fellow in his arms, because he was quite small like a cat, and I accepted the gift with thankfulness. At first I gave him milk for he could not yet eat flesh, but when he grew larger he was no more to be satisfied with milk only, so I had to give him rough meat, and he ate nearly one sheep every day, but the King supplied me with the needful food for him. After three years he grew into a beautiful, fine animal and was really a kingly lion. He liked to play just like cats do and was very amusing indeed. We often played with him, and let him loose from his chain, and gave him liberty to run about. My daughter, who was about three years old, rode now and then on the lion's back, but I was obliged to be at her side to hold her with my right hand, while I led him with my left. He was very tame indeed, but when he got his meals, he did not like that anyone should look at him. His voice was so

HAGOS, THE LION.

powerful that he made the air tremble, as well as the cows, sheep, and goats, who were near him. He grew larger and larger until he looked just like the adjoining picture. I called him Hagos, and he followed me like a lamb. When I was taken prisoner by King Theodore, the lion was also taken and killed, and his skin was carefully prepared, and presented to one of his brave Generals, who wore its skin on his shoulder to show his fearlessness, and power, and victory.

The King gave us more liberty to preach the Gospel than any Protestant missionary or priest had ever had in Abyssinia before. The word of God was distributed in the common Amharic language, religious books and tracts were translated, and children were taught in our schools. The Gospel was also made known by private conversation among rich and poor, at the King's court, as well as in the poorest hut. On the basis of our friendship with the King, the other mission stations, under the direction of Mr. Flad, among the Falashas at Tchenta, and of Messrs. Staiger and Brandeis, of the Scotch mission at Darna, were likewise working satisfactorily, and all were very thankful for the blessings which attended our mission work.

We were also at peace with the Abuna Salama, who made me trustee of his household property for a considerable time; indeed, mine was the only house in the country, besides his own, that he entered, as custom prevents him from going into any place where there is a woman. So much is this the case that the women cover and hide even in the temple when he comes near.

CHAPTER VII.

NOW I will narrate the facts which gave rise to all the difficulties, captivity, trials, bloodshed, and horrors, which ended with the costly English expedition, and the suicide of King Theodore, which have never been thoroughly described, though so many books, journals, and pamphlets have been published about them. I think I may say that I am able to describe these things better than any of the Europeans who have been in Abyssinia, not that I am more diligent than others, but on account of my having been in the immediate presence of the King, where I could see how things went on. I made use of my position and privileges as much as I could, and often at the risk of my own welfare, and I acknowledge with humble thankfulness to God that I was many times able to prevent the excited King from executing the European prisoners, especially in the last time at Magdala, when every-one's life was hanging on the minutest thread. But Mr. John Bell's place I could not occupy for I was not a soldier, nor could I follow the King continually like he did, nor could I as a missionary mix myself with politics, but wherever I could give good counsel to the King I did not neglect my duty as a messenger of peace.

King Theodore, in the commencement of his career, was accompanied by two good guardian angels. The first was his wife, the Queen Toua-betch; the second was the prime minister, John Bell. The Queen, according to Abyssinian custom, took great care of the King in regard to food. He was not allowed to accept anything to eat or drink from any other hand but hers, and she was wise enough to keep the King continually sober, saying, "A King must not drink intoxicating liquors." Besides this, she read the Bible with him, thus seeking to keep him in the fear of God. John Bell was his wise and good counsellor, who enjoyed his full confidence, while at the same time exerting a beneficial influence upon the King. He was thus able to guide the King by peaceful suggestions for the internal welfare of his country, as well as with regard to foreign powers; but alas! the Queen died, and John Bell was killed in battle. The King was left alone, and no one was found to take John Bell's place.

Then the King married the daughter of King Ubie of Tigré, whom he conquered, but the new Queen did not give the same constant attention to the King as the former Queen had done. In consequence of this the King grew displeased, and gave way to intoxicating drinks, and then began to care for other women also, although not nearly to such an extent as has been reported. I cannot say that I ever saw him drunk, but even the moderate use of drink seemed to inflame his naturally excitable disposition, and caused him to be guilty of injustice and iniquity.

It was in the year 1862, that the English Con-sul, Captain Cameron, came to Abyssinia, accom-panied by his secretary, a Frenchman named Bardel. These two gentlemen spent the rainy season in Gondar, the capital, during the absence of the King, who was at war with the Wollo

Gallas. When the King returned from his expedition he received the two diplomatists with great honour, saying that he wished to enter into more intimate friendship with England and France, and he proposed to both to send them back to their respective Governments with nice letters, asking the Queen of England and the Emperor Napoleon III. of France, for friendly interest in Abyssinia. It is entirely untrue, however, that the King asked for the hand of Queen Victoria in that letter. The King supplied these two gentlemen with money for the journey, and told them emphatically, " Please carry these letters personally to your Governments, and bring me back the answers."

Captain Cameron and M. Bardel left Abyssinia, and for some time all went well. Arrived at Massowah, M. Bardel went by steamer *via* Egypt to France, whilst Captain Cameron sent his letter by post to the Foreign Office in London, and went to the Boggos, Mensa, and Keran country, in the Soudan, which was in rebellion against King Theodore on account of the slave trade, which is carried on to a great extent in these wild regions. He thought of remaining there until a letter reached him in answer to King Theodore's, which he hoped it would do before the rainy season, when no European is able to remain in these low-lying tropical regions without exposing himself to deadly malaria. The expected answer to King Theodore did not come, and on account of the bad climate he was obliged to go up to the high land of Abyssinia without it. There he met with the King, who was sadly disappointed at Captain Cameron's unfruitful journey. I was just then with King Theodore, and had often to translate for them. This disappointment was the first cause of mischief which made King Theodore become suspicious of Europeans, and this feeling was soon strengthened by other things, as the sequel will show. Captain Cameron, being perfectly sure in his own mind of a favourable reply from his Government, said to the King, "Your Majesty, I will give my head if after two months the answer to your letter is not here." Time passed on, however, and there was still no answer. This brought the King into such a rage that he could scarcely see any European without distrust and excitement. This was the FIRST cause of mischief.

Meanwhile it came to pass that M. Guillaume Lejean, a French Consul, came to Abyssinia, and lodged in my own house. He was respectfully received by the King; but the Frenchman's behaviour was vacillating and undignified. The King asked M. Lejean if he would like to stay in his country, or whether he was going away. He answered, "I should like to stay, if your Majesty permits me to do so." King Theodore replied, "Oh yes, you may stay until my friend M. Bardel, your fellow countryman, returns, whom I sent to your Government with friendly negotiations." This M. Lejean gladly accepted, but after a few weeks he changed his mind, and asked leave to return. The King, surprised at this, said, "Please wait until M. Bardel comes back;" to which M. Lejean replied, "Your Majesty, M. Bardel is a miserable liar and deceiver, and will never come back." The King said, "I want to keep you here until we know who is the liar." M. Bardel came back, and M. Lejean proved to be the liar : so the King said, "I have liars enough in my country, let M. Lejean depart from here." When M. Lejean arrived at the Abyssinian boundary, and was safe out of King Theodore's hands, he sent an insulting letter to him. That was the SECOND cause of mischief in setting the King against the Europeans, and it took the more effect from the answer of Napoleon III., through his Minister of Foreign Affairs, Drouyn de Lehuys, not being satisfactory.

Not long before this Dr. Stern, in company with Mr. and Mrs. Rosenthal, came to Abyssinia to visit the Jewish Mission station at Tchenta in Dembea, and to settle Mr. and Mrs. Rosenthal as helpers with Mr. Flad in proselytizing the Abyssinian Falashas, of whom a considerable number were already baptized. When Dr. Stern had completed his visit and was about to leave the country, he obtained the requisite permission from the King, but afterwards remaining longer, he fell into his hands, just as he was returning from an unsuccessful expedition. Dr. Stern not being acquainted with the etiquette of the Abyssinian Court, made some other mistake also, which so excited the King that he caused him and his servants to be beaten, and kept under guard during the night. Before morning Dr. Stern called the Frenchman M. Bardel, and said to him, " I have a book with me entitled, ' Wanderings among the Falashas of Abyssinia.' It is in that box. Please bring it to me. I am afraid to keep it because there are some things written in it which will not please the King." M. Bardel took out the book, but instead of giving it to Dr. Stern, translated all the passages written against the King, with some letters which he also found of the same nature, and made them all known to the King. This, as might be supposed, put King Theodore in a terrible fury, and became the THIRD cause of mischief which helped to bring iron chains and captivity to the Europeans. The following are specimens of the objectionable passages ; " King Theodore is not a descendant of the Royal Dynasty, but only the son of a poor woman who sold a kind of

GONDAR, CAPITAL OF ABYSSINIA, WITH THE KING'S PALACE.

medicine. He is a cruel, blood-thirsty man, like a wild animal." Many other equally bad things were written. Moreover the King was further exasperated by no answer having arrived from England, so that he appointed a day of judgment for all these cases, exclaiming with a loud voice to the guilty transgressors, before thousands of people; "You Europeans came into this country, and I loved, honoured, and respected you, because I thought that all Europeans were like my beloved John Bell, who always spoke the truth; but you are liars. I did you good, but you returned me evil; you spoke and wrote against me in your reports, and gave me a bad name before the world. God shall be judge between you and me." The King's throne was erected in a large plain near Gondar, and surrounded by thousands of people. The Abyssinian Codex, or law book was consulted. Dr. Stern and Mr. Rosenthal were sentenced to be executed and the gallows erected before their eyes. As I was in favour with the King, I went with a trembling heart and implored him, with tears, not to execute this judgment. As I knelt before him, he looked fixedly at me, and took my hand in his, saying, "Don't be afraid, my friend, my child. For your sake, and Mr. Bell's, I will not kill them, I will not only grant you Stern's life but even if you asked a finger off my hand, I would give it you, because you are true, and I love you." Their lives were spared, but Captain Cameron, Dr. Stern, Mr. Rosenthal, with their European servants, and the missionaries, Mr. Martin Flad, Mr. Staiger, and Mr. Brandeis, were all put in chains.

In the year 1864, Captain Cameron, Dr. Stern, and Mr. and Mrs. Rosenthal, with their European servants, were sent prisoners to Magdala; whilst Mr. and Mrs. Flad, Mr. Staiger, and Mr. Brandeis, were allowed to dwell in the country near Gaffat as semi-prisoners. The condition of every European became very dangerous under these circumstances, for the King had lost all confidence in Europeans, even in me, whom he called his best friend. As I was appointed agent for the English envoy, Mr. Rassam, who arrived about this time, I was put into a most critical position, because it was very difficult to deal with the King, and I often got myself into great danger for daring to speak in favour of the prisoners. My attempts to ameliorate their condition, and suggest measures of peace between the King and his prisoners, to provide them with money, and assist their messengers between the coast and Magdala, were acknowledged with gratitude by Mr. Rassam, in his " Mission to Abyssinia," vol. ii., pages 292 and 340.

CHAPTER VIII.

THE English Government were alarmed at hearing of the captivity of the English Consul Captain Cameron, of Dr. Stern, and Mr. and Mrs. Rosenthal, and sent Mr. Hormutz Rassam, Dr. Blanc, and Lieutenant Prideaux, to King Theodore to negotiate the deliverance of the prisoners on friendly terms. They arrived in Abyssinia at the beginning of 1866, and were ordered to reside at Quarata, near the beautiful lake of Tzana, 6,000 feet above the sea.

King Theodore received the British mission with great honour, and treated them royally indeed. Mr. Rassam presented the official letter from Her Majesty Queen Victoria to King Theodore, in which she asked him to deliver the captives to Mr. Rassam, in whom he might place full confidence, and through whom he might convey all his wishes. But the Amharic translation was inaccurate : it said, "We give you Mr. Rassam as a good confidential gentleman, and all and everything which your Majesty desires he will do for you." Thus the King was wrongly informed, which gave rise to future difficulties, which was the FOURTH cause of mischief.* The King often said, "The great Queen of England has sent me a confidential,

---

* See also Dr. H. Blanc's "Narrative of Captivity in Abyssinia," pages 129, 130.

good man, through whom the old friendship between England and Ethiopia shall be renewed and cemented. He is more valuable to me than all the European prisoners. Let them go where they like if my dear friend Mr. Rassam remains with me." King Theodore then gave Mr. Rassam 10,000 dollars, and sent to fetch the prisoners from Magdala, handing them over to him at Quarata, where another trial took place. They acknowledged their guilt, and asked pardon. The King said, "I have given the prisoners over to Mr. Rassam, and they belong to him, he may send them wherever he likes."

The fatal misunderstanding between the King and Mr. Rassam consisted in the inaccurate translation of the Queen's letter, which led the King to suppose that he was to remain with him in Abyssinia, whilst he sent off the prisoners to Europe. I pointed out this error to Mr. Rassam, but he thought it would be of no consequence. I was obliged to stay with my fellow missionaries, and came to Quarata too late to interfere in the matter.* If Mr. Rassam would have remained with the King, he could easily have sent the prisoners to Europe in charge of Dr. Blanc and Lieutenant Prideaux, whilst he stayed on some time longer in Abyssinia; and thus he could have spared the further captivity of all the Europeans, and much bloodshed, loss of life, and other indescribable horrors and miseries connected with the English expedition, which cost besides £10,000,000 sterling. King Theodore was very friendly with Mr. Rassam, and really loved him. Mr. Rassam, too, knew how to deal with the King better than any other foreigner; but when he insisted on ac-

---

* See my book, "Ten Years in Abyssinia," in German, pages 52 and 53, in which this story is clearly related.

companying the released prisoners back to Europe, he greatly disappointed him, though the King, wishing to find out certainly whether Mr. Rassam wished to stay with him or not, let him do as he thought best.

The prisoners were sent away along the east side of Lake Tzana, whilst Mr. Rassam himself, with Dr. Blanc and Lieutenant Prideaux, crossed the lake in canoes on the 13th of April, 1866, to take leave of the King, who was residing at the time at Sagie. I accompanied them, and as soon as we arrived at the Court I saw at once that matters were completely changed. Mr. Rassam and his party were taken prisoners, and an order sent to bring back the released captives, who were on their way to the frontier. They were all brought to Sagie, and from this date, Mr. Rassam, Dr. Blanc, and Lieutenant Prideaux, were joined to the rest of the prisoners, and a new period of troubles, perplexities, and captivity began. Mr. Rassam, however, was kindly treated by the King during his imprisonment. Many things happened at Sagie, and among them the repeated trial of the first prisoners, and Mr. Flad's departure for England to obtain instruments and workmen for the King. Executions of natives, and other atrocities also took place daily, increasing the misery of the long season of captivity and perplexity, but they cannot be described in detail.

After a while cholera broke out in the camp at Sagie, and the King was obliged to leave the low country for Debra Tabor and Gaffat, 9,000 feet above the sea. It was a very difficult journey, because the first rains had set in, and I had my wife and little daughter Rosa with me. We had to travel in the midst of a crowd of 100,000 soldiers, women and children. Some sick, dying,

and even dead, were carried in the crowd, and many
others lay dead on the ground, the multitude passing over them, so that the smell became fearful, and
the lamentation for the dead was heart-rending.
Some of my servants fell ill and died on the road.
After a few days' journey we arrived at Debra
Tabor, and from thence we went to our mission
colony, whilst Mr. Rassam was left there with his
fellow prisoners.   When we reached our house my
wife was seized with a violent attack of cholera,
followed by typhus fever, which was so dangerous
that she was brought to the very brink of the grave.
In despair I ran to the King, asking that Dr.
Blanc, who was a prisoner at Debra Tabor, might
be allowed to come to my house and prescribe for
her in her alarming and unconscious condition,
which request was granted.   The cholera prostrated
all our servants, and some of them died.   Indeed,
the angel of death was daily claiming its victims at
Gaffat.   The anger of the King caused many
executions, and much bloodshed, so that every hour
our lives were in danger, either of being attacked
by the cholera, or the cruelty of an excited
monarch.   All seemed to go wrong, and every
house was filled with forebodings of greater suffering yet to come.   Dr. Blanc told me candidly to be
prepared for the worst with regard to my dear
wife, and that little Rosa was not to go to her any
more, though she repeatedly asked for the child.
My heart was breaking, and it seemed to me that
every tree and shrub were mourning for the
immense loss of life.   During that time of great
misery, Mr. Rassam and his fellow captives were
brought to Gaffat, and subsequently sent to prison
at the natural fortification of Magdala.   My wife
began to recover, and was soon able to get up
again.   By degrees the cholera passed away, but

the anger and hatred of the King towards all the Europeans, and also towards the natives, increased every day, and the continuance of our lives and mission work was no more to be depended on, for we were in danger and uncertainty every hour.

On the 13th of April, 1866, King Theodore sent a large number of soldiers to my house at Gaffat, and ordered me to gather my fellow missionaries at three o'clock in the afternoon. This was the King's message : " I have heard that you are in correspondence with England (of course by M. Bardel's instigation), therefore you are prisoners." In an instant our houses were surrounded by soldiers, and every one of us taken in charge. I remember still, as if it had happened but yesterday, being carried away from my home, with my dear wife and our little daughter Rosa, who was only three years old, following me in despair. A rough soldier pushed my poor wife backward with such force that she fell heavily against a rock, bruising her head in the fall. Her wild lamentation, " Let me die with my husband," and Rosa's childish voice, crying out, " Papa, papa, come," penetrated my heart like a sharp arrow; but I was powerless to help or comfort them, being carried away with my brethren by the wild soldiers to Debra Tabor, where we were kept under strict guard. The next morning we were obliged to go down again the one hour's journey to Gaffat, but were not allowed to enter the colony. We were then asked to give up all our property, dress, furniture, money, and books. Debtera Sahaloo, teacher of my boys' school, was brought before the King, and his hands and feet were cut off. He was faithful unto death, and preached the Gospel even during the indescribable agony of the next two days. We gave up everything pertaining to the Mission colony and to ourselves, my wife concluding the whole by taking the golden saddle, which the King once presented to me, and throwing it out from the upper window, so that, without her meaning to hurt them, it fell rather heavily upon the soldiers' heads. *Sic transit gloria mundi.*

It was late in the evening when we were transported with our families to Debra Tabor. This was the end of the Abyssinian Mission colony at Gaffat, where we had worked and suffered for six long years, and where I had lost four dear sons; but, by the Lord's goodness, spiritual children were born unto me in return. It was very touching to see how our school children followed us into prison with the Gospel in their hands, and how they served us, bringing water and milk, whilst our own servants ran away in fear. We had nothing wherewith to support these children, so some went back to their relations, but a few remained with us, of whom three died on the road to Magdala.

At Debra Tabor we were as beggars, but we comforted ourselves with thinking that in death nothing is needed but faith in Jesus Christ, and to Him alone we lifted our hearts, and committed our souls. At first we lived in tents, but were afterwards ordered to enter small huts, in which we could scarcely stand upright, and a thorn fence, ten feet high, was placed round about us. Thus were we kept in misery, having scarcely enough to eat, and were continually in danger of our lives; but—

> " Let not sorrow dim your eye,
> Soon shall every tear be dry ;
> Let not fears your course impede,
> Great your strength, if great your need."

One day the King said to me, " You European people are very clever, but you conceal your capacity. Now I want you to make me a gun which will discharge a ball of 1,000 pound weight. If you say that you do not know how, I shall regard you all as liars, and you know what I have done with those that deceived me." I felt sadly perplexed, thinking, if I say we cannot do such a thing, the King may kill us all at once, and also those at Magdala; and if on the other hand I say we can do it, and then fail, it may bring the same danger upon us. So after some reflection I replied, " We will try our best to do it;" and the King was satisfied. It was very discouraging to have the story reported to us, that the King had told some of his courtiers that he intended to use the Europeans as slaves, and after they had succeeded in casting the great gun, meant to kill them on the plain of Debra Tabor. I made a drawing of the gun according to the plan he wished, and showed it to the King, after which I made the model. Great preparations were made for casting the gun. Thousands of people were engaged, and two large furnaces were built. At this time the King, being excited by the fear of a European expedition for the release of his prisoners, vented his anger on his own people also, and when they tried to run away, was after them like a lion upon his prey. I often wished I was chained with the other prisoners at Magdala, out of sight of the formerly good-hearted, but now so cruel, monarch. Once he made a short journey to Dembea for some days, and during that time we could breathe more freely; but he soon returned with 80,000 cows, and killed them round about our camp, leaving their carcases exposed to the sun and air, which after a few days caused much sickness among the people.

Many in the King's camp had nothing to eat, some were actually starving, and a considerable number of soldiers ran away, but were caught again, and massacred with their poor wives and innocent children. It was under such distressing circumstances that we had to make arrangements for the casting of that memorable gun. The King came several times daily to us, and sometimes I had long conversations with him, but was all the while trembling, because he would change so suddenly, and then it seemed as if he could not rest without shedding blood. At last the day came for casting the great gun. The two furnaces were heated to melt the metal, and thousands of people assembled. The King stood between the two furnaces, and taking hold of my hand, he said, " Now tell me what is to be done, and I will give orders to carry out thy will." Wherever I went the King accompanied me, holding me fast by the hand, which made me the more afraid, for I thought if the gun should prove a failure, he may perhaps put us all into the burning fiery furnace. When I saw that the metal was sufficiently heated, I asked the King to give orders to open the channel of the furnace, and the heated brass ran like a fiery serpent into the large mould prepared for it. After twenty minutes it was full, and the King was glad, and called the gun "Sebastopol." It was opened after three days and found well cast. Because there was no shot large enough for it, however, this gun was never used for the destruction of men, but on the contrary, was the means, in the hand of God, for saving our lives, and those of the prisoners in Magdala.*

After this it was again debated whether the Europeans should be killed, but the King said, " No, let them live and make a wagon for the

---

* See also Dr. H. Blanc's "Narrative of Captivity in Abyssinia," page 323.

gun." A large wagon was constructed, and when it was finished one of the chiefs said, "Now, your Majesty, we have what we wanted, and you have made yourself an everlasting name, because nothing was done like this in Ethiopia before, but only under your glorious reign. We are no more in need of these white asses," meaning the Europeans. But the Abyssinians could not transport this heavy piece of artillery, and were needing our suggestions and superintendence not only for its transmission, but also for making the road, which humanly speaking, preserved our lives once more.

The King continued so fearfully exasperated that he kept on killing many more of his own people. Some were burnt alive, others shot, hanged, and otherwise tortured to death. Once I remember three hundred poor victims being killed by starvation. It was a horrible sight. Executions in every possible way were devised. Men, women, and children, in high position or of low degree, both friends and enemies, all were treated alike when the King's anger was kindled; and nothing seemed to prevent him from doing his worst towards us but, in God's hand, the making of the great gun and subsequent wagon and road. One day he began to kill the servants of the missionaries, Messrs. Staiger and Brandeis, and he was just going to kill their masters also, when I implored him for counter orders. He yielded, saying, "*Eshy* (all right), for thy sake I will not do it." This was by no means the only time that I had the privilege of being the means of saving the lives not only of European missionaries and political prisoners, but of Abyssinians also. In those days we could realize the truth of the words in Psalm xci., "A thousand shall fall at thy side, and ten thousand at thy right hand; but it shall not come nigh thee."

We were seven months at Debra Tabor, where we
lost our fifth son, in consequence of the hardships
which we suffered. Night and day we were in
danger of our lives. Besides this, we were forced
to work like slaves, as the children of Israel did
for Pharaoh in Egypt, in order to satisfy King
Theodore's ambition to perform something which
no one before him had ever accomplished in
Abyssinia.

CHAPTER IX.

DEPARTURE FROM DEBRA TABOR—ARRIVAL
AT MAGDALA.

THE sad news reached England of the imprisonment of Mr. Hormutz Rassam and his colleagues, together with the re-capture of the old prisoners, and the Government decided to undertake a military expedition, in order to set them all at liberty. When King Theodore heard of the arrival of the expedition at Zullu (Ansley Bay), near Massowah, he resolved to leave Debra Tabor for Magdala. On the 1st of October, 1867, we left with the royal camp; but the King was unable to travel faster than one or two miles daily, as he had to have the roads made for his heavy artillery. Though the distance, therefore, between Debra Tabor and Magdala is only 200 miles, it took us six months to make the journey, on account of the broken character of the land through which we had to pass. The whole journey was stained with cruel bloodshed, which I had better not describe.

Owing to the bad food and the great heat I was taken seriously ill with dysentery, my strength gave way, and I was confined to bed. In this miserable condition I was transported from place to place. One night during my illness, when I was unconscious at intervals, as my dear wife was watching by me, fearing that in this sad condition I could not live long, she suddenly heard the tramp of soldiers coming towards our little tent. They unceremoniously entered, saying that the King had sent them for me. My wife replied, "My husband is so ill, he cannot walk." "Never mind," they shouted, "we will carry him." My wife saw at once that something fresh had happened, and she sat down and burst into a flood of tears. The soldiers carried me off by force, my poor wife wishing to follow, but they pushed her away, and dragged me along, through bushes, thorns, and jungle, till I reached the King, who was sitting before his tent. His complaint was : "I have heard that thou desirest to run away with thy brethren. I replied, "No, your Majesty, and I could not do so even if I wished." Heavy iron chains were then brought to put upon me, but the soldiers said to the King, "We can keep him without chains, for he is too ill to stir." So I lay on the damp ground, without bed or covering, till morning, and I saw the dew upon the grass had frozen during the night. In the morning the King saw that I was very ill, and sent me back to my family ; but next evening I was seized again, and banished far away from my wife and child, under the cruel treatment of a Pasha. I was not nursed or cared for, but left to die, and I wished and asked the Lord that He would end my great sufferings. However, it was not His will that I should die, but live. A woman was sent to me by my wife, who administered a medicine composed of linseed and cress seed, pounded together and mixed with water. This preparation I began to take, and from that time I got better, until my health was to a great extent restored.

After much trouble the King arrived with his camp at Beit Hor, on the edge of an immense gorge, 3,000 feet deep, and 7 miles wide. This

CHARACTER OF THE ABYSSINIAN HIGHLANDS.

stupendous wall of rock is on the edge of the Talanta Highlands, and forms one side of the deep gorge in which the Tshitta river is hidden. Though scarcely able to do anything, I had to act as engineer, and plan the road down to the bottom of this gorge and up on the other side to the height of Talanta. The other missionaries helped, and it was made, under our superintendence, by thousands of men. After a short time the artillery and the whole camp passed safely across to the plateau of Talanta. There the King rested for a while, and it was here that I suggested to him sending a message of peace to the Commander-in-Chief, Sir R. Napier, now Lord Magdala, whose expedition was already near. This brought me into the greatest danger of my life. The King wanted to fire his pistol at me, but the Lord stayed his hand. He then threw his spear, which flew against me, and missing my body, entered deeply into the ground.

Having thus narrowly escaped death, I was imprisoned under very close guardianship. After a few days the King said to me, "I think it will be better for me to be thy guardian, for my people might play me a trick, steal thee away from the camp, and carry thee to the rebels or to the English army." So he ordered my tent to be pitched near his own. It was a double silk tent, of beautiful colour both inside and out, which the King had presented to me some time before when I was in favour, and which I had never used for fear of arousing jealousy, till I was now imprisoned in it.*

After this the King, hearing the English army was approaching, proceeded to Magdala, but before reaching that place there was another road to be made, 4,000 feet deep, down to the River Beshielo,

---

* This tent can be seen at Katherine Backhouse's residence, Ashburn, Sunderland.

which is a tributary of the Blue Nile. On the other side of the river the road had to be made up to Magdala. This was hard work, but the King accomplished this great task, which often reminded me of Napoleon's road across the Simplon from Switzerland to Italy. King Theodore often worked hard himself, and thus encouraged the whole army, in dragging up the heavy pieces of artillery. For the large gun Sebastopol it took in some places 800 men to move it forward towards the contemplated fortress of Magdala.

The English army approached nearer and nearer every day, and the King was duly informed of their proceedings, which made him furious, and thus increased his cruelties and bloodshed. The least unpleasant thing was enough to make him give out a dreadful order for execution. The misery, starvation, and sickness in the King's camp were fearful; and we Europeans were often reminded by the people to make ourselves ready for death. They would say, "In a few days your turn for being killed will come also." One day the King called me and said, "Take this telescope and look over the gulf of the River Beshielo. There thou wilt see thy brethren, who have come from England to kill me. I am pleased to see those red jackets. I am glad that I have moved England to bring me the answer which Consul Cameron, the liar, promised to bring." The King became gloomy and dark as night, restless and angry as Saul, and I trembled with fear as I lifted up my heart to Him from whom alone the needed help cometh. None of the Europeans, who were imprisoned some with and others without chains, ventured to think that there could be any escape from the lion's mouth without a wonderful interposition of Divine grace, of which we did not deem ourselves worthy. We therefore prepared to die, and strengthened each other by prayer.

The missionaries had their camp at Islamgie, not far from the gate of the fortress of Magdala, while the political prisoners, Mr. Rassam and his party, were shut up in the fortress. One day the King called me, saying, " Let us go to Magdala. Call thy brethren and let us go together. I want to see my friend Rassam." I was very troubled at this, because I thought that King Theodore was going to hurl us down over the perpendicular wall of 400 feet, where many poor victims had been thrown during the last few days. Arrived at the fortress, the King released the prisoners from their chains, and called Mr. Rassam and his party, except Messrs. Stern and Rosenthal, and had a friendly conference with them in our presence. King Theodore said to Mr. Rassam : " As I have confidence in you, I present to you here my son Prince Ala-mayu. Take care of him, and be to him a father, for I know that my end will soon come, and that the time is near at hand when you shall stand by the side of my dead body. Then you will think, ' O King Theodore, how great was thy sinfulness !' But please do not judge me, because God will judge each one of us. I shall be judged as a king. Thou wilt be judged as an ambassador. Waldmeier will be judged as a missionary. And the poor beggars will be judged as beggars. God is my witness in heaven, and Waldmeier and his party on earth, that I am thy friend. I will pay thee another visit after God has shown us what He is going to do." With these words the conference terminated, and we returned to our huts and tents.

CHAPTER X.

EARLY in the morning of the 9th of April, gloomy clouds arose on the western horizon, and soldiers as well as others were afraid for the future; more especially ourselves and the political prisoners, of whom it was said by the natives, "These are the cause of the Anglo-Abyssinian war. They, of course, must be massacred." Mr. Rassam and his party, and my comrades and I were near each other that day, because the King called Mr. Rassam to come down from the fortress. King Theodore was restless and excited. He called me and said, "Let us go together and see what thy friends, my enemies the English army are doing." We soon reached an elevation, and he, looking through his telescope, exclaimed, "The English army is really proceeding rapidly, and it seems to me that they use the same road which thou planned and made, and for which we had so much trouble in breaking the hard rocks." The King had ordered the making of the road, and it turned out ultimately for his own destruction, and for the victory of the English army. "What a fool I am to have made the road," said the King, "but it appears that God wants to have it so." He returned very angry, and did not speak as usual when we went to our tents.

At four o'clock that afternoon the Abyssinian

MAGDALA.

prisoners began to cry out "*Exeo! Exeo!*" which means, "God have mercy on us." The King on hearing this, asked in great anger, "What is this?" When he was told that the prisoners were crying so, on account of being half-starved, he went himself in a great fury to the prison, and gave orders for a horrible butchery. The hands and feet of 335 of the poor victims were cut off, others were killed by the sword, and others shot, but ultimately all were thrown over a precipice 200 feet deep, where they were dashed to pieces, and became the food of vultures and hyenas. The place of execution was quite near to our tents and huts. The Abyssinians said that the King had become insane, and had begun his butchery with the natives, and intended to conclude it by executing all the Europeans. The heart-breaking cries of the victims, and the gushing rivulets of blood running down the slopes, were enough to make the strongest feel faint. We sighed, we prayed, we trembled, we wept. We tried to comfort each other; but who could help us? No one but our Father in heaven; because we ourselves and every native of Abyssinia would not have given a farthing for our lives. Night coming on, caused a stoppage in this horrible work, and we commended ourselves anew into the hands of our heavenly Father.

On the 10th of April, at six o'clock in the morning, two royal messengers came running hastily towards my tent, asking me to come at once to the King. We were much afraid, and the melancholy behaviour of the messengers made us the more anxious. However I went at once to the King, whom I found in a very dangerous mood. It seemed that he had called me for something about which he suddenly changed his mind. In consequence of this he let me stay in silence before him, whilst he looked moodily on to the ground, and after a short time he entered his pavilion. In about an hour he re-appeared, dressed in his court robes of gold and silver, and stood on an elevation overlooking the camp, giving orders that Mr. Rassam and his party should at once be brought up to the fortress of Magdala. This was a very threatening sign, and I feared that all was working together to bring about a horrible end to the Europeans who were in the King's power. While King Theodore was still standing, a messenger came with a letter from the Commander-in-Chief of the English army. I informed the King that the leader of the English expedition had sent him a letter. He replied. " Let the letter be kept in the messenger's pocket, and he can go back to his master, because I shall not receive it at all; it would not change my mind." The King then ordered his artillery-men to take charge of all the large guns, and bring them to Fala, a mountain plateau, from which he could easily look down upon the advancing English army.

King Theodore then said to me, " Go and take leave of thy family, because to-day thou wilt have the honour to die with a King." I went and said farewell to my dear wife and Rosa, not thinking that I should ever see them again in this world. Then I had to follow the King, who kept me barefooted all the while under guard; and as I walked along he saw the tears running down my face, and was surprised that I could not realize the joy and honour of dying with a King. It was not a long distance from Magdala to Fala, but it was a Via Dolorosa. When we arrived at Fala the King mounted his horse, and gathering about 7,000 men before him, began the following speech : " My children, be not afraid of these English soldiers, because they are

like the Philistines who made war against David;
but, remember, David smote them, and in the name
of God I shall conquer. Am I not a son of David
and Solomon? Has not God anointed me King of
Ethiopia? Am I not the old hero in the battle,
the pillar of fire to those who are afraid? Who
can bear my countenance? Has not God given me
victory after victory? To-day you shall see that I
who brought the English army to Abyssinia, shall
also obtain the victory over them. As our Abuna
Salama is dead, and according to our rules he should
absolve those who might fall in battle, I absolve,
in the name of God the Father, the Son, and the
Holy Ghost, every soldier who may lose his life in
battle against the Europeans."

After the King had finished his address the
whole Abyssinian army rushed down upon the 600
or 700 English soldiers who were already arrived
in the valley of Arogie and Damm Vouse. These
consisted of detachments from different regiments,
under Colonel Cameron, and Majors Chamberlain
and Pritchard; and the Madras Sappers, under
Major Prendergast. All the rest of the troops
were still coming up the Beshielo Valley. King
Theodore looked down from Fala, and got into a
fearful mood, so that I prepared myself for death
at all events. The King at once ordered his
artillery-men to charge the large guns (40 lbs.);
but it happened that one of these pieces of artillery
got a double charge, and therefore burst. The
King was standing quite near it, and we were only
about four yards distant when the disaster took
place. The King became furious and trembled
with rage, gnashing his teeth in his fury. All the
remaining guns were fired upon the English troops,
who in return opened fire upon the Abyssinians
with their breech-loader and Snider rifles, at the

rate of six volleys a minute, so that the latter were beaten at once, and mown down like grass by the bullets which fell upon them. The rest of the army turned back towards Fala, and the victory was won, but not by the Naval Rocket Brigade, nor by the Mountain Gun Battery of light steel guns. All these were as nothing, and would only have brought the English into trouble; but the victory was won by the breech-loading rifles.

The principal fighting was over, and only now and then we heard some guns, and saw rockets like smoky serpents flying over the battle-field. A cold rain came on, and behind the clouds the evening sun was setting in its golden garment. As I and my fellow prisoners watched it we never thought to see it rise again, because the King and his official staff had decided to execute all the prisoners in the coming night. As the remainder of the Abyssinian army came back, they reported the loss of a large number of soldiers. Many fathers, husbands, sons, and brothers, returned no more to their families in the camp of Islamgie, which caused a most dismal howling and lamentation from the relations of those who had fallen in the battle. The King repaired to his tent in the dusk of the evening, but he knew not what to do. His anger had made him almost insane, and he allowed his chiefs to strengthen him in the horrible plan he had formed of our execution. Exactly that day two years before, my fellow prisoners and I were taken captive at Debra Tabor.

During the night of the 10th of April, Mr. Flad and I were summoned before the King. Every one was afraid for us, and as we went along we trembled with fear, and could only silently look up to Him who knew and felt the agony of our hearts. But the King, instead of

being angry and exasperated as we expected, was
on the contrary very friendly and agreeably disposed. He said, "Make yourselves ready, and I
will send you with a message to Mr. Rassam."
The message was as follows: "I, the King of
Ethiopia, was under the idea that I was the only
strong man in my country, but as God has shown
me stronger men than I am, I ask thy advice in
order to bring about a reconciliation between myself and the Commander-in-Chief of the English
army." We conveyed the royal message to Mr.
Rassam in the fortress of Magdala, who proposed
to the King to send a messenger to the Commander-
in-Chief, proposing measures of peace. When we
returned to the King we found him totally changed,
and in an excited mood. We reported Mr. Rassam's message, and the King said, "There is no
hurry about sending to the English. Let God do
what He pleases. Now go to sleep." We were
quite prepared to obey this last command, for we
were completely exhausted from constant sorrow
and the hourly fear of being killed. We were only
allowed a short time for rest, as at four o'clock in
the morning the King again sent for us, and asked
our advice on the matter of peace. We advised
him to adopt Mr. Rassam's proposal, and he consequently sent Mr. Prideaux, Mr. Flad, and an Abyssinian named Alamy, with a petition for reconciliation and peace to the English Commander-in-Chief.

About nine o'clock the King went to a hill from
whence he looked through his telescope into the
English camp, exclaiming, "Oh, wonderful sight
in Abyssinia! This day an English army is on
Ethiopian soil!" The King waited impatiently for
an answer, but none came until three o'clock in the
afternoon, which brought him again into excitement and anger. We were afraid to present the

letter to the King, but were obliged to do so, as it was written in English, and we had to translate it into the Amharic language. The contents were as follows :—

"To His Majesty King Theodore.

"Your Majesty fought yesterday like a brave man, but you were conquered by our arts and power. We trust now that no more blood will be shed between us. If, therefore, your Majesty will submit to the Queen of England, and bring all the Europeans who are in your Majesty's hand and deliver them safely this day into the British camp, I will guarantee honourable treatment for yourself and all the members of your Majesty's family.

"Signed by the Commander-in-Chief,

"ROBERT NAPIER."

"What is the meaning of honourable treatment?" exclaimed the King, in a convulsion of excitement. "I know," he said, "it means to treat me as a prisoner. I, Theodore, a prisoner! That shall never be. Go away from me." Then we retired to a distance of fifty yards. The King then wrote a letter to the English Commander, giving full expression to his revengeful, angry, and despairing feelings, and sent it by the same messenger who had brought him the letter from the English camp.

The royal anger had now reached a fearful height, and the Abyssinian courtiers also were filled with deadly hatred against all the Europeans. They were prepared to destroy us, and only waited with impatience for the slightest sign from the King to carry out his cruel commands. Mr. Rassam and his party were still kept in the fortress, so that they had no idea of what was going on, although we could fully realize their great danger at this

moment, and our own also. Each one of us lifted
up his heart in prayer, asking the Lord to help us
safely through the valley of death. The King sat
upon a stone looking gloomy and dark as night.
By and by he suddenly roused himself up, took a
little water, and began to pray, making the sign of
the cross upon his breast, and bowing himself three
times low towards the ground. After this he took
a double barrelled pistol from his belt (but not the
one presented to him by the Queen of England),
and attempted to shoot himself through the head.
His courtiers and favourite officers ran to him in
fear, for they never saw their King in such a mood
before. They seized hold of his hands, but at that
moment the pistol discharged itself, and whizzed
harmlessly into the air, wounding only his ear.
"Oh, your Majesty," they exclaimed, "you have
not to die, but these Europeans, who are the cause
of this war, they must be massacred, now, *now*,
NOW." Then his courtiers tried to take from the
King his deadly weapons, which he refused to give
up. At last Ras Ingeda succeeded in getting them
under his care.

These blood-thirsty counsellors then began to
propose to the King the way in which they eagerly
desired to massacre the Europeans without exception, together with their wives and children. One
said, "There is a great wood house with a straw
roof, large enough for them. There we will burn
them alive." Another said, "No, let us cut their
hands and feet off, and let the English come and
take them away." A third said, "Let us hang
them all on yonder tree." And a fourth, "No, let
us kill them by guns, and then we will all run
away." I heard myself these horrible counsels,
and even more shocking plans for our execution
were proposed, the very hearing of which was like

a premature death. We poor persecuted victims were like sheep brought to the slaughter. Our prayer was, " Oh, Father in heaven, help us ! Take away the bitterness of death from us. Not our will but Thine be done. Strengthen us in these our last moments. Forgive us all our sins for Christ's sake, and lead us to the better land." We were surrounded by angry soldiers whose relatives were yesterday killed in the battle, and they were so eager and greedy for the destruction of our lives, that they began to sharpen their swords, for the King's order was expected at once. In a short time the royal messenger arrived, and our danger was at its height. It seemed as if the last moment must have come, and the cruel soldiers beamed with delight at the prospect of carrying out their deadly plans. I was summoned before the King, who looked at me and my brethren who were standing behind for some minutes without saying a word. Then he began : " *Sit down, be not afraid. I was advised to kill you and all the Europeans, but you have not done anything against me, and I shall not kill you. My death is near at hand, and I do not like that you should go before and accuse me in the presence of God. Go, and get your friends Rassam and party, and accompany them to the English camp.*" These were the wonderful words of the King. It was he who saved our lives, humanly speaking, for all the Abyssinian chiefs wanted to massacre us ; and the English expedition could not interfere in any way at that time without putting us in greater danger. But it was our own prayer-answering Father in heaven who thus influenced the King's mind, and brought about our deliverance, using the English expedition as a means to bring our sufferings to a conclusion.

Mr. Rassam and his party soon arrived, but the

King had previously said, "Please do not let me see my enemy Stern;" so I ran to meet Mr. Rassam, and told him to hide Dr. Stern, which he did. On the way the King called Mr. Rassam to his side, and took leave of him, saying, "Farewell, my friend, if we see each other no more in this life, we shall meet again beyond death. I trust thou wilt remain my friend, even when thou art out of my power. If, however, thou shouldst change thy kindly feeling towards me, then thou wilt hear, either of my death, or that I have become a monk." The King had always over-estimated Mr. Rassam's power, and after his deliverance he still imagined that his influence with the Commander-in-Chief would yet bring matters to what he considered a successful issue. On that memorable day, Mr. Mayer, Mr. Saalmüller, and I accompanied Mr. Rassam and his party, at sunset, into the English camp, where we arrived at half-past eight o'clock, and were received with a hearty welcome and joyful hurrahs. We were brought before Sir Robert Napier, who greeted us cordially, and gave orders for our lodging; but we could not sleep well, as there were still our own families and nine Europeans in King Theodore's hand.

The 12th of April was Easter day, and early in the morning, according to Abyssinian custom, cows and sheep were slaughtered for the celebration of the feast. The King sent a letter by Mr. Bender, asking the Commander-in-Chief of the English army to receive 1,000 cows and 500 sheep as a token of peace and friendship. Messrs. Flad, Mayer, Bender, Saalmüller, and I had been sent by Sir Robert Napier to King Theodore in the morning, in order to ask him to deliver our families and the rest of the Europeans to the English Commander. We were not long on the way, but knowing the changeable moods of the King, our hearts were filled with anxiety, hope and fear by turns taking possession of us, as life and death seemed again on the balance. We found the King sitting on a stone near the road, in a tolerably good mood. We delivered our message from Sir Robert Napier, which was to the effect, that he desired all the Europeans should repair to the English camp; and Samuel, Mr. Rassam's dragoman, and Detchatch Alamy told the King that when the Europeans were all gone to the English army, the cows and sheep would be received with thankfulness. After this the King gave orders that our families and all the other Europeans were to depart in peace. How joyfully I went to my dear wife and Rosa, who were still in fear and trembling, to tell them to come off with me as quickly as possible to the English camp! Then I went to take leave of the King, who exclaimed, with tears in his eyes, " Farewell, my dear friend, I loved thee as I loved John Bell." In the afternoon, at three o'clock, all the Europeans arrived in the British camp. Their number, including children, was fifty-nine persons. After so many years of trial and perplexity, of fear and danger of our lives, to find ourselves again in liberty and peace was almost too much for our hearts to realize. It seemed more like a dream, and we could only grasp its reality by degrees. " When the Lord turned again the captivity of Zion, we were like them that dream. Then was our mouth filled with laughter, and our tongue with singing. Then said they among the heathen, the Lord hath done great things for them. The Lord hath done great things for us; whereof we are glad."—Psalm cxxvi. 1–3.

Preparations were made early in the morning of the 13th of April for storming Magdala, and by nine o'clock the whole army was on foot. Mr. Flad and I were chosen by the Commander-in-Chief to accompany the army, and show them the best roads and the most advantageous position for the attack. I had to go with General Charles Staveley, to help to get the position of Salassie, a mountain opposite Magdala, and near enough for good guns. After this I received orders from General Merryweather to disarm all the Abyssinian soldiers, which was very hard work. In the midst of the stir and confusion I saw four men carrying a wounded soldier towards me. This proved to be the same man who treated my poor wife so rudely, pushing her on to the ground, when I was taken prisoner two years before at Gaffat. He had requested his companions to carry him to me, so that he might entreat my forgiveness. He was mortally wounded, but said, "I cannot die before I am reconciled with Mr. Waldmeier."

During that time the English army was preparing for the attack on Magdala. The storming of the fortress began in the afternoon, and the rocky mass, though undefended, received many blows in vain. The English artillery did their business very badly. I was quite ashamed that the Abyssinians should see such failure. The only advantage gained over the natives was again by the breech-loader and Snider rifles, which showered a hail of bullets upon the enemy. King Theodore stood with fifty of his faithful officers on the brow of his fortress, and saw how the English were advancing, whilst his own soldiers were running away. His armour bearer said, "Your Majesty, let us lay down our arms and surrender?" "No," said the King, "Let us not fall into men's hands, they have no pity; let us fall into God's hand." He then took his pistol and shot himself through the head, falling instantly dead on the ground. Fifteen minutes afterwards the English soldiers entered Magdala, and Sir Robert Napier, Mr. Rassam, and I stood by the dead body of the King. I was asked, " Is this the body of King Theodore?" I replied, " Yes," and turning to Mr. Rassam, reminded him of the King's words a few days before. After this the dead body was carried into Mr. Rassam's house, thus paying him the promised visit. On the 14th of April King Theodore was buried in the church at Magdala. The native prisoners were released, who up to this time had been in chains in Magdala; and the English flag was hoisted on the fortress for the first time. Queen Terrowork, the daughter of King Ubie, was also a prisoner in Magdala. She was at once set free, and I was charged to accompany Her Majesty to the English camp, with Prince Alamayu, who was then six years of age. Magdala was subsequently partly blown up by powder and destroyed.

The stirring events of these few days filled the world with the wonderful news : " Conquest of the English expedition! Prisoners set free! King Theodore dead! Magdala destroyed!" These great deeds were not accomplished by the skill, arts, or power of the English army, because, with the exception of the breech-loading rifles, there was little to admire in the warlike proceedings; and if King Theodore had not concentrated his forces at Magdala, and been surrounded by enemies in his own kingdom, and forsaken by his own army, it would have been impossible for a foreign power thus to gain the victory over him. Just as surely as the Egyptian army, under European officers, was annihilated in the year 1877 by King John of Abyssinia ; and as Hicks Pasha's army was utterly destroyed at El Obeyed, in Kordofan, by the

Mahdi's power; so would the Abyssinia expedition have failed, even under Sir Robert Napier's wise arrangements, if the whole country had not revolted against their King, and favoured the English army both on their coming in and going out. Besides this, King Theodore was unfairly treated with regard to his gift of 1,000 cows and 500 sheep which were a sign of peace and friendship, and which Mr. Samuel reported would be thankfully received as soon as the Europeans should all have reached the English camp. It was on this understanding that he allowed the Europeans to depart, but on their arrival the cows and sheep which accompanied them were sent back, while King Theodore still believed his present to have been accepted. He was, therefore, greatly surprised when the English forces approached Magdala by storm. He said, " I delivered the prisoners to the English expedition on being informed of the acceptance of my present of 1,000 cows and 500 sheep as a sign of good will; and now they come and fight with me again." In this matter the King was deceived, which was also acknowledged in the account of the Abyssinian expedition in the *Illustrated London News*.

I do not judge the conduct of Captain Cameron, Mr. H. Rassam, Dr. Stern, the French Consul Lejean, and other Europeans in Abyssinia, but leave that to the readers of my statements. Surely this tragic story of England's dealings with Abyssinia will be helpful to civilized Christian nations the world over; also to missionaries and politicians in being more careful in their dealings with uncivilized, or half-civilized, countries. I am fully convinced that this Anglo-Abyssinian war, with all its bloodshed, and enormous expense, might have been spared, by a nobler way of dealing with King Theodore, and that the prisoners might have been set at liberty without such an accumulation of danger, fear, and perplexity.

The British army in Abyssinia consisted of 12,000 English and Indian soldiers, 20,000 servants and transporters, 8,000 camels, 12,400 mules, 8,000 oxen, 200 donkeys, and 45 elephants. The time occupied was eight months from the starting of the expedition until its termination, and the total expenditure was £10,000,000 sterling; £6,000,000 being paid by England, and the remaining £4,000,000 by India. 50 lives were lost by accident, sickness, and war. When the English expedition was preparing for Abyssinia, Joseph Abdelnur Faker, of Beirut, was ordered to go up to Brummana and buy as many mules as he could to send to Abyssinia. Who would have thought at that time that one of the released prisoners from Abyssinia should come up to Brummana and establish a mission there?

> "God moves in a mysterious way,
> His wonders to perform."

Although the expedition was not sent to Abyssinia purposely to release missionaries who went there on their own responsibility; but rather to liberate the English Consul, and the British Envoy, Mr. Rassam, and his party; yet the missionaries, and all Europeans of different nationalities, who were kept by King Theodore in bondage, were thus set at liberty by English intervention; and heartfelt were their thanks and gratitude, first to Almighty God, who was the overruling power, and then to the English expedition, and its noble leader, Lord Napier of Magdala.

CHAPTER XI.

DEPARTURE FROM MAGDALA.

ON the 16th of April we left Magdala, the scene of our fears and joys, our bondage and deliverance, and crossed, for the last time in our lives, to all human probability, the wild river Beshielo, and its stupendous gorge of 4,000 feet in depth. We arrived on the 18th at the plain of Talanta, where the British army was gathered, and on the 20th Lord Napier had a review of his troops, addressing them in the following words :—

"Soldiers and sailors of the army of Abyssinia : —The Queen and the people of England entrusted to you a very arduous and difficult expedition, to release our countrymen from a long and painful captivity, and to vindicate the honour of England, which had been outraged by Theodore, King of Abyssinia. I congratulate you with all my heart on the way in which you have fulfilled the commands of our Sovereign. You have traversed, often under a tropical sun, or amidst storms of rain and sleet, 400 miles of mountainous and rugged country. You have crossed many steep and precipitous mountain ranges to the height of 10,000 feet, where food supply was at times scanty. In four days you passed the formidable chasm of the Beshielo, and came within sight of our enemies; and when some of you had been for many hours without food or water, you defeated the army of

King Theodore, which poured down on you from its lofty fortress in full confidence of victory. A host of many thousands laid down their arms at your feet. You have captured and destroyed upwards of thirty pieces of artillery, many of great weight and efficiency, with ample stores of ammunition. After you forced the entrance of his fortress, King Theodore himself who never showed mercy, distrusted the offer of it held out to him by me, and died by his own hand. You have released not only the British captives, but those of other friendly nations. You have unloosed the chains of more than ninety of the principal chiefs of Abyssinia. Magdala also, where so many victims have been slaughtered, has been committed to the flames, and now remains only a scorched rock.

"Our complete and rapid success is due firstly to the mercy of God, whose hand, I feel assured, has been over us in a just cause, and secondly, to the high spirit with which you have been inspired. Indian soldiers have forgotten the prejudices of race and creed, to keep pace with their European comrades. Never did an army enter upon war with more honourable feeling than yours. This it is which has carried you through so many fatigues and difficulties. Your sole anxiety for the moment was to arrive where you could come close to the enemy. The remembrance of your privations will pass away quickly, but your gallant exploit will live in history. The Queen and the people of England will appreciate and acknowledge your service. On my part, as your commander, I thank you for your devotion to duty, and the good discipline you have maintained throughout. Not a single complaint has been made against our soldiers, of fields injured, or villagers wilfully molested either in person or property. We must not, however,

GROUP OF TRACHYTE MOUNTAINS IN TIGRE.

forget what we owe to our comrades, who have been labouring for us in the sultry climate of Zullu, in the Pass of Kameylea, or in the monotony of the posts, which maintained our communication. One and all would have given everything they possessed to be with us, and they deserve our heartfelt gratitude. I shall watch over you safely to the moment of your re-embarking; and to the end of my life I shall remember with pride that I have commanded you.—R. NAPIER."

On the 21st we left Talanta, and crossed, with a detachment of the expedition, the deep chasm of the Tshitta river. On our arrival at Beit Hor we took leave of all our native friends, relations, and scholars, with whom we bowed in prayer before the throne of grace, committing each other to our heavenly Father's care. Hailu Mariam, my Timotheus, took his Bible, and went to his native heathen Galla country as a preacher of the Gospel. Our parting was hard and sorrowful indeed, for we felt that on earth we should see each other's faces no more. We travelled southward on the high land, and then descended into the deep valley of the great river Takkassie, with its hot mineral spring. This river separates the eastern province of Tigré from the western one of Amhara, and after a long and precipitous decline, flows down from the Abyssinian Alps into the low country of the Kunama tribes, and runs directly northwards through the midst of Soudan, under the name of Atbara, till it unites with the Nile about twenty miles above Berber. Between the Nile and the Atbara was the old kingdom of Meroë, where are still remaining two ancient temples and an avenue of sphinxes, which date back to the time of King Tirhakah, of the twenty-fifth Ethiopian dynasty (Isa. xxxvii. 9), whose name is inscribed at Medinet

Abu. This river, though very large and powerful, in summer loses itself in the sandy plain of Soudan, to re-appear at intervals, which shows evidently the existence of a subterranean connection on a more water-tight clay bed under the sand. In July it receives the tropical rainfalls of Abyssinia, and in August the Atbara and Blue Nile swell into two mighty streams, which cause the fertilizing inundation of the Nile in Lower Egypt. Passing on our way the Alps of Lasta, Doba, Wodshera, Enderta, and Haramad, we arrived at Senafie, in Tigré. We saw in the distance the Bahet Mountain, where not long ago most interesting plants belonging to the Lobeliaceæ were discovered, ten feet in height, with a fleshy stem, bright green leaves, and a candle-like spike of blue blossoms. The only localities known where this plant grows are in Abyssinia, 13,000 feet above the sea. From Senafie we descended through the bed of the river Komayle to the port of Zullu, forty days being occupied in travelling from the heights of Magdala down to the Red Sea. The difference of climate was very great, from 10,000 feet above the sea at Magdala, where we had cold frosty nights and rain, and Zullu on Ansley Bay, where the thermometer stood at 130° (Fahrenheit) at noon, and the heat was intense.

The small strip of land between the Red Sea and the Abyssinian Mountains is called Samhara, and there towards the south are the natural salt pits which supply the whole of Abyssinia. The water of the Red Sea contains more salt than other sea water. At high tides and storms it overflows its banks, and the water runs over the plain, forming great pools on the lower land. The great heat condenses the water, and the salt remains crystalized on the ground like ice, one or two inches in

RHYNCHOPETALUM MONTANUM (LOBELIACEÆ).

thickness. The Danakeel Gallas cut the salt into blocks, one inch thick, two inches wide, and seven inches long, and carry them to the highlands for sale in the markets. These pieces of salt are used as small money in the whole of Abyssinia. I was always in the habit of exchanging twenty-six pieces of salt for one dollar.

After having been half roasted in the great heat, I was glad to embark with my dear wife and Rosa, and the other prisoners, for Suez. From thence we went by rail to Cairo and Alexandria. During the whole journey we were supplied with the necessary provisions and assistance by the order of Lord Napier, who paid each one's travelling expenses to his respective country. When the English Commander-in-Chief left the Abyssinian territory, he presented to Kasa (the present King John) one mountain battery of steel guns and smooth bore muskets for one regiment, in acknowledgment of his kind assistance to the expedition. The people of Abyssinia were astonished that the English left the country to itself, and did not take possession or even nominate a Government for it; but it would be too costly for England to take up Ethiopia at the present time. In the future, however, I feel sure that some European Power will exert its dominion over that healthy and fertile country, with its intelligent inhabitants.

CHAPTER XII.

PRESENT CONDITION OF ABYSSINIA.

AS many people will like to hear how matters are progressing in that distant and interesting country since the English expedition left, I will quote from a letter which I wrote some time ago in *The Friend of Missions*. Since the death of King Theodore, the Abyssinian kingdom, or empire, has been divided into two parts. The first includes Tigré on the eastern, and Amhara on the western side of the river Takkassie, under the name of Abyssinia, over which King John now reigns. The second is called the kingdom of Shoa, south of Abyssinia, and is under the dominion of King Menelek, the son of King Hailu Melekot, of Shoa. He was at school at Magdala when I was there, and I often saw him afterwards with King Theodore. One day, however, he ran away from Magdala, and went to Shoa, where he subsequently ascended his father's throne. Kasa,* with his superior arms, soon subdued all rebellion, was crowned King of Abyssinia, and assumed the name of John. He annihilated the Egyptian army in the year 1877, by which means he obtained a large supply of good guns, and plenty of ammunition. One year later, wishing to enlarge his dominions, King John declared war against King Menelek, who

---

* Kasa was his name when he rebelled against King Theodore, but *he* calls himself now, John, King of kings of Abyssinia.

JOHN, THE PRESENT KING OF ABYSSINIA.

was already in trouble because his own wife had revolted against him, though her rebellion was soon quelled, and the Queen and her party forgiven. Meanwhile, King John was fast approaching with his destructive army, and the news filled the hearts of the Shoa people with terror. Nevertheless, King Menelek stayed at Letsche, and hoping to end the matter peacefully without bloodshed, he sent his ambassadors to King John to ask for peace, but they were sent back with a refusal, and the Abyssinians, having already crossed the frontier, began to plunder and kill. The people of Shoa naturally expected that Menelek would gather an army and fight against the enemy, but he remained quietly in Letsche, only putting his treasures in safety. Ultimately negotiations were re-commenced between the two kings, John insisting that Menelek should acknowledge him as his chief, and his country should be tributary. Menelek was forbidden to cross the northern boundary of Shoa, and was also expected to give soldiers to King John. The following conditions of peace were accordingly drawn up between the two kingdoms on the 4th of March, 1878 :

1. King Menelek must pay tribute to King John.

2. He must supply King John's army with provisions when in his dominion.

3. He must cease to be called King of kings of Ethiopia, and only be called King of Shoa.

4. He must give King John assistance in any time of need.

5. King John must give Menelek help in time of need.

6. King Menelek shall rule the Wollo Galla Mohammedans, who are located between Shoa and Abyssinia.

7. King Menelek must build Christian churches

in the Wollo Galla country and introduce Christianity there.

8. King Menelek must give free passage to King John's army as far as Debra Lebanos, a convent in Shoa.

Agreed to, and signed by the two kings on the 14th March, 1878.

King John, now Emperor of Ethiopia, crowned Menelek with his own crown, as King of Shoa, on the 26th of March, 1878; and proclaimed by his herald, "I have crowned my son Menelek, as King of Shoa; honour him, as you honour me."

In consequence of the agreement between the two kingdoms, King John, who was fully under the power of priestcraft, was anxious to establish one form and creed of the Christian religion, throughout the whole Abyssinian Empire. This was previously tried by King Theodore with regard to the Abyssinian Jews and Mohammedans, but he could not succeed. There is a dogmatic difference between the Christians of Shoa, and those of Abyssinia; as the Shoa people believe in three births of Jesus Christ—the first from the Father, the second from the Virgin Mary, and the third by the Holy Spirit at His baptism in Jordan; whilst the people of Abyssinia accept only two births of Christ, viz., the one from the Father and the other from the Virgin Mary. On this occasion, a large Council was held in Shoa, and those who believed in three births were compelled to renounce their views, and adopt the creed of King John. The Shoa people call this belief *Kara Haimanot*, or the knife creed, because, they say, it cuts off one birth of Jesus Christ. At that council it was also concluded that Christ was perfect God, and not a man. Against this doctrine three monks began to protest, saying that Christ was perfect man and perfect God, and

AN ABYSSINIAN MAMHER, OR TEACHER OF THEOLOGY, WITH HIS STUDENTS.

they quoted before the King, the passage in Phil. ii. 6 —8 : " Who being in the form of God, thought it not robbery to be equal with God : but made Himself of no reputation, and took upon Him the form of a servant, and was made in the likeness of men : and being found in fashion as a man, He humbled Himself, and became obedient unto death, even the death of the cross." King John and his theological *Mamherotsch* (teachers), upon hearing this, became very angry ; and the King exclaimed, " I do not permit anyone to insult my Lord Jesus Christ, by saying that He was also a perfect man, according to the sayings of these monks :" and he gave orders to cut out the tongues of these three monks, which was done instantly. The accompanying picture illustrates the usual dress of the Abyssinian priests, who are the only people in the country who wear white turbans, and constantly have the cross in their hands. The students dress in sheep skins, and with their little baskets, beg from house to house, singing psalms and the Ave Maria. Mohammedans, Jews, and heathens, were forced to adopt Christianity without instruction, and those who resisted were beaten and killed. King John and King Menelek then travelled together through the Wollo Galla country, plundering, killing, burning and baptizing ; an astonishing way of propagating Christianity.

Soon after this, Mr. John Mayer, my brother missionary under King Theodore, returned to Shoa, in connection with the St. Chrischona Mission. This induced King John to ask King Menelek to send all Europeans away ; but the latter answered, " I do not like to shut my country against Europeans, because I love them." This he has really proved, for he sent Mr. Mayer and his fellow workers to the heathen Baly Gallas to preach the Gospel, and at the same time he supported and protected them, as they were still under his dominion. Till quite lately Mr. Mayer sent me very encouraging accounts of his missionary success there. King Menelek also wrote me a long letter, asking me to come to him to preach the Gospel among the Gallas. There were also Swedish (from the Stockholm Fosterland's Stiftelsen Expedition) and Roman Catholic missionaries working among them. King Menelek had also European workmen engaged in his kingdom, who were not connected with any mission, but were well treated and paid for their services, and he gave them full liberty to leave whenever they wished. The King also did what he could to suppress the slave trade.

King John, on the contrary, is an enemy to all Europeans, and shuts his country against them. He does not allow any missionary to enter his dominions. The Bibles and Testaments printed by the British and Foreign Bible Society in the common Amharic language, which were distributed between 1858 and 1868 by Bishop Gobat's missionaries, were diligently sought for by the King and burned. It is reported that King John is much more cruel than King Theodore. He goes about plundering villages with his large army, destroying the homes of the poor peasants, and butchering men and women for trifling causes. He is a conqueror and a wild warrior, but not able to rule with justice, nor to improve the condition of his country and people. Though King Theodore was hard, the people of Abyssinia much wish that his time could come back again. Poor Abyssinia is more than ever a country of bloodshed and horrors. Oh ! when will Ethiopia stretch out her hands unto the Lord and have peace !

At the beginning of 1886, King John wrote a

WOMAN OF SHOA.

letter to King Menelek to Entoto, asking him to expel at once all the Protestant missionaries and Europeans from his country, or to force them to embrace the Abyssinian form of Christianity. King Menelek, who was kind and good to all the Europeans, was greatly disappointed at these forcible measures, but, as his vassal, he dared not disobey King John. So he recalled Mr. Mayer, who was still superintending the Baly Galla Mission, and told him that he was very sorry to convey to them King John's order, but as the missionaries could not embrace the distorted Christianity of the Abyssinians, they must leave the country. Mr. Mayer went back to his mission station, where all the people and school children were gathered together, and informed his family, fellow-missionaries, and all the people, that the whole missionary party must leave the country. For several days the people were howling and weeping, and it was heart-breaking for all thus to separate probably for ever. The missionaries then travelled through Fare towards Tajurrah. The Swedish missionaries joined them, and many other people, and on the 10th of February they entered the wilderness, and were exposed to many dangers. The caravan consisted of 1,000 men and 1,000 camels. Mr. Mayer writes under date of May 27th, 1886 : " I am very sorry to hear from the people that King Menelek again allows the traders to carry on their horrible business of the slave-trade. This sad news was confirmed by the fact that several slave dealers brought 600 young Galla girls, with many boys, and joined our caravan towards Tajurrah. When we arrived at Kurfa, on February 28th, we were told that a caravan had been attacked by robbers the day before, when twenty-two persons were killed. We went round about in the neighbourhood a little, and found the twenty-two bodies in different places, but half eaten up by the hyenas. After leaving this horrible place we arrived, at the beginning of April, at a deep ravine, and then upon the Salt Sea of Asal. For one hour we walked upon this salt sea, just as we should walk on a frozen lake in Switzerland. The heat was intense, and the land, of course, without vegetation. Arrived in Tajurrah, which is occupied by the French, the Governor received us very kindly, and sent us on one of his war vessels to Aden. One of our missionary brethren had to remain behind, because our money was stolen by some Haussa Gallas, and the French power was too weak to compel them to give it up. Out of what they had stolen, however, they gave us back a little, which was just enough to pay our passage from Aden to Jerusalem, where I now am, poorer than I ever have been in my life; but the Lord will provide."

NATURAL FORTIFICATION OF DEBRA DAMO IN TIGRE.

CHAPTER XIII.

AFTER the hot journey on the Red Sea, and across the sultry sandy plain between Suez and Cairo, we spent a short time at the latter place, where we were very kindly received by Mr. H. Rappard, son-in-law of Bishop Gobat, and now Inspector of the St. Chrischona Mission. Then we returned to Jerusalem to Bishop Gobat, by whom we had been sent out as missionaries. There I gave a public account of our mission in Abyssinia, and of our sufferings and wonderful deliverance. We brought a number of our Abyssinian scholars with us to Jerusalem, and they were put into Bishop Gobat's School, and Mr. Schneller's Orphanage, after which they were sent to St. Chrischona and trained as missionaries. They have now gone back to Abyssinia in connection with the London Society for Promoting Christianity among the Jews, to preach the Gospel to the Falashas, as no Europeans are allowed to enter Abyssinia. These native missionaries are doing excellent work; but it is a pity that, according to the old agreement, their converts still have to be baptized by Abyssinian priests, and thus become members of the Abyssinian church. The good Bishop Gobat was often attacked by the High Church party, for having sent out lay missionaries to Abyssinia, and not ordained clergymen; but it would have been impos-

L

sible for the latter to have organized a mission in that fanatical land. The pious Bishop himself, did not highly value human ordination for a country like Abyssinia, where it might be more damaging than helpful to young theologians, who seek to become true followers of Jesus Christ. He preferred sending out lay missionaries, who would be able to work with their own hands, as Paul did, at the same time that they were engaged in preaching the Gospel. It was this mechanical work which enabled us to reach all classes of the people, and was the means in God's hands of prolonging the lives of the political prisoners, and finally saving us from a cruel death, for that great blessing of preaching the Gospel to others also.

Mr. Bender and his family, with Mr John Mayer and his family, subsequently returned to Abyssinia; but Mr. and Mrs. Bender were soon called to their heavenly rest; and Mr. Mayer went from Abyssinia to Shoa, where, as before stated, he was for some time engaged in a most interesting work among the Baly Gallas, into whose language he has already translated the New Testament. Mr. Saalmüller remained in Jaffa, in connection with Dr. Hoffmann's Mission; and Mr. W. Staiger came to Beirut in connection with the Mission of the Free Church of Scotland. As our heavenly Father had so wonderfully delivered us out of thousands of dangers, I desired more than ever before to dedicate the remainder of my life to the Lord's service, and decided to remain in the Eastern mission field. At Jaffa, on my way to Jerusalem, I made the acquaintance of Miss Arnot, who proposed to me to go to Beirut and help Mrs. Elizabeth Bowen Thompson's work in the British Syrian Schools. For this purpose she wrote to Beirut, and thus unconsciously prepared the way for my future mission work. In all these things can we not distinctly trace the hand of the Lord leading His children?

During our stay in Jerusalem we lodged at Bishop Gobat's house, and generally spent the evenings with him and his family. One evening we were speaking much about Abyssinia, when Mrs. Gobat, with a vivid recollection of her own experiences in that country, asked whether we were not afraid of the hyenas there, because our houses were surrounded by wild beasts at night, and they were continually howling and disturbing our rest. Whilst we were speaking of these animals, a drunken man passed by, making a loud noise, but as the shutters were closed and we could not see him, we only heard his voice. Rosa, our little daughter of five years old, hearing the cry of the drunkard, said in the Abyssinian language: " Papa, the hyenas of this country do not cry like those in Abyssinia."

When we left Jerusalem, Bishop Gobat also gave me letters of introduction to Mrs. Bowen Thompson, and to Mr. and Mrs. Mentor Mott, who received us into their own house at Beirut, and treated us very kindly.

After having passed through so much sorrow and anxiety from being, as it were, continually on the verge of death, it was no wonder that our health began to give way, and it was deemed expedient that we should remove quickly into the cooler climate of Mount Lebanon. Here we were introduced to Mr. and Mrs. Benton, of the American Mission at B'hamdoun, and Mrs. Benton took great care of my dear suffering wife, for which we were very thankful. After some days we went with Mrs. Bowen Thompson and Mrs. Mott to Ain Zahalta, where there is a branch of the British Syrian Mission. At that place I left my wife and

Rosa for some time, to the kind care of Mrs. Thompson and Mrs. Mott, whilst I went home to Europe to take measures for the re-establishment of the mission in Abyssinia.

When I reached my home in Lörrach, after ten years' absence, my uncle and aunt, who had adopted me as their son on the death of my parents, did not recognise me. I said to them, " I am come from a far off land, and am weary and hungry, will you not give me rest and comfort?" " Oh, yes," they said, " only please to wait a little ; " and still, not having recognised me, they continued, " we have a son away as a missionary in Abyssinia, but we do not know where he is now." Then I could no longer disguise myself, and replied, " I am that son, just come from Abyssinia." Surprised and deeply touched, they wept for joy ; and my aunt said, " Let me look into thy eyes. Yes," she cried, " they are the eyes of Theophilus, but where is thy fair hair, that hair of which I was so proud, where is it gone ?" Then I explained that having to stand in the sun before King Theodore, without being allowed any protection, my head had become so swelled and painful that in a few days the hair fell off. " Never mind," she answered, " with hair or without, we are thankful to see thee once more before we die." The old meeting which was held in our house before I left home, was still continued, and on account of my having just returned from Abyssinia, it became so crowded that we decided to build a new room, which also soon became too small. Then a large house was erected for the sum of £2,000, which is used for meetings as well as for a regular place of worship.

During my stay in Europe, I wrote a book in German (afterwards translated into Swedish, French, and Arabic), called " Ten Years in Abyssinia ;" and

I went about the country lecturing, and seeking to interest God's people about that benighted country. I had a call from Geneva, to engage in temporary home mission work there, and wrote to my wife, asking her to come to Europe. Only a few days after this an offer came from the Committee of the British Syrian Schools, in London, asking me to assist Mrs. Bowen Thompson, as Inspector of her Schools in Beirut, Damascus, and Mount Lebanon. News from Abyssinia also informed us that circumstances were not favourable for our return to that country, so I accepted Syria from the Lord as my second mission field, and sent a telegram to my wife, who was then at St. John's Hospital in Beirut, telling her to remain. The telegram arrived just as her luggage was being carried on board the Austrian steamer. So she remained in Beirut, which was good for her, as her health was still weak after the birth of a little son, three months before. Here I should like to acknowledge the great kindness of Sister Sophie Gräff, in taking such good care of my dear wife.

After an absence of ten months, I returned in May, 1869, to my wife and to the work of the British Syrian Schools. I hired a house near to the head quarters of Mrs. Thompson and Mrs. Mott, and began to enter upon my duties as Inspector of the branch schools; but, as I did not know the Arabic language, I had to study very hard, and my being nearly forty years of age made the acquisition of this very difficult language much more arduous.

CHAPTER XIV.

IN May, 1869, I arrived at Beirut in Syria, where I joined the mission work of the British Syrian Schools, and received much kindness from Mr. and Mrs. Mentor Mott, and Mrs. Elizabeth Bowen Thompson, who introduced me to the work.

Beirut is beautifully situated in the plain of Phœnicia. It is unquestionably a very ancient city, and is probably referred to in the Bible, though it seems uncertain whether it is identical with the Berith mentioned in Judges viii. 33. It is certain, however, that the worship of Baal was followed both here and at Byblus, the ancient Gebal or Jebeil (Ezekiel xxvii. 9). It is difficult to identify Beirut with Berothai of 2 Sam. viii. 8., from which David took exceeding much brass; for as there are no traces of copper mines in the neighbourhood, it is not easy to see how there should be much brass there, unless it had been accumulated by traders from Cyprus. We know, however, that the Phœnicians colonized Cyprus, and developed a lively trade between the two countries in the time of David and Solomon. It was during this time that the copper mines of Cyprus were being worked, and the precious metal may therefore have been taken thence to Berothai, from which place David brought it to Jerusalem. It is reported that the Phœnicians came to Cornwall,

PORT OF BEIRUT

from which place they took tin for mixing it with copper, and thus making brass at Beirut. Tyre, Sidon, Beirut, Byblus, and Tripoli, were important cities along the Phœnician coast of the Mediterranean; and though Tripoli is not so old as the others, they are all very interesting on account of their antiquity. In all these cities idolatry was practised, and the gods of the Phœnicians worshipped. The god Chronos ($X\rho\acute{o}\nu o\varsigma$), subsequently known in that neighbourhood as Baal-Berith, was worshipped in Beirut, and also the goddess Astarte, who was represented as a woman standing on a crescent, like the Virgin Mary in some Christian churches.

On the heights of Lebanon, which command a general view of Beirut and Phœnicia, we still find ruins of ancient temples, as at Deir el Kalla, near Beit Mary. An ancient Phœnician aqueduct was constructed, through which the water from Ain Arrar, four miles north-east of Brummana, was conveyed in stone tubes to the old city round Deir el Kalla, traces of which can still be easily seen. The aqueduct is called by the people, the "Kana Zobeida," or Channel of Zenobia, though it is mentioned in the history of this country that it was made by the Phœnicians, and only repaired when out of order by Zenobia, Queen of Palmyra. I do not think that this aqueduct carried the water of Ain Arrar to Beirut, as some writers say, but the water was only carried to the temple and city of Deir el Kalla by the way of Babdat and Brummana. The bridge of Zobeida also, not far from Mansourieh, over the River Magoras which falls into the sea at Beirut, is a wonderful work of ancient architecture, 160 feet high. The water of the Magoras was taken high enough up, and carried by a canal along the right side of the river over the bridge of

Zobeida, and then through a tunnel and at low places over arches to Beirut. These water-works the inhabitants of Beirut could easily protect, but the aqueduct between Ain Arrar and Deir el Kalla on Mount Lebanon was beyond their control. The rivers which came down from Mount Lebanon and united with the sea were regarded as holy by the Phœnicians, like the river Damur, south of Beirut; the Magoras, at Beirut; and the Lycus, north of that city; as well as the Nahr Ibrahim, or the river Adonis. All these rivers were worshipped in the olden time, and temples were consequently erected near them.

Some say the name of Beirut was derived from the word *Beer* which means a well, and there are many at this place; but Sauchoniathou, the oldest Phœnician historian, says that the wife of the god Elyon of Byblus was called Βηρούθ (Beyrouth), and as Beirut was so near Byblus its people followed the same kind of idolatry, and called it after the name of the goddess. The Jewish king Herod Agrippa I. preferred to reside at Beirut, and he beautified the city by constructing a most splendid amphitheatre and many other public buildings. Josephus relates that Titus celebrated his victory over Jerusalem, together with the birthday of his father Vespasian, by gladiatorial plays in this amphitheatre, when hundreds, and perhaps thousands, of captive Jews were thrown to wild beasts and thus perished.

From the third to the sixth century Beirut was a celebrated seat of learning. Many schools and colleges were there, open for thousands of students from far and near, especially for the study of jurisprudence, and Beirut was then called the nurse of the sciences and the mother of the laws. On May 20th, 529 A.D. Beirut was totally destroyed by a terrible earthquake which visited the whole Syrian coast, and destroyed many cities and villages, in which 250,000 men lost their lives. It is wonderful that the visits of any of the apostles to Beirut are not mentioned anywhere, though the city early embraced Christianity and became a bishopric. Pamphilus, a native of Beirut and Presbyter of Cæsarea in Palestine, was a learned theologian and very active in the propagation of the Gospel ; he died the death of a martyr, 309 A.D.* Beirut flourished under the Christian Emperors until the Emperor Justinian, who united himself with the Maronites of the northern Lebanon against Abd el Malek, the Mohammedan leader, and gained the victory over them, though Beirut remained in the hands of the Mohammedans. According to Ritter, the earthquake of 529 A.D. and the conquest of Beirut by the Mohammedans have brought its former glory down to a very poor place.

In 1110 Beirut was taken by the Crusaders, who built a beautiful church there, and dedicated it to St. John ; but when the city fell again into the hands of the Mohammedans, this church was converted into a mosque. The Christians, under Mohammedan oppression, became degraded, and Beirut on the whole fell back into ignorance and superstition.

According to the French Consul, M. H. Guys, who was residing in Beirut from 1824 to 1838, this city had then only 15,000 inhabitants, of whom there were nearly 7,000 Mohammedans, 4,000 Greek Orthodox Christians, 1,500 Maronites, 1,200 Greek Catholics, 400 Armenians, 200 Jews, 800 Druses, and 400 Europeans. It now contains 100,000 inhabitants. No other city in the Turkish Empire has had such rapid growth and development. It has

---

* See Mr. Edward Backhouse's " Early Church History," page 360.

become the seat of the European trade, and the residence of the European and American Consuls. Beirut has large and beautiful gardens, especially of mulberry trees. Its soil is fertile and produces all the tropical fruits and vegetables. Its climate is healthy, and its position, with old Lebanon in its immediate background, rising to the clouds, makes it one of the nicest spots in the world.

Mount Lebanon means the White Mountain, like Mont Blanc in Savoy. Two reasons for this are obvious. The first is the snow, which is very conspicuous on the highest summits during the winter months, and can be easily seen from Cyprus. We cannot say that the snow covers these mountains the greater part of the year, for we only see it from late in the autumn until the early spring, except on Mount Hermon the snow can be seen the whole year round. But this mountain, though included in Anti Lebanon, is not called the White Mountain, but Sion or Jebel E'Sheikh (the chief mountain). The second reason is the whitish appearance of the limestone rocks, of which most of Mount Lebanon is formed. The vegetation of Lebanon goes up to 6,000 feet; beyond that height it is destitute of anything like trees and shrubs. Nothing can be seen but the white sterile limestone rocks during the greater part of the year. It is also interesting to remark that the limestone in the lower regions along the sea coasts becomes rather dark, while in the higher regions of Lebanon it remains white, which is caused probably from the purifying friction of the rain and snow upon the pale heads of Mount Lebanon.

The whole of Palestine and Syria, in regard to its geological formation, consists principally of limestone; but on Mount Lebanon we also find a soft sandstone formation of red and yellow colour, containing a good deal of iron ore and iron pyrites upon clay beds. These soft sandstone localities are common between the limestone hills of Lebanon, and rest, no doubt, upon a limestone foundation, however deep it may be found. They show themselves just at the foot of the mountain not far from the sea shore, as well as on every height of Lebanon, up to 6,000 feet. In some parts these beds of sandy soil are from three to six miles in length, and two to three in breadth ; some are larger, some smaller. Upon this soil we find much cultivation, especially of mulberry trees. The uncultivated parts are covered with fir trees. In these localities we find a number of coal mines, besides excellent iron ore, which was used formerly for the manufacture of the celebrated Damascus steel. The largest of the coal mines is found two miles south-east of Saleema, near Kornail, and it was well and systematically worked during Ibrahim Pasha's occupation of Syria in the year 1836, under the English engineers Brattel and Hornhill ; but when Ibrahim Pasha was defeated, the mining work was stopped and the mines are closed up to this day.

The double mountain ranges of Lebanon and Anti Lebanon, which run ninety miles in parallel lines from the sources of the Jordan towards the north-eastern boundary of Syria, are divided from each other by the high plain of Bukaà, in which the ancient ruins of Heliopolis (Baalbec or Baal Gad) are located. Mount Lebanon runs along the Mediterranean coast, and is far more beautiful than the Anti Lebanon, which possesses no special attraction besides its southern summit of the Mount of Transfiguration, upon which the tower was built which looketh towards Damascus (Cant. vii. 4). Not without cause did Moses, the man of God, pray to go over and see the good land that is

beyond Jordan, that goodly mountain (Hermon)
and Lebanon (Deut. iii. 25). These beautiful
mountains were included in the Promised Land,
but Israel never took possession of them. Mount
Lebanon has a great attraction for the people of
the East as well as to Europeans. Its healthy
bracing air, when coming from the sultry feverish
plains of Palestine, Egypt, and Phœnicia, is truly
beneficial. When walking in the morning or evening amidst the hills and fields of Mount Lebanon,
one is at once reminded by the fragrance of the
flowers, of the pine and fir trees, and of the myrtle
and other aromatic shrubs, of the Song of Solomon
iv. 11, where it says, "The smell of thy garments
is like the smell of Lebanon." Also, " I will be as
dew unto Israel ; he shall grow as the lily, and cast
forth his roots as Lebanon. His branches shall
spread, and his beauty shall be as the olive tree,
and his smell as Lebanon " (Hos. xiv. 5, 6). Solomon delighted in Lebanon and its forests, and took
much of the fir, pine, cedar and oak wood, in order
to build the interior of the temple, and his palaces
at Jerusalem. The prophets speak with glowing
interest of Mount Lebanon, " The glory of Lebanon
shall come unto thee, the fir tree, the pine tree, and
the box together, to beautify the places of My
sanctuary " (Is. lx. 13). " The glory of Lebanon
shall be given unto it, the excellency of Carmel and
Sharon ; they shall see the glory of the Lord, and
the excellency of our God " (Isa. xxxv. 2). The
80,000 hewers who were sent by Solomon to Mount
Lebanon, to cut down the cedar, fir, pine and oak
trees, must have inflicted a great damage on its
forests, from which they have never recovered. Now
there is no supply of timber on Mount Lebanon
for the temple in Jerusalem, nor is there any need
for it, for the large forests have long since passed

RUINS OF PALMYRA.

away, and the temple of Jerusalem is no more ; but there is a spiritual sanctuary into which we have to bring the spiritual glory of Mount Lebanon.

Within the limits of this part of Lebanon we find localities of very great interest. About three miles south-west from Brummana, near Beit Mary, are the ruins of an ancient Phœnician temple, with the inscription, "Iovi Bal Marcodi." This Bal Marcodi was no doubt Baal-Berith, who was worshipped by the Phœnicians of Beirut, and also by the Israelites who were fond of imitating the heathen idolatry of the Phœnicians (1 Kings xi. 5). At Apheca (Afka), between the lofty summits of Munitrah and Sanneen, at the sources of the famous river Adonis (Tammuz), we find the ruins of a very ancient temple of Venus. This temple was built by Kingras, king of the Giblites, who are mentioned in Joshua xiii. 5, and 1 Kings v. 18, and was used for the abominably licentious worship of Venus and Adonis.

The feasts of Tammuz, or Adonis, were held at Byblus (the ancient Gebal) by the Giblites, as well as in the temple of Venus at Apheca, and at Baal Gad or Heliopolis, in Damascus, Palmyra, Babylon, Phœnicia, Egypt, and Jerusalem. The death of the beautiful god Adonis, who was killed by a wild beast at the sources of the river which is known by his name, was lamented by Venus, and by all the beautiful women and girls of Mount Lebanon, Byblus, and Cyprus. At the beginning of the winter when the rain came down in torrents from Mount Lebanon, the floods carried off much red iron ore, and gave the waters of the river a reddish colour which was supposed to be the blood of Adonis, whose death was said to have taken place in the autumn. But with the return of spring Adonis was said to rise again from the dead in all his beauty. Both seasons, therefore, were commemorated in the feasts of Tammuz, at which the women and girls played the greatest part. At the first they made a great lamentation, for which the women in the East are wonderfully capable ; and at the latter they broke forth in exceeding joy and pleasure, fancying that Adonis the object of their love had risen from the dead, and in order to gratify Venus and Adonis they indulged themselves in sensual pleasures.

> "Tammuz came next behind,
> Whose annual wound in Lebanon allured
> The Syrian damsels to lament his fate
> In amorous ditties all a summer's day ;
> While smooth Adonis from his native rock
> Ran purple to the sea, supposed with blood
> Of Tammuz yearly wounded." *

We see with sorrow how attractive these heathen feasts were to the children of Israel, for they were early introduced at Jerusalem. In the prophecy of Ezekiel we read, " He brought me to the door of the Lord's house, and behold there sat women weeping for Tammuz (Adonis)."—Ezekiel viii. 14.

The temple of Venus at Apheca on Mount Lebanon, where this demoralising heathen worship was carried on till the beginning of the fourth century, was with many other heathen temples utterly destroyed by Constantine the Great.

As I look from Brummana northwards I can see through the telescope at a distance of twenty-three miles the ruins of ancient Gebal. The Giblites in ancient times were clever stone squarers and ship builders and rendered King Solomon great service through the medium of Hiram, King of Tyre, in building the temple and palaces at Jerusalem (1 Kings v. 18). These Giblites may, therefore, have

---

* See "Paradise Lost," I. 446.

been the means of introducing the heathen feasts
and worship of Tammuz to Jerusalem (Ezekiel
viii. 14), because in Byblus (Gebal) the worship of
Adonis was so greatly honoured that we find the
following inscription upon old coins : Ἀδωνίδος ἱερά
(holy Adonis), Βύβλου ἱεράς (holy Byblus). The river
Adonis, which was holy to the Giblites, enters into
the sea only half an hour south of Byblus or Gebal.

About five miles to the north of Brummana
down at the sea coast is the Nahr el Kelb (the
Lycus or Dog river) which runs down from the
heights of Jebel Sanneen to the Mediterranean. I
often visited the exceedingly interesting historical
monuments which were discovered there by the
French Consul, M. H. Guys, in the year 1808, consisting of six Assyrian and three Egyptian tablets
containing the pictures of the respective kings
chiselled out life size upon the hard limestone rock,
with Egyptian hieroglyphics and Assyrian cunei-
form inscriptions commemorating the journeys,
battles, and victories of Ramses, Sesostris, and
Pharaoh Necho of ancient Egypt, and of Shalman-
ezer, Tiglathpileser, Eserhaddon, and Nebuchadnez-
zar of Assyria. Many other Persian, Greek, and
Roman potentates passed by this old road who are
all gone into oblivion; but the Assyrian and Egyptian kings whose names we find in the Bible have
perpetuated their deeds by these monuments, which
thus become an excellent illustration of the facts
recorded of them in the Holy Scripture. In my
journey through Egypt I saw many tablets similar
to those at the Dog river, representing Ramses II.
with the winged Discus and the mystic Tau, the
symbol of eternity and happiness, which so
much resembles the Cross which is the type
of Christian life and eternal happiness.

I was greatly astonished when I came from the

tropical Alps of Abyssinia to find two kinds of trees in Syria which I had nearly daily before my eyes in the former country. The first is called in the Amharic language *Shola* and in Arabic *Shumi-zet*. It is a sycamore tree with large branches stretching out nearly horizontally from the trunk, at about a man's height. This tree I found also at Jericho, and by the Jordan, and its low branches must have been convenient for good Zaccheus to mount. It bears wild figs (Amos vii. 14). The second tree of Abyssinia which I found at Beirut was the Wansa, in Arabic *Maksas*. It has beautiful foliage and edible yellow berries. These two trees had many sad and joyful associations to me from their connection with Abyssinia. Sometimes we had lodged under them, and sometimes I had seen them crowded with the dead bodies of those whom King Theodore had executed. In the interior of the Galla country these two trees are regarded as holy, and are worshipped by the heathen.

There are some kinds of trees which we find growing both on the plain between Mount Lebanon and the Mediterranean Sea, and on the average height of Mount Lebanon, which is about 3,000 feet above the level of the sea. Among these is the mulberry tree (Morus alba), which is cared for and loved very much by the natives of the northern part of Syria, and not without cause, for it provides the inhabitants with the means of living, and beautifies their country with its shining, fresh, dark green foliage. A few other trees we also find in nearly every locality, as the fig tree, pomegranate, olive, almond, cypress, poplar, quince, apricot, fir, pine, laurel, service, acacia, different kinds of willow, vine, and pear tree. Other kinds of trees grow only in the low, hot plain along the coast, such as the orange and citron, which we find in

CEDARS OF LEBANON.

abundance at Beirut, Sidon, and Jaffa. Mandarin oranges, which have been only lately imported, are growing with success; and cactus, bananas, tamarisk, sycamore, and palms are common. The mimosa (Acacia Egyptiaca, the Arabic musk), which is at home in Soudan, where it yields gum Arabic in abundance, has also been introduced; but in Syria it does not produce gum, and is only liked on account of its yellow aromatic blossoms. It likes great heat, and grows well at Jericho and by the Jordan.

The trees which grow only on the heights of Mount Lebanon are the evergreen oak, often by mistake called Terebinth, the common oak, the walnut, plane, different kinds of Terebinth, the storax, apple, cherry, plum, and the stone pine or Pinus pinea, which bears edible fruits. The cedar tree occupies the highest place in the vegetation of Mount Lebanon. As one looks at these majestic trees one understands the full beauty of the illustration: "The righteous shall flourish like a palm tree, and spread abroad like a cedar of Lebanon." These beautiful and stately trees, which the Lord had planted, are now reduced to two small groves, one of which is in the southern part of Lebanon at Barouk, and the other larger grove is in the northern part at B'sherry, at a height of 6,000 feet.

The following flowers and shrubs grow abundantly on all the heights of Lebanon, as they do in other parts of Bible Lands. The Cistus salvifolius and prickly broom are always to be found near each other, under and between the pine trees. Many kinds of blue anemones and deep red violets grow in millions from December to the end of March. crocuses, tulips, cyclamens, and irises, grow in abundance early in the spring; and later on different kinds of lilies, myrtle, oleander, rhododendrons, wild flax, mallow, lavender, Adonis æstivalis, Ranunculus, lupins, Solanum sanctum, Acanthus, meadow saffron, Capparis spinosa, periwinkle, Bongardia, wild pea, scabius, gladiolus, hollyhock, Salvia Indica, Rubus sanctus, burnet, Plumbago, buglos, veronicas, heaths, and many other species.

The flora of Syria is rich and beautiful from February to the end of April or to the middle of May; but with the beginning of June the grass and its flowers are dried up by the scorching heat of the sun, and pass away; but on the heights of Mount Lebanon they last a little longer.

CHAPTER XV.

WHEN the American missionaries began their good work in Syria, in the year 1823, they chose Beirut as their central station, and so it became again what it had been before, a centre of learning, not of Roman law, but of the law of God which makes wise unto salvation. Simple schools were opened for boys and girls. The Arabic language was studied, religious conversations and meetings held, a new printing press was sent from America, the Bible was translated, printed, and circulated, and many other books and tracts were printed and distributed. Seminaries for both sexes were opened, a large Protestant church was built, and in the year 1870 the Syrian Protestant College, including medicine and surgery, received its first students, and on the 7th of December, 1871, the corner-stone was laid for the New College which is the crown of the Protestant mission work in Syria. All these powerful agencies exercised great regenerating influences upon the people at Beirut, and through the whole of Syria. They aroused the sleepy clergy of the different Oriental churches into jealousy, which provoked them also to open schools. More than all, the Jesuits got up in excitement and left their mountain school at Ghuzir, on Mount Lebanon, to make Beirut their central station. They built an immense castle-like college in connection with an excellent press where they printed their new version of the Bible in three volumes. There are now 8,900 scholars under daily instruction in the different schools and colleges at Beirut.

BEIRUT SCHOOL STATISTICS.

	Schools.	Teachers.	Boys.	Girls.	Total.
Protestant Schools, high and common	30	116	761	2281	3042
Orthodox Greek	15	33	928	425	1353
Papal Greek (Melchites)	3	11	227		227
Maronites	10	25	820		820
Syriac	1	2	80		80
Jewish	3	7	125		125
Jesuit, high and common	14	29	1024		1024
Sisters of Charity	4	31		1110	1110
Sisters of Nazareth	2	18		340	340
Mohammedan	11	23	805		805
	93	295	4770	4156	8926

PROTESTANT SCHOOLS OUTSIDE BEIRUT.

	Schools.	Teachers.	Boys.	Girls.	Total.
American Mission, high and common	80	115	3200	780	3980
Anglo-American Friends' Society on Mount Lebanon	10	12	272	72	344
British Syrian Schools	20	40	50	2000	2050
Irish Presbyterian Mission at Damascus	10	11	396	30	426
Free Church of Scotland on Mount Lebanon	10	13	280	100	380
Society for Promoting Female Education in the East	1	4		60	60
Reformed Presbyterian Mission at Latakieh	7	10	300	100	400
	138	205	4498	3142	7640
Protestant Schools at Beirut	30	116	761	2281	3042
	168	321	5259	5423	10682

These, of course, will be an immense power for the future elevation of the social, religious, and political condition of the people in Syria.

In Beirut are ten public printing presses, and nine regular journals are printed, with a circulation

of 10,000. The population of Syria is estimated
at 2,055,000 :

Mohammedans	...	...	1,000,000
Nusariehs	...	...	250,000
Maronites	...	...	250,000
Greeks	...	...	235,000
Roman Catholics	...	...	80,000
Druses	...	...	80,000
Bedawin Arabs	...	...	60,000
Jews	...	...	30,000
Ismaeliyehs	...	...	30,000
Armenians	...	...	20,000
Jacobites (Monophysites)		...	15,000
Protestants	...	...	5,000

2,055,000

I must remember the British Syrian Schools
in Beirut, Lebanon, and Damascus. These schools
were founded by Mrs. Elizabeth Bowen Thompson, in the year 1860, just after the bloody Druse
massacre of the Christians on Mount Lebanon;
and before saying anything about her work,
it may be well briefly to explain the causes of that
fearful event. Christians and Druses formerly lived
in peace and friendship with each other. The
Druses mainly occupied the southern, and the
Maronites the northern part of Mount Lebanon;
but there were also a number of villages which
were inhabited by both.

In the year 1756 two Emirs of the Shehab family,
who were Mohammedans, became Maronites, and
other Shehab Princes followed, which was felt to
be a disgrace to their religion, and caused much
trouble. The Turkish Pashas did not lose any
opportunity of securing animosities among the inhabitants of Mount Lebanon, knowing well that if
the people there should ever be bound together by
feelings of mutual confidence the danger to the
continuance of Turkish supremacy would be great.
The Christians were greatly oppressed by the

Turkish Government. In 1833, Mohammed Ali and his adopted son Ibrahim Pasha conquered Syria and tried to elevate that degraded country. He was afterwards defeated by the help of the English fleet, and Syria again fell back under the destructive power of the Turks. Since then the Sultan has always done his utmost to secure Mount Lebanon by creating enmity between its different tribes, especially between the Druses and Maronites. The last, being under French influence, boasted much of their position, and pushed their hatred too far. It is said that the Maronite Patriarch received from France £20,000 in order to strengthen their community against the Druses, which embroiled them also with the Sultan and excited him against them. The ambitious Maronite patriarch and his whole clerical suite were the instigators of the animosity against the Druses, which ultimately resulted in an affray at Deir el Kamar, in the year 1841, and then in a general civil war and massacre in the whole of Lebanon. This weakened the whole country and secured the supremacy of the Sultan over all Syria, and he rejoiced to stand as conqueror though his position was gained through the worst passions of human nature. In the year 1845 the Maronite clergy gathered their adherents and led them to the bloody and devilish work of massacring the Druses. The bishops, to their shame be it said, were the officers in the war, carrying their crucifixes in their hands and destroying everything before them till they were defeated at Muktara. The feeling of hatred was thus firmly planted in the hearts of these two mountain peoples, and the growing tendency to revenge was cleverly fostered on both sides by the Turkish officers, who, seeing that the Druses were far superior in warfare to the Maronites, invited the former to an intimate fellowship and union with the Sublime Porte.

Said Beg Jumplatt, the most influential chief of the Druses, obtained a Firman from Constantinople appointing him an Imperial Equerry. The Druses were flattered with golden promises by the Sultan, and they began to think much of themselves, while the Christians were ignored and despised by the authorities. The Druses were used by the Turkish Government to break the power of the Maronites, and, if possible, to remove all Christians from Lebanon. In 1859, the signal for a very serious affray took place at Beit Mary, half-an-hour south-west of Brummana and now under the care of our Mission, by which every sensible man could clearly see that a civil war was going to follow. The Maronite patriarch, bishops, and priests, excited their adherents against the Druses, and all the Maronite and Greek Christians began to prepare themselves for war. So did the Druses, whose delight it is to shed the blood of idolaters, as they call Christians, and in this they were fully encouraged from Constantinople. The Druses began to try their weapons upon the Christians here and there, and killed some of them, which passed off without the slightest notice by the authorities. Small fightings in different localities, in which the Christians were always the losing party, took place. On the 30th of May, 1860, the Druses, with fire-signals arranged with the Turkish soldiers, began the massacre in terrible earnest. In a few hours all the villages were in flames. Christian men, women, and children, fled away in the utmost consternation. Said Beg Jumplatt took the full command of these dark and bloody horrors, and in a short time Lebanon was in conflagration and stained with blood. Druses from Hauran came to unite

with their brethren in Lebanon; and the Turkish
forces, under pretence of maintaining and securing
peace, played the worst part in the tragedy.

The horrors committed at Jesseen, Zachleh, Deir
el Kamar, Hasbaya, Rasheya, and Damascus, were
fearful. But the culmination of horrors took place
at Hasbaya, where the Druse Lady, Sitt Naaify,
the sister of Said Beg Jumplatt, got the Christians,
under the pretext of protection, into the large
castle, where their arms were taken away from
them. Wives, mothers, and daughters, went up to
Sitt Naaify, and threw themselves madly at her
feet, imploring her to release their husbands and
fathers; but she was as cold as a piece of marble,
and gave order that all the Christians should be
massacred. Before this awful order was carried
out, Ali Hamadi went up to the blood-thirsty
woman, and said to her, " Are all the Christians to
be massacred? Please think of their families, the
widows and orphan babes, and take compassion.
Spare those fine young men. Execute the leaders
only, and set free the rest." But she said, " Impossible! Not a Christian is to be left alive from
seven years old to seventy!" The trumpets
sounded, and Druses and Turks entered the castle
and massacred the Christians with hatchets, bill-
hooks, swords, and guns. As the Christians
bowed their heads under the executioners' swords,
they exclaimed, " In Thy name, Lord Jesus;" but
the murderers responded, " Don't you know that
God is a Druse?" After the bloody work was
over, and about 1,000 victims lay in the courtyard
of the castle, Sitt Naaify entered, and seeing all
these mutilated corpses lying in six inches of
human blood, she said, " Well done, my faithful
Druses! This is just what I expected from you!"
Before there could be any interference from the

Powers in Europe to stop this horrible butchery, 11,000 Christian men were massacred, and 24,000 widows and orphans were in consequence in the greatest destitution. Thousands of them were flocking to Beirut for refuge and help.

Mrs. Bowen Thompson heard of the great misery of these widows and orphans in Syria, and being herself a widow, she sympathized deeply with them. So she left her native land, and in the love of Jesus went out to the Syrian field of desolation to help the poorest of the world by maternal and spiritual comfort. She arrived at Beirut in October, 1860, and began her great work among the widows and orphans, which ultimately developed into the most interesting mission of the British Syrian Schools.

Being engaged as Inspector of the branch schools of this Mission, I had to visit the schools regularly at Beirut and many villages on Mount Lebanon, as well as at Damascus. There were over twenty schools, with an average attendance of more than one thousand children. The Training Institution at Beirut where 80 girls are trained for teachers would need special description, if space could allow, because it is the central point of the British Syrian Schools. The best side of this very interesting work is that it consists not only in giving secular instruction, but it trains the Syrian girls in sound Gospel truths, which lead them to Jesus Christ, the Prince of Peace. This is specially needed in Syria where the people are so ready to shed each other's blood. It was exceedingly interesting to see the children of the murderers sitting closely together with the children of the murdered and learning the love of God, as it has been made manifest through Christ Jesus. I was not privileged to work long with Mrs. Bowen

Thompson, who was like a pious mother over her whole work. When my dear wife was ill and I was suffering from fever, Mrs. Thompson came and knelt down at her bedside and offered up fervent and effectual prayers which were answered by our Father in heaven. She worked so hard during her nine years missionary efforts in Syria, that her health was greatly impaired and she had to leave for England on the 17th of September, 1869. She reached her sister, Susette Smith's residence, at Blackheath College, London, on the 7th of October, and on the 30th she wrote her last letter to her dear Syrian children, as follows :

"When I was a little girl I always wanted to go to Syria, and I wrote a little book to interest other little girls about you, and to lead them to Jesus. It has given me great pleasure that my friend, Mr. Saleem Bistany, has translated this book into Arabic. I now send it with a very few simple words to say that the same advice which I gave you long ago I give you now. Read the word of God, and make it your study. When you open the book put up the prayer which you find in Psalm cxix. 18, ' Open Thou mine eyes, that I may behold wondrous things out of Thy law.' I pray to God to give you the Holy Spirit to help you to remember what you read, to teach you your need of it, and how to make use of it, so will you become acquainted with your own hearts, and the Holy Spirit will lead you to the heavenly Friend, who will bless you and will bring you to glory, such as is not seen on earth. I know how fond little children are of pictures, to teach them about countries, and trees, and birds, and about people who have lived in former days, so now I send you a picture, one of the loveliest that can be conceived, for it is one of the loving Jesus receiving children when others thought they were too young, and wanted to send them away. ' Suffer little children to come unto Me, and forbid them not, for of such is the kingdom of heaven.' Some people worship pictures, but this is very wrong, and I wish my children to learn the second Commandment. I hope to see you again in heaven. Farewell. God bless you.

" Your affectionate friend, and Syrian mother,

" ELIZABETH MARIA THOMPSON."

On the 14th of November, 1869, dear Mrs. Thompson's departure to the better land was drawing nigh. The last words she uttered were, " Glory be to the Father, the Son, and the Holy Ghost! Jesus! Jesus! Rest! rest! Arise! Amen!" and she was transplanted to the celestial regions. On the 18th of November the sad telegram reached us in Syria which caused indescribable grief and sorrow. Dear Mrs. Thompson was a living sacrifice for the glory of God. She lived not for herself but for Him who called her out to the great harvest field in Syria. Gerald Smith's words respecting her are true :

> " Mourn for the widow's and the orphan's friend !
> Mourn that a life so dear so soon should end.
> With wisdom, grace, and love divinely blessed,
> She raised the fallen, shielded the oppressed ;
> The blind she led to touch the Word and see,
> And healed the strife of creeds by charity.
> Damascus mourns her ; Hermon's daughters weep ;
> Their mother in the Lord has fallen asleep !
> Her native land has claimed her mortal part,
> Jesus her soul, but Syria has her heart !"

Mrs. Mentor Mott was appointed by her late sister to follow her as the Directress of the British Syrian Schools, assisted by her husband, Mr. Mentor Mott, and her sister, Miss Lloyd. I had the branch schools and the teachers under my care, and did my best to co-operate with Mrs. Mott in the whole work. My daughter Rosa was in the Training Institution, and was well cared for.

Mrs. Mott carried on her sister's great work with much wisdom, energy and devotedness, and I was pleased to see the disinterested way in which she did not gather her children and workers under the organisation of the Established Church of England, of which she, her husband, and Miss Lloyd were members, but she led her large flock every Sunday to the American Presbyterian Mission Church at Beirut.

In the year 1869, the British Syrian Schools were visited by Eli and Sybil Jones, Richard Allen, Charles Wakefield, and Captain Pim, who were greatly pleased with the work. I was told that they were Quakers, or Friends, who were good people on the whole, though wrong in rejecting the outward ordinances. This interested me much, and as I had never become acquainted with such people before, I the more desired to see them, and learn their religious principles. Their addresses, especially those of Sybil Jones, were so powerful and edifying, that our hearts were touched, and I began to think that their religious principles must be of a superior nature. I went to the hotel where they lodged, and made their acquaintance, and from that time I have believed that the Quaker principles are the right basis for a true spiritual Church. When these dear Friends left the country, their blessed influence remained upon my heart, though they had not the slightest idea of it, nor had I any hope of seeing them again.

In the spring of 1871, another Quaker, Stafford Allen, with his son Francis Allen, visited Syria, and they also visited the British Syrian Schools, where I got acquainted with them through Captain Pim. It was so arranged that I had to accompany Stafford Allen, his son, and Captain Pim, to Baalbec and back. Having already a great leaning towards the principles of the Society of Friends, I inquired more deeply into them, and had very blessed intercourse with Stafford Allen all the way along. He also seemed to take great interest in me, and it was on that journey that we were bound together by an everlasting friendship. He said to me when he left the Syrian shores, " If thee come to London, please visit my house, and stay with me, and my dear wife Hannah will take care of thee." I was then very far from guessing that Hannah Stafford Allen would become the mother of the Friends' Lebanon Mission.

On the 15th of March, 1872, I left Beirut with my dear wife and two children for Europe, while our daughter Rosa was left at Mrs. Mott's Institution. When we reached our home at Lörrach, I left my wife and the two small children, Theophilus and Augusta, with my relations there, and went to England, where I arrived on the 13th of April at Blackheath College, the residence of Mrs. Mott's sister, Mrs. Smith, who was the principal person in England connected with the British Syrian Schools. Mrs. Smith introduced me to Colonel Boileau, the Secretary of their Mission, and with him I visited many towns up and down the country, holding public and private meetings, in order to increase the interest in the British Syrian Schools. In the year 1879, after the death of her husband, Mrs. Smith came out to Syria in order to help Mrs. Mott in the great work. She was engaged for six years in the work in Beirut, and fell asleep in Jesus on the 25th of January, 1885. Her loss to the British Syrian Schools is great, because she was a mother in Israel, well beloved.

On the 17th of April I visited my friend Stafford

Allen, whose acquaintance I made in Syria. He introduced me to his wife, Hannah Stafford Allen, and I was glad to see her heavenly countenance, with the lustre of peace and love upon it. From that time, during my stay in England, I was privileged to make her house my home. Here I got initiated by degrees into the principles of the Society of Friends, and the Friends' Meeting at Stoke Newington became a great blessing to me. Robert and Christine Alsop, Rebecca Thursfield, and Hannah Stafford Allen, were used of God to lead me more and more into the spiritual principles of the Society of Friends. The more I began to know them the more I began to love them, and often did I say to myself, "Oh! what a precious thing it is to come out from the bondage of ritualistic slavery into the liberty of the children of God." I will not judge for others, but to me Quakerism was just the very thing which gave rest to my conscience, and peace to my soul.

After I had completed my lecturing with Colonel Boileau, on behalf of the British Syrian Schools, I rested a few days in my new English home at Stafford Allen's, and departed on the 4th of July to Germany, where I met my family. After having had different meetings in Germany and Switzerland, we left again for Syria, where we arrived on the 3rd of September, and I again resumed my duties in the British Syrian Schools. I visited all the schools in Beirut and on Mount Lebanon. The schools at Hasbaya and Mucktara interested me very much. At Hasbaya I met with that terrible Druse lady, Sitt Naaify, who looked gloomy and downcast, but somewhat redeemed her melancholy appearance by a sharp and friendly look at me, and the promise that she would do her best for the welfare of Mrs. Mott's school there. At Mucktara I met

AN ARAB SCHOOL.

the widow of Said Beg Jumplatt, the leader of the
last massacre and brother of Sitt Naaify. This
lady received me very kindly, and I lodged in the
Druse castle of Jumplatt, which was for some time
the summer residence of the English Consul. I
felt, however, very queer among the Druses, and
would rather have slept in a simple countryman's house than in the gloomy Druse castle, which
is stained with blood.

At Zachleh, the largest village on Mount Lebanon, where the poor Christians were plundered and
killed in the time of the massacre, Mrs. Mott has a
very flourishing school, and some Bible women also
at work there. In Damascus, too, where the civil
war committed the most fearful horrors and bloodshed, Mrs. Bowen Thompson, at the sacrifice of
her health, founded her last work of an educational
character, which is still in a most satisfactory condition. Moslem, Druse, Christian, and Jewish girls
were alike instructed there in the glorious Gospel
truth, while M. Frankel, of the Jewish Mission, had
divine service every Sunday on the premises of the
British Syrian Schools. At Damascus I made the
acquaintance of the excellent Dr. Wright, now
editorial Secretary of the British and Foreign Bible
Society in London. I went, too, to see the celebrated Abd el Kadir, of Algiers, and also Dr.
Mushaka, who is one of the most learned self-
taught men. He was a Greek Catholic, but seeing
the errors of his church, became a Protestant, and
wrote an able book of 340 pages, in which he exposed the errors of the Roman Catholic church.
He also entered into a written controversy with the
learned Patriarch Maximus, in which Maximus
was silenced by the truth which Dr. Mushaka so
well handled. I had many happy and blessed hours
with Dr. Mushaka, because we could sympathize

with each other, as both of us had been under the Popish yoke, but were now happily escaped from bondage into the liberty of the Gospel. I also visited Mr. Crawford, of the American Mission, who has worked faithfully at Damascus for many years, under great perplexities, oppositions, and trials; but, after much toil, his work has been richly blessed.

Through my work in the British Syrian Schools I became well acquainted with the religious condition of Damascus, Mount Lebanon, and Beirut. I found the southern part of Mount Lebanon well supplied with mission schools and missionaries, while in the northern part, especially in the neighbourhood of Brummana, there was no resident missionary. I often looked eastwards in the evening when the setting sun threw its golden rays over the mountain, and I could see clearly many villages and hamlets in which priestly assumption kept the people in darkness and superstitious bondage. I thought in my heart, why should we teachers and missionaries be accumulated at Beirut, while only eight miles to the east nothing is done for the enlightenment of the benighted mountaineers. This idea came often before me, and each time it left a deeper impression upon my soul. I began, therefore, to inform myself about those lofty mountains and their inhabitants, and was told: "The inhabitants of Brummana and its neighbourhood are the greatest liars and thieves in the world. They are Maronites, Greeks, and Druses, and the evil report of them has filled the country, even unto Egypt. Everyone is afraid of them. The American missionaries wanted to establish a Mission amongst them, but they were expelled from the place in 1831, and the Bibles and Testaments which they distributed among the people were publicly burnt. You will not be able to organize a Mission there." What a fine report, I thought; surely that is just the place for a mission station! I made it a subject of earnest prayer, and went on with my work as usual in the British Syrian Schools. When, after a long time, the subject was matured, and my doubts and fears removed, I felt in my soul that I was called by the Lord to go up to those bad people at Brummana. My position in the British Syrian Schools was outwardly a very comfortable one, and I had nothing to complain of in any respect. I could not reasonably expect such a comfortable home on the mountains, among good society, and with such comparatively easy work; but the consultation with flesh and blood and outward comfort had to be set aside, that I might follow the order of God, which was day and night before me in the following words, "Go up to those mountains of Brummana." On the 9th of April, 1873, I gave in my resignation to the Committee of the British Syrian Schools, six months before my service was to be concluded in that mission field.

Here I desire to give an abridged description of the Druses, and Orthodox Greek, Greek Catholic and Maronite churches, among whom I was working in Beirut, Mount Lebanon, and Damascus, so that the reader will more easily understand the oppositions and difficulties which beset the path of a missionary in Syria.

CHAPTER XVI.

THE SECRET RELIGION OF THE DRUSES.

THE religion of the Druses on Mount Lebanon
was kept strictly secret from its origin at
the beginning of the eleventh century until
1838, when Ibrahim Pasha conquered Syria. Some
of his soldiers, when at Hasbaya, entered into the
Kalwat, or Druse place of worship, and took away
a number of the principal books which, till then,
had been carefully hidden there. Parts were subsequently translated into some modern European
languages, and from that time the mystery of the
Druse religion was unfolded to the public. The
best works about the Druses and their religion are
Dr. Wartabet's " Researches into the Religions of
Syria," published in 1860 ; Colonel Churchill's "Ten
Years' Residence on Mount Lebanon," in 1885 ;
Dr. Philipp Wolff's " Die Drusen und ihre Vor-
laüfer," in 1845 ; Sylvestre de Sacy's " Exposé de
la Religion des Druses," in 1838 ; G. W. Chasseaud's
" The Druses of Lebanon, their Manners, Customs,
and History," in 1854 ; and Petermann's " Reisen
im Orient über die Drusen," in 1860.

Many of the Druse books, which are all in
manuscript, found their way to Europe, to the
Vatican in Rome, to Paris, Vienna, Munich, Ox-
ford, and Upsala ; but as there are few competent
scholars in the Arabic language in these cities, the
contents of the books remain mostly on the shelves

of the libraries, and scientific men have to be satisfied with that which is already translated. Ventura, who wrote a history of the Druses, in the Appendix to his "Memoir of Baron de Tott," in 1786; and J. G. Worbs, author of the "Geschichte und Beschreibung der Drusen, in Syria," in 1799; and other travellers in Syria before 1838, could not ascertain the real truth of the Druse religion, because nobody of any other religious denomination had ever seen or possessed a Druse book, and on this account many misrepresentations were made both about the people and their religion.

The Druses consider there have been ten incarnations or manifestations of God to the human race, by different human forms, at different times, and in different places, but only within the limits of the Fatimite Dynasty. The first was in El Alec; the second in El Bar; the third in Abu Zakaria; the fourth in Ali; the fifth in El Muell; the sixth in El Kaim; the seventh in El Mansour, who founded Bagdad, 762 A.D.; the eighth in El Muezz; the ninth in El Azeez; and the tenth in El Hakem, who, according to Ibn Khillikan (vol. 2, p. 165) is also called Abu Ali El Mansour. The last five incarnations were kings of Egypt and Northern Africa.

El Muezz, who traced his descent to Fatimah the daughter of Mohammed, was the strongest among them, and it was he who founded the city of Cairo in the year 972, and conquered the whole of Syria and Palestine as far as Damascus. His son, El Azeez, succeeded him, and married a Christian woman, whose brothers he appointed patriarchs in Alexandria and Jerusalem in the year 978. Their son El Hakem ascended the throne when he was eleven years of age, and distinguished himself by his cruelty and folly. He persecuted Christians, Jews, and Mohammedans alike, and caused indescribable atrocities; killing more than 18,000 men by his fanaticism and bloodshed. He destroyed the places of worship of all other denominations, and among them many Christian churches. He also pulled down the church of the Holy Sepulchre at Jerusalem, in the year 1009. He was a second Nero, and caused fearful sufferings and loss of life. His bloodthirstiness and folly in persecuting the Christians, caused them to cry desperately for help and protection to their brethren in Europe, who responded to their earnest entreaty by the first Crusade to the Holy Land.*

At El Hakem's court, at Cairo, were two Persian priests named E' Dorazy and Hamse, who were the founders of the Druse religion. E' Dorazy publicly declared his master, El Hakem, to be an incarnate God, and asked the people to worship him. This excited the people so much that E' Dorazy was at once killed by them. But his adherents were ever after called by his name, Druses. Hamse wrote his books in secret and published them after El Hakem was dead, or killed by his sister, Sitt el Mullook, in a most secret way.

Ali Dahir, the son of El Hakem, succeeded him on the Egyptian throne, and at first claimed the same submission and honour which had been granted to his father. But Hamse, the Prime Minister, who was a Persian magician, said to Ali Dahir, "We cannot grant thee the same honour and submission which we paid to El Hakem, because he was a god and not a man; he was not born, nor could he beget children." Ali Dahir was greatly displeased with this, and said to Hamse, "Am I then an illegitimate bastard?" Hamse

---

* Charles Knight, "English Encyclopædia," under Fatimite; and "Zeitschrift des Deutschen Palestina," Vereins, vol. 7, p. 264, 1885.

said, "Thou hast said it." Ali Dahir was greatly exasperated, and gave vent to his anger by repudiating all the religious doctrines taught by his father and Hamse, and by persecuting all those who adhered to them. He killed many of them, and those who were not reached by his sword fled to Banias, Damascus, Mount Lebanon, and the Wady e' Tyme, near Mount Hermon in Syria, in the year 1103. There they found already a kind of Batenites, a Persian sect with whom the Fatimites already sympathized, who pretended that every outward thing in this world has its secret interpretation, and that every passage in the Koran has a mystical meaning. Their name in Arabic means possessors of secrets. These Batenites came originally from Irack (Ispahan in Persia), and settled down especially in the Wady e' Tyme, near Hasbaya, in the neighbourhood of the sources of the Jordan. The persecuted Hamsites or Druses naturally found a good deal of sympathy among them, and then it was that the Druse religion took hold of these Batenites.

The Selihites, who were descended from the Hymyarites, emigrated into Hauran in the time of Christ. They came from Yemen, in Arabia, and made a covenant with each other for which they were called Tannoukhites, from an Arabic word meaning Confederates.* Afterwards some of them came to Mount Lebanon, where they are still called by that name.

In the history of the Arabs, as well as in Knight's "English Cyclopædia" (vol. 1, col. 418), we find that Amru Ben Amer Musyka, one of the nobles of Yemen, also emigrated northwards, on account of the predicted *Seil el Arim* or Torrent of the Mound, that is to say, a flood caused by the burst-

---

* See Wetzstein's "Hauran," p. 105.

ing of a famous reservoir. After his death, his son Jofna established himself and his descendants in Syria. They likewise were known as Tannoukhites, and it seems probable that they were already Christians when they left Arabia, as one of the tribes in Yemen who embraced Christianity was called Tannoukh. We know, too, that King Aberha, of Abyssinia, had conquered Yemen about the fourth century, and during the seventy years in which he and his son ruled over that country, they propagated the Christian religion by force, as is still the custom of Abyssinian kings. Some of these Arab tribes who settled on Mount Lebanon appear to have held some Christian heresy like Manicheism, which has some similarity with the religion of the Batenites. It is known in the history of Mount Lebanon that the Yemenites settled at first in the district of El Meten, on its western slopes, and as they were quite different from the other Arabs who had preceded them, and who liked tent life, they constructed solid stone houses, and the castle of Musyka, so named in honour of their first leader, was their central stronghold. In 1844, Consul Von Wildenbruck, of Beirut, discovered the ruins of the old castle of Musyka, one hour's distance to the east of El Meten, in the district of El Meten. Its colossal bevelled stones, fourteen feet long by five feet high, indicated great age. All these Yemenites came to Mount Lebanon before Mohammed began to preach his religion. When that religion afterwards overran the East, they became Mohammedans in order to accommodate themselves to it. In the eleventh century, however, they embraced the religion of the Druses, and have since stuck to its deluded principles with wonderful firmness. These Yemenites or Tannoukhites also built a large castle at Abeih, which is now in a neglected condition.

WANDERING ARABS.

There are not many Druses there now, for their chief centres are Baakleen and Mucktara, where their princes are residing. Since their massacre of the Christians in 1860 the Druses have diminished, and many have emigrated to Hauran. It is said that there are not more Druses in Mount Lebanon, Wady e' Tyme, Damascus, and Hauran, than 70,000 souls.

Hamse, in his books, declared El Hakem to be God who had appeared for the tenth time in human form, and himself to be the most glorious of all created beings, the cause of causes, the centre point, the universal intelligence, the true Christ, the leader of believers. But, while asserting that El Hakem is everlasting God, Hamse admitted that God cannot condescend really to adopt man's form, but His human appearance in El Hakem was only a phantom. This resembles the doctrine of Docetus, Basilides, Valentinus and Marcian, who could not comprehend that Jesus Christ was God in human form, but a mere phantom.* "God," said Hamse, "is so sublime that even the best attributes by which we endeavour to define Him, would interfere with the glory of His unity."

Hamse, as a Persian magician, naturally based his new religion upon the two principles of good and evil. The first he regarded as absolute and eternal, the latter relative and emanated. He held that these two principles clothe themselves with successive human forms, which explains the belief in Metempsychosis. The universal intelligence embodied in Hamse is the first and most glorious existence which was created by El Hakem, or God. It was the concentration and representation of every good, through which everything was created, except itself, which emanated from God, in conse-

---

* Neander's "Church History," vol. 1.

quence of which it is the pure light in opposition to the gross darkness. From the light—that is the universal intelligence, the true Messiah, even Hamse—four kindred spirits emanated, which were manifested in human form in the time of El Hakem, by Ismael, Mohammed, (not the founder of Mohammedanism,) Salmân, and Beha Eddeen. These were called the ministers of truth who have to proclaim the way of salvation. They are also called Matthew, Mark, Luke, and John, for they believe that just as Hamse may represent Christ, so these four kindred spirits may represent the four Evangelists. Just as the soul of the universal intelligence and light was in Hamse, and through Hamse in the four ministers of light and truth, so is the darkness and all evil found in Mohammed, the founder of Islamism, whom they call the devil, the opposer of every good, who has also his four ministers of darkness who are known in human form as Ali Ibn Aby Talib, Aby Baker, Omar, and Othman. As God has manifested Himself ten times to the human race, the universal intelligence with its four ministers of truth and light, as well as the devil with his four ministers of lies and darkness, have likewise appeared in human form, and they will also appear in the great judgment day, when the devil with his ministers will be punished eternally.

Here we meet a good deal of the reformed Persian Religious Philosophy of Zoroaster in the Zend Avesta. The Persians believed in one eternal God over all, infinite in regard to space and time, and too great and glorious to be defined by the human intellect. Basilides, of Alexandria, says that God cannot be explained, ἄρρητος ἄκατον ὅμιστος (no language is able to define Him). The Persians also believed in two principles, the good and the evil, which are opposing each other by their respective agencies and creations. The good principle they called Ormuz, and the bad Ahriman. The first is represented by light and fire, and the second by darkness; but as the light is of an eternal nature it must finally obtain the victory over darkness and all evil. The adherents of Zoroaster were persecuted by the Mohammedans in the middle of the seventh century, and took refuge in Gujerat in India, where their descendants are still to be found, as the well-known Parsis. These Persians, who came from the same common stock as E' Dorazy and Hamse, had some tendency to receive the Druse doctrine, and many Druses say that they have brethren in India and China. Muktana Beha Eddeen, who was next to Hamse in compiling and increasing the religious books of the Druses, sent some of his books to India and others to Constantinople.*

We have seen that the universal intelligence was said to be the most perfect and glorious of all created beings, pure light from the pure light of God. But when the universal intelligence became proud in looking upon his superior glorious attributes, he fell at once from his glory, down to the deepest woe, and from him the devil or adversary emanated, who was not in existence before. He was entire darkness, and empowered with every attribute of opposition in order to fight with the universal intelligence, who cried to God for help in the conflict.† God, having pity, caused four good ministers to emanate from the universal intelligence; but the adversary asked God also for

---

* See Herzog's "Theological Encyclopædia."

† In Mani's doctrine, who took so much out of the Persian Religious Philosophy to make up his own, we find that when the first man was in conflict with the powers of darkness, he began to be in danger, and implored God for help, who sent him the eternal Spirit to lift him up to the kingdom of light.

the same number of ministers, in order to defend himself against them. His appeal was granted, and four evil ministers emanated from him, because it pleased God to create for every positive a negative, through the whole creation.

Metempsychosis is a principal doctrine of the Druse religion. They believe that the souls of men are emigrating from one human body into another, which is the case with all men, good or bad. The souls of Hamse and his four ministers, as well as the souls of the devil and his four ministers, have been wandering from the beginning from one human body into another. The spirit of Hamse, for instance, was in the time of Moses in Jethro, the priest of Midian, and in the time of Jesus Christ in the body of Zachariah, and the souls of the four ministers were in the four evangelists. In the time of Mohammed the spirit of Hamse was in the body of Salmân El Phârisy, and the souls of his four ministers in Mukdad, El Ghaffary, Omar ben Yasser, and Nedshashy. The souls of the devil and of his four ministers of errors emigrated into the bodies of Adam, Noah, Abraham, Moses, Aaron, Joshua, Jesus Christ, Peter, Mohammed, Ali Said, and Kaddah. As the Druses believe in the eternity of matter, like the Zabeir of Babylon, they consider that the emigration of souls is wonderfully arranged by God to reward the good and punish the wicked. "Look at that poor sick and destitute man," said a Druse to me, "he must have committed much mischief in a former life. And look at the rich Sheikh Mousa, he has no doubt been a good man before he was born." When speaking with the Druses about Metempsychosis they say, "Did not Christ say that John the Baptist was Elijah? and did not the disciples of

Christ say in regard to the man who was born blind, 'Who did sin, this man or his parents, that he was born blind?'" "Basilides, in his Religious Philosophy in the second century, could not complete his system without using the doctrine of Metempsychosis which was believed by the old Egyptians. Basilides says that the souls of men wander from one human body into another in order to be punished or rewarded just as they conducted themselves in former bodies, till there is such a development for good that the purified souls can appear before God. All sufferings of men he attributes to their bad and sinful conduct in former bodies."* In the Philosophy of Plato we meet the doctrine of Metempsychosis, and the Druses regard Plato, Æsculapius, and Pythagoras, as incarnations of Hamse, the universal intelligence. Hamse, no doubt, studied the Egyptian Gnostics, and used some of their material to build his own system.

As one result of their belief in Metempsychosis, the Druses are not at all timid of danger in times of epidemic sickness or war. They have no fear of death, for in this they are perfect fatalists like the Mohammedans. They say, "There is no death for us Druses at all; *that* is for the Christians to be afraid of. Death for us is just to go from one house to another according to the will of God." Hence we can understand their heroic conduct in the time of battle and massacre. If Druses are travelling to distant places and meet other Druses they test them by the question, "Where do your farmers sow the seed of Ehlilish?" This should be answered by, "Our farmers are sowing the seed of Ehlilish in the hearts of believers." Then they bring them two pots and set them before them. In one is water and in the other is nothing. If the

* Neander's "Church History," vol. 1.

strangers take the full pot and pour it into the empty one they show that they believe in the transmigration of souls and they accept them as fellow believers.

The Druses are divided into two principal classes, namely, into the Akkals, the wise, learned, and initiated; and into the Juhhals, the unlearned and stupid. This is also an ancient practice, which Hamse, Muktana Beha Eddeen, and other Druse writers have borrowed from old religious systems of the Persians, especially from the Gnostics and Mystics, who divided their adherents into two classes, namely, into Esoteric and Exoteric. The first are the πνευματικοί, the Electi or spiritual and learned; the second are the ψυχικοί, the Auditores or unlearned. Most of the Philosophers, Mystics, and Gnostics, say that the most spiritual part of religion is the property of only a few, that it is difficult to find God, and is much more difficult to lead another to Him.*

The Druses say that they have only a few Akkals who are in possession of the whole wonderful and good Mystery of the Druse religion. This causes them to divide themselves into three classes, which agrees again with Basilides. He calls the first πνευματικοί, the second ψυχικοί, and the third ὕλη. The first, say the Druses, are the good and spiritually minded Akkals, who live near God. The second are those who are mixed up with too much earthly things, but may yet be saved. The third are the real Juhhals who perish entirely, because they disobey the law of God, and are subject to the will of the flesh, for which they are condemned to hell. It is generally acknowledged that the Druse Akkals live a good moral life, and are much better than many Christian priests. They never take any intoxica-

---

* See Plato.

ting drink or smoke tobacco. They dress very simply. They do not use bad language. Their chief work is to read and study and learn by heart the 111 epistles of Hamse, which are divided into six volumes. They conduct their meetings, which are held on Thursday evenings, on elevated isolated places, in very simple buildings, where the Akkals, and Juhhals, and women, gather together. The superior Akkals, after having taught and admonished the audience, have a special meeting among themselves, to speak about the political signs which must occur in order to announce the coming of Hamse and El Hakem. For the Druses expect, most certainly and watchfully, the coming of their Christ from China about this time, as the 900 years which Hamse said would pass before his re-appearance in human form have now elapsed. I asked one of their Akkals: "If the anticipated revelation of El Hakem and Hamse does not soon take place, what will become of you?" The Akkal said, "Our nearest way is to Protestantism." "But how can you think of embracing Protestantism," I answered, "while the Protestants believe in the crucified Saviour Jesus Christ?" The Druse Sheikh said, "That is the very stumbling-block for us, because our books tell us that your Christ, who was crucified by the Jews, is a false Christ, and the true Christ, even Hamse, was then in Zachariah; but if he does not appear in a few years our whole religion is a mistake, and in this case we cannot do better than unite with the English Protestant Church; but we are sure that the true Christ will soon appear." The Druses have been often misrepresented by some travellers and writers as being worshippers of the "calf," which is not true at all. On the contrary, they call Ali Ibn Aby Talib the "ox," and Mohammed the "calf," to denote their

stupidity as incarnations of the evil spirits.   The
Druses are enemies of all kinds of idolatry.   This
was one cause of the enmity between them and the
idolatrous Greek and Maronite Churches of Mount
Lebanon, which partly resulted in bloody massacres
like that of 1860.

The Druse Akkals encourage the instruction of
their own women.   They teach them to read and
write, and reveal to them the holy secrets of their
religion.   I often visited the house of an Akkal,
and was astonished to see what interest the Druse
women manifested in religious concerns.   In this
they differ very much from the Christian women of
Mount Lebanon, who are usually too ignorant and
indifferent to carry on religious conversation of any
kind.   The middle class between the higher Akkals
and the lowest Juhhals, are not much instructed in
religious concerns.   The principal thing which they
know is the difference between the false and the
true Christ.   It is a curious fact that the same doctrine in regard to the true and false Christ took
hold in the twelfth century of some people in the
south of France, who were called the Albigenses
and Chaterers, who pretended that the true Christ
was not the one who was crucified by the Jews,
but the one who walked on the sea of Galilee, and
entered through the closed door to the disciples,
saying, " Peace be unto you."   They believed also
in a relative dualism of good and evil, and in
Metempsychosis.   Some Church historians like
Neander think that these singular doctrines were
brought to Europe by the Crusaders.   The Druses,
the Albigenses, the Manicheans, and the most of
the Gnostics and Mystics, have always been very
fond of the Gospel of St. John.

The Druses believe that God created all visible
and invisible things through the universal intelli-

EMIR EDEEN, A DRUSE AKKAL OF MOUNT LEBANON.

gence, and that from the good and evil which emanated from it He formed men as we find them now, a composition of light and darkness, good and evil, right and wrong. As the Druses believe in Hamse, from whom the true light is derived, they naturally think they must possess more light than other people, through which they can comprehend the truth, and obtain the victory over darkness and lies. The Druses believe that God in the beginning created the same number of people, male and female, of all ages, occupations, and capacities, as there are found now, neither less nor more, for each body a soul, and for each soul a body, and that when any man dies, his soul emigrates into a body which is born just at the very time. This they call farewell, or to dress in another shirt. As the souls of the Druses are wandering from one Druse body into another Druse, so it will be with the souls of other denominations. They circulate in their wanderings from body to body within the limits of their respective religions. No man, therefore, from any other religion can become a Druse, and no Druse, they think, can truly become a member of any other religious society. If this should appear to take place outwardly, it is only to accommodate themselves to circumstances, while they remain unchanged in their hearts. In such a case they say their own religion is like the body of a man, and other religions are like clothings. The body remains the same, but the dresses may be changed according to circumstances, fashion, and climate. In the year 1837, when Ibrahim Pasha invaded and conquered Syria, many Druses changed their religion outwardly, professed themselves Christians, and were baptized, just in order to escape military conscription; but when Ibrahim Pasha was defeated and returned to Egypt, the

Druses who were baptised returned to their Druse religion.

The final destruction of the world is not believed in by the Druses, because they believe in the eternity of matter. The glorious reign and perfect happiness of the Druses begins with the re-appearance of El Hakem and Hamse and their hosts. The Druses calculate from the appearance of El Hakem in Egypt, in the Mohammedan year A.H. 400, until his re-appearance at Mecca 900 years after. Now we live in the year A.H. 1302; so we see very clearly, that according to the Druse books, the 900 years have fully and literally elapsed, and the advent of the Druse Saviour has not occured. The sign of the coming of El Hakem and Hamse, they say, will be the overthrow and destruction of the Chinese Empire, and the great war between the European Christian powers and the Mohammedans, who have profaned the holy city of Jerusalem. The armies of the different Christian kings will then march towards Mecca, and fight there with the Mohammedans. An Abyssinian king, who is called John, an incarnation of the devil according to the books of the Druses, will at that time come down from his mountains, with his great army of Christian soldiers, cross the Red Sea, and proceed towards Mecca in order to assist the European Christian kings in destroying the Mohammedans.* While this war is going on the startling news from the east will reach them, causing great perplexity and fear, that the Druse god El Hakem, and Hamse, and his four ministers, with their innumerable armies are approaching from China. The Christians and Mohammedans will then say to each other, " What can

---

* As the present King of Abyssinia is called John, the Druses prognosticate the coming of their Saviour about this time.

we do better than unite and make peace with each other and surrender ourselves to this great and wonderful king of glory, El Hakem?"*   El Hakem and Hamse will then take possession of Mecca with tremendous power, and all the Christian kings and their armies, together with the Mohammedans, will tremble with fear and perplexity because the day of judgment is at hand.   On the tenth day of the month Thi El Hijjah (that is, September), should this judgment be carried out.   El Hakem will appear in the same human form in which he appeared 900 years ago in Cairo, and will take his seat on the roof of El Kabba, the black stone of Mecca, and will tell the Christian, Mohammedan, Jewish, and heathen nations who are gathered before him, "I have appeared in the human form ten times before to teach you my condescension, that you should believe in me, the true God, and Hamse who is the true Christ; but you would not hear my commandments, on which account you have to bear the punishment of your folly." Then El Hakem will cause a tremendous thunder storm and earthquake, by which the Mohammedans, Christians, Jews, faithless Druses, and heathen will be swept away from the surface of the plain, together with the city of Mecca, leaving no trace whatever behind them.   After this fearful judgment the Druse God with Hamse and his four ministers will proceed toward the north-west to Hauran (Bashan), to gather all his believers and give them great rewards for their faithfulness.   Then they will proceed to Mount Lebanon where the Druses will leap

---

* In the system of Mani we find a similar passage, to the effect that when the powers of darkness were fighting with each other they pushed each other to and fro until they came to the portals of the kingdom of light. Then they said to each other, "What can we do better than unite with each other in order to enter into the wonderful kingdom of light!"— Neander's "Church History," vol. 1, division 2.

for joy, join the celestial army, and proceed to Egypt. They will carry the old Antagonist, the devil, with them, who is Harrat ibn Tarmakh, from Ispahan in Persia, whose soul was in Adam and wandered from one person into another until it entered into Mohammed, and, finally, into John, King of Abyssinia. On the road to Egypt, between Ramleh and Ledd, the devil will be killed, by his head being cut off into a golden vessel. In great pomp and triumph, El Hakem will then proceed to Cairo in Egypt, with the whole of his army. Arrived at Cairo, another judgment will take place of all the people who were not present at the destruction of the Christians and Mohammedans at Mecca. The Mohammedans, Jews, and Christians, will be punished by being obliged to carry heavy blocks of lead, iron, and glass in their ears, which will burn them in summer, and freeze them in winter. But the greatest punishment is for those Druses who at first believed, but after the disappearance of Hamse, fell back into unbelief.

The Druse God will continue to dwell personally among his people in Cairo on the throne of his glory and power. Hamse, the true Christ, will receive power and glory and be like an emperor; his four ministers will be like kings, and each Druse will be like a prince. The four ministers will travel over the whole world, and take all the gold and silver and all the treasures from the rich men and kings, and kill all the unbelievers who shall be still left in other places. Then they will come back again to Cairo, where all the riches will be accumulated for the enjoyment of the Druses. The Druses will dwell in upper rooms in beautiful palaces, and the Christians, Jews, and Mohammedans, will be their slaves, and will have to work very hard for the Druses without wages. They will also have very little to eat and not enough to drink, though the Nile is quite near. They will not have any clothing, and they will have to pay a heavy tribute to the Druses besides their service day and night. The greatest trouble for them, however, will be a horrible smell diffusing from their skins, which will not trouble the Druses but only themselves. Each Druse will live one hundred and twenty years without his natural force abating, and then a sweet dream will come over him, in which his soul will be transferred without pain into another Druse body, who will just at that time be born without pain, and in that body he will live again one hundred and twenty years, and so on always, world without end. The condition of the Christians, Jews, Mohammedans, and Heathen, will also remain the same. They will always remain the slaves of the Druses, and their souls will migrate from one miserable body into another, under great agony and pain, to all eternity.

This account of the principal doctrines of the Druse religion is the result of much study and conversation with Druses. The Druses are a fine intellectual people in every respect, and they deserve a better religion than this poor delusion.

CHAPTER XVII.

THE name of the Greek Orthodox Church, to which some of the Christians in Bible Lands belong, owes its origin to the Greek Empire ultimately embracing that form of Christianity as the religion of the state. The Greek Orthodox or Oriental Christians in Syria and Palestine call themselves Rome or Romany, but this name has nothing to do with the old city of Rome in Italy, which was the centre of the Western Churches, but has its origin in Constantinople, which was founded by Constantine the Great, in 326 A.D., and called New Rome, in opposition to the more famous city of the west.

Greek civilization prepared the ground for the readier propagation of Christianity. The Gospel was preached, and the New Testament written in classic Greek, and in this language we have also the oldest Christian literature, consisting of treatises on Christian doctrine and its defence against heathen philosophy and idolatry. We find already in the first and second centuries a number of congregations in Greece and Asia Minor, like Corinth, Ephesus, and Sardis, where the Gospel was powerfully presented in opposition to Roman and Greek mythology and philosophy, and Egyptian and Syrian Gnosticism. With the decline of Greek and the progress of Roman influence, the east and west became divided, not only politically but religiously. The Bishop of the Greek Church at New Rome, proud of the antiquity and merits of his Church, looked for a certain supremacy over all the Churches; while the Bishop of Old Rome, favoured by political advantages, did not feel disposed to submit, but wished to assume universal supremacy. Yet the Western or Roman Church had no violent rupture with the Eastern or Greek Church. Dogmatical disputes between the Eastern and Western Churches began under the Emperor Zeno in the fifth century, and were settled for a time by the Council of Chalcedon, in 451 A.D., which pronounced the equality of the Bishops of Rome and Constantinople. In spite of this arrangement, the Bishops Pelagius II. and Gregory I. of Rome had new difficulties with John Yejunator, who assumed the title of Ecumenical Patriarch at Constantinople, in the year 587 A.D. Long controversies took place, not only in the Greek Church herself, but with her rival Church of Rome, on certain doctrines which were being developed in the Eastern Churches with regard to Monotheletism, which asserts that Christ had no human will, but only a Divine, and Monophysitism, which maintains that He had but one nature, not human, but Divine.

The Trullo Synods at Constantinople in 680 A.D. settled these theological disputes for a short time, for in their eighteen sittings Agatho, Bishop of Rome, so ably presented the truth that the Monothelite leaders, Makarius of Antioch and Gregory of Constantinople, were defeated, and were afterwards expelled by the Emperor Constantine Pagonatus. Makarius fled to Kessrawan on Mount Lebanon, where he taught the people the Monotheletic heresy. Jacob Baradoi, who travelled in great poverty and self-denial through the whole of Syria and Asia Minor, induced the people also to adopt the Monophysite doctrines, and they were called after him Jacobites.

The time from 726 to 842 A.D. was occupied in the Greek Church with continual disputes with regard to the worshipping of pictures and images, in which the strong inclination to religious symbols, so characteristic of the Greek mind, appeared. These disputes caused fierce fightings between the friends and enemies of pictures. They condemned each other publicly and privately, and the acts of one Council contradicted those of another. Troubles and weakness to the Church thus arose from within, while sufferings from without were caused by the Mohammedans, who abhorred the Christians on account of their idolatry. The Western Church was protected by its geographical position from the attacks of the Mohammedans, and, besides this, till the seventeenth century it was not so much inclined towards picture or image worship. It was a most unfortunate fact, that after the pictures had been removed from the Greek Oriental Churches by the Emperor Theophilus, his wife Theodora, through the influence of the priests, replaced them after his death. On the 19th of February, 842 A.D., the Greek Church degraded herself by publicly acknowledging the worship of pictures. She then began to call herself Orthodox, and the Feast of Orthodoxy ($\dot{\eta}$ $\pi\alpha\nu\dot{\eta}\gamma\nu\rho\iota\varsigma$ $\tau\tilde{\eta}\varsigma$ $\dot{o}\rho\theta o\delta o\xi\acute{\iota}\alpha\varsigma$) is still held to commemorate this dogma of the infallibility in doctrine of the Greek Orthodox Church.

The Greek Church having thus exalted herself as being in sole possession of the right Christian doctrine, looked down upon Rome and the Western Churches, and attacked them for having adulterated the true faith by teaching that (1) the Holy Spirit proceeds from the Father and from the Son;

(2) there must be fasting on the seventh day of the week, but in the first week of Lent, milk and cheese may be allowed ; (3) the priests must not marry ; (4) unleavened bread should be used in the Eucharist ; (5) animals that were strangled may be eaten, and also meat on fast days by those who are ill ; (6) bishops may wear rings on their fingers, and shave their beards and cut their hair ;* (7) children may be baptized by only dipping them once in water ; (8) the sign of the cross may be made in other ways than that prescribed by the Greek Church. Many other such miserable and minor things were brought against the Bishop of the Western or Romish Church, who in return attacked the Bishops of the Oriental Churches and their errors. On both sides the controversies were carried on, not only with hierarchical envy, but with political intentions. The gulf of division grew larger and larger, and the very means which, from time to time, were used to unite these Churches, tended further to separate them. Rome went on developing in unity and power, both within and without, while Constantinople remained behind, being too obstinate in its pride in its own orthodoxy to make any right progress.

The accumulating hatred between both parties took hold of every little difference in doctrine to use in fighting with each other. Thus the use of un-leavened bread in the communion in the Western Churches, and of leavened bread in the Eastern, was the chief cause of their official separation in July, 1054, when the excommunication of the Greek Church was publicly read by the Papal legates at Constantinople in the venerable church of St. Sophia, which is now a Mohammedan mosque. It is as-

---

* The Greek Orthodox priests never cut their hair or beards, but let them grow as long as they will, which gives them a very ugly appearance.

tonishing that while the Roman Catholic and Greek Orthodox Churches should both be in the same fundamental error in departing from the simplicity of the Gospel of Jesus Christ, they should continue to quarrel in wild fury over insignificant differences of religious ceremonies till the gulf which separates the two largest portions of the Christian Church has become so wide that there is never likely to be unity between them. The Crusaders who were such a concentrating and cementing power for the general good of Christendom did not succeed in uniting the Greek and Roman Churches in their great object of rescuing Bible lands from the Mohammedans. These caused fearful destruction and loss of life in the Greek Churches, which were under their immediate political power, and the union of the Eastern and Western Churches, which was prevented by the obstinacy of the former, would have limited the sword of Mohammed.

The Reformation in the sixteenth century also passed by without being able to influence this corrupt and obstinate Greek Orthodox Church. The Lutheran Theologians of Tubingen tried to give an impulse towards Reformation. The Catechism of Luther and Confession of Augsburg were translated into Greek, and in 1575 much correspondence took place between the Lutheran Theologians and the Patriarch Jeremiah, of Constantinople, but without the expected results. Much hope, however, was entertained when Cyrillus Lukaris occupied the patriarchal chair, for he adopted the evangelical principles of the Protestant Church, and confessed them publicly in 1629. Like Luther, he saw the corruption and errors of his Church, and did his utmost to develop a Reformation. But while Luther met with success in the tendency to progress, the liberty of religion and of conscience, and

CONSTANTINOPLE.

general enlightenment, in which the Reformation
could strike root, Cyrillus Lukaris found his old in-
flexible Orthodox Greek Church unwilling to be
taught better things. Cyrillus stood alone, and the
Greek clergy and the Jesuits together brought his
work to nothing. He was persecuted and troubled
in every form, until his enemies succeeded in influencing Sultan Murad to put him to death in 1638.

The present Greek Church has, like the Roman
Catholic Church, seven Sacraments : (1) Baptism,
(2) Chrisma, or holy anointing, (3) Eucharist, (4)
Repentance, (5) Holy order of Priests, (6) Marriage,
(7) Extreme Unction. The Greek Church also
believes that all the canons and rules issued by their
seven ecumenical councils were inspired by the
Holy Spirit, and it prefers them to the Old and New
Testament. It believes in transubstantiation in
the Eucharist, intercession of saints, auricular
confession, and the power of the priests to
absolve sins. It cultivates picture worship, Mariolatry, and thousands of foolish superstitions which
have grown reverend to them through their
antiquity. It believes in one limbo near hell for
the wicked, and another near heaven for the saints.
The Greek Orthodox Church is divided into three
great sections, the first in Greece, the second in
Russia, and the third in Syria. All reject the Pope
in Rome as Antichrist, in which they are right.
The first two are governed by their own independent Synods. The Greek Church in Syria is
governed by four patriarchs, namely, those of Constantinople, Antioch, Jerusalem, and Alexandria.
Both the higher and lower clergy are mostly men
of little education, but desperately obstinate, and
proud beyond measure of their Orthodoxy, repudiating every effort for the reform of their polluted
Church, and pressing always for its restoration,

rather than its reformation. The Greek Orthodox Church is just at present in very great need of churchmen, and a number of churches on Mount Lebanon are without priests, because the young men of some education do not like to dedicate themselves to the priesthood, and the old priests are dying away. On this account the Greek Bishop often persuades men to become priests who are not at all qualified for such an office. At Brummana, quite lately, a shoemaker who did not like to work offered himself as a priest to the Greek Bishop at Beirut, who received him, gave him a little instruction for some weeks until his hair and beard were grown long enough, and then conferred upon him the priestly office and priestly dress. The shoemaker, therefore, came back in the priestly costume of the Orthodox Church, but as stupid and more ugly than he was before. The Orthodox clergy are generally unlearned, while their people are more enlightened. It is the opposite with the Maronite clergy who are generally learned, but their adherents are very ignorant. When the American missionaries entered the Syrian Mission field in 1823 they entertained the idea of reforming the Oriental Churches, especially the Greek Orthodox. They soon had to give up their plan on account of the above mentioned causes, and had to be content with working among private individuals, and affecting the whole population through the education of the young. By great perseverance in the midst of persecution and counteracting circumstances, they have succeeded in organizing Protestant Churches in Syria, which are composed mostly of converts from the Greek Orthodox Church. It must be always borne in mind, however, that the missionaries have to work with much more difficulty, and with less success, among the deluded, degraded, and dead Eastern Churches, than among the heathen. It needs a long time of much patience and faithful work, before the accumulated rubbish of many centuries of superstition and human invention is removed from these Eastern Churches, and they are converted into Spiritual Temples of God.

CHAPTER XVIII.

WITH the decline of Greek influence and the increasing power of the Roman Empire the Bishop or Pope of Rome availed himself of the most favourable political condition of that time to assume the supremacy over all the Christian Churches. At the council of Chalcedon in 451 A.D. the Papal legates, who assumed great authority over the rest, occupied the left side of the house with their party, while Dioscuros, Patriarch of Alexandria, and his party took the right side. The Papal legates defended the Doctrine of the Western Churches in acknowledging two natures and two wills in Jesus Christ. The Emperor Marcian with his wife Pulcheria, who was his guiding star, agreed with the Theological views of Pope Leo and his legates, which made a very great impression upon the whole assembly, and many members of the Oriental Churches left their places and went over to the left side where the Papal legates presided. From that time until now, this part of the Christian Oriental Church has called herself the Melchite (Royal), or Catholic Church. The Pope made continual claims on the Greek Catholics as being under his supremacy, but though they had united with Rome in the Doctrine of two natures and two wills in Christ in order to please the Emperor Marcian, they did not agree in the future with all that he demanded. The Greek Catholic Church, therefore, continued to govern itself while struggling on one hand against the hierarchical despotism of the Pope, and on the other against the Monophysite and Monotheletic heresies of Alexandria and Palestine. By degrees the Pope greatly reduced his expectations with regard to the Greek Oriental Churches, but he never gave up his mission to them, nor neglected to do his utmost by various councils to bring about the union of all the Churches under the Roman Pontiff.

In modern times the Jesuits have been a powerful agency for working in Papal interests among the Greek Orthodox and Melchite Churches. About the year 1650 some Jesuits were sent to Syria with the object of performing mission work. They settled at Antioch, Beirut, Damascus, Jerusalem, and other places. At Antioch the Greek Patriarch gave them full liberty for their work; but not till after many years of Jesuitical intrigue and fascination did they succeed in influencing the Greek Orthodox Bishops of Tyre, Sidon, Beirut, Baalbec, and Tripoli, with their flocks, to submit to Papal supremacy. All those who thus submitted to the supremacy of the Pope called themselves Greek Melchite Catholics, and said that they originated in the Council of Chalcedon; but more correctly they are, to large extent, the fruits of the Jesuit Mission in Syria. For some time the Greek Catholics had to suffer a great deal of persecution from the Greek Orthodox patriarchs and bishops, but since the year 1760 they have enjoyed religious liberty. There are about 50,000 Greek Catholics in Syria, who acknowledge the Pope as the visible head of the Church, but they do not unite with the Roman Catholic Church so fully as the Maronites do, because they remain attached to the old Greek Orthodox Church in many things. The Greek Catholics, for instance, use leavened bread in the Eucharist, and in this point, which was the first cause of final separation between the Greek and Roman Churches, the Pope gave way wonderfully, in order to be acknowledged by the Greek Catholics as head of the Church. They have the same Missal and Horologion, and the same order of rituals, as the Greek Orthodox Church. They use the old Greek language as the sacred language of the Church, and allow their priests to be married before their ordination. They call the Virgin Mary Θεοτόκος (mother of God), and cultivate the same Mariolatry, and picture and image worship, as the Greek and Roman Churches. In baptism they differ from both the Romans and Greeks, because they neither use immersion nor sprinkling, but pour water over the candidate in the name of the Father, Son, and Holy Spirit, believing that this is the washing of regeneration, without which nobody can be saved. They believe in transubstantiation in the Eucharist, and differ only in the exact moment when the great change takes place. They always used to have their religious feasts at the same time as the Greek Orthodox Church, but in 1857 they began to celebrate their festivals according to the Roman calendar. This causes a difference of twelve days between the Western and Eastern Churches. The Western Church celebrates Christmas on the 25th of December, but the Greek Orthodox on the 6th of January. There was a great controversy among the Greek Catholics themselves about this point. Some of them agreed with the Patriarch and celebrated their festivals with the Roman Church, and some did not agree to this and kept their feasts with the Greek Orthodox Church. On this account they split into two parties, but both retain the name of Greek Catholics, because both look towards the Pope as the visible head of the Church. We see from all this that the Greek Catholics are partly attached to the Greek Orthodox Church and partly to the Roman Catholic. One of their liberal clergy told me once: "Our doors are open to Rome, to Constantinople, and to London," indicating that they are liable to be influenced by the Pope, by the Greek Orthodox Church, and by the Protestants.

A number of Greek Catholics have become Evangelical Christians, and some of them have proved most efficient and useful members of the Protestant Church, like Dr. Michael Mushaka at Damascus, who publicly and privately taught the truth, and attacked the errors of the Popish Church.

CHAPTER XIX.

SOME historians think that the Maronites de-
rive their name from an abbot named Maroon who lived near the Orontes in the sixth
century and preached Monotheletic doctrine, whom
they regard as a great saint, though the Pope condemns him as a heretic. Others say that it was
from John Maroon who lived and taught on the
Northern Lebanon some years later. Towards the
middle of the seventh century the Emperor
Constantine Pagonatus, persecuted the Maronites
on Mount Lebanon,* and also stationed 12,000 men
from the Persian emigrants, called Mardi, on the
Northern Lebanon, for the purpose of opposing the
Mohammedan invasion.† It is from these people of
Persia with whom they united in fighting against
the Mohammedans that the Maronites are also
called and call themselves Mardites. When Justinian II. removed the 12,000 Mardites from
Lebanon to Armenia, the Maronites continued the
contest with the Mohammedans and fought so well
that for a long time they secured their independent
position. The Monotheletic Maronites on Mount
Lebanon had to endure hard and long persecution

---

* See Dittmar's "Universal History," vol. 3, p. 213 ; and Herzog's "Theological Encyclopædia," vol 10, p. 180.

† See Chambers' "Encyclopædia," vol. 3, p. 679 ; and Auguetil Dupperon's
"Recherches sur les Migration des Mardis, Ancien Peuple de Perse."

MARONITES ASCENDING MOUNT LEBANON.

by the Byzantine Emperors Justinian I., Justinian II., Constantine IV., and Marcian, on account of which many of their priests and bishops emigrated to distant countries, especially to Armenia.

After the Maronites had been Monotheletics for more than 500 years, according to the statements of William of Tyre and Bishop Vitry, they began to listen to the delegates of Pope Innocent in the year 1215. In the time of the Crusaders the Maronites joined the Christian army from the West, and thus came more in contact with the doctrines of the Papal Church. In 1445 special effort was made through the Council of Florence to unite the Greek Catholic and Maronite Churches under the supremacy of the Pope. The Maronites seeing some political advantages in uniting with Rome approached it step by step. Messengers from Rome induced promising young men to go there from Mount Lebanon, and after being educated gratis, they were sent back to their native country as Papal agents. Pope Gregory XIII. dedicated a large amount of money to erecting at Rome, in 1584, a Collegium Maronitarum, exclusively for young Maronites. From this College a number of learned and distinguished men took degrees; like the Patriarch Georgius Amira, and Professors Gabriel Sionita and Abraham Ecchellensis, from Mount Lebanon, who were finally engaged in the great work of the Polyglot Bible at Paris; also Joseph Simon Assamani, from Tripoli, the author of the "Bibliotheca Orientalis," in 4 vols., which is regarded as an authority in Oriental History. By the powerful agency of this College in Rome the Pope could soon exert full influence and power over the Maronites on Mount Lebanon, where he likewise founded high schools for the education of their youths. At the end of the fifteenth century the

Maronites fully acknowledged the supremacy of the Pope, and united with the Roman Catholic Church, not from religious conviction, but from the political motive of desiring the assistance of France and Austria, which was really accomplished when the French Emperor Louis XIV. granted them letters of protection. This political agreement between France and the Maronites is still kept up with increased interest by the French Consuls. By their union with Rome the Maronites have been freed from the Monotheletic heresy, but have adopted instead all the errors of the Roman Catholic Church which make them much worse than they were before, and more fanatical than the Roman Catholics themselves. The number of Maronites in the whole of Syria is estimated at 250,000. They have only one Patriarch residing at Kanobin in Kessrawan, who is subject to Rome, and governs all the Maronite bishops and priests, and all the convents with their monks.

In order to strengthen the Maronites against other denominations, as well as to purify them from their old tendency to errors, the Pope has four agencies engaged to accomplish his designs. These are, first, the Jesuits; second, the Franciscans; third, the Lazarists; and fourth, the Capuchins. The first are trying to catch the people by introducing more scientific knowledge, while the second, third, and fourth are engaged in elementary education and good works for the poor. They have an enormous influence among the Oriental Christians, who have a natural tendency to outward show, and much inclination to be helped instead of doing their utmost to help themselves, and thus be independent.

On the appearance of Protestantism in Syria in the year 1823, by the American Missions to the

Oriental Churches, the Jesuits, well aware of the power of Evangelical teaching, lost no time in instructing the Maronite patriarch, bishops, and priests, and all other Popish Christians to oppose the missionaries by counteracting and neutralizing their influence by every possible means. The missionaries had, therefore, a very hard time in thus beginning their work among a superstitious and ignorant people, under the fanatical Maronite clergy. The following story out of the annals of the Syrian Mission field of the first Protestant convert and martyr on Mount Lebanon illustrates their difficulties as well as the triumph of truth over fanaticism and superstition.

CHAPTER XX.

WHEN the American missionaries began to occupy Syria as their Mission field they engaged Assad Shidiak, an intelligent young Maronite, as their teacher in the Arabic language. Before this he was secretary to the Maronite Patriarch, Joseph Habeish. Through contact with the missionaries Assad Shidiak learned to know the Holy Scriptures and the truth as it is in Jesus Christ. The Patriarch was informed that Assad was employed by Protestants, and sent him a letter asking him at once to abandon his engagement with heretics and come to him, unless he would be put under excommunication. Assad delayed for some time but finally went to him at the convent of Alma,* where the Patriarch inflicted all kinds of trials upon him. From this place he wrote the following letter to the missionaries at Beirut :—" I pray God the Father, and His only Son, Jesus Christ our Lord, that He will establish me in His love, and that I may never exchange it for any created thing, but that neither death, nor life, nor things present, nor things to come, nor height, nor depth, nor riches, nor honour, nor dignity, nor office, nor anything in creation, may be able to separate me from His love. I beg you to pray to God for me."

---

* Alma is a convent a little north of Brummana.

After some time Assad ran away in the night from his prison in the convent at Alma to the missionaries at Beirut, and at their request he gave them the following report of his sufferings, which is taken from a book called "The Martyr of Lebanon:"

"Since many have heard that I have become insane, and others that I have become a heretic, I have wished to write an account of myself and let every reader judge whether I am mad or slandered, whether I am following after heresy or after the truth of the orthodox faith. Every serious man will confess that true religion is not that of compulsion, nor that which may be bought and sold, but that which proceeds from believing the Word of God, and endeavouring to walk according to it to the glory of God; and that those who are contentious, and do not obey the truth, but obey unrighteousness, are far from true religion. This is the standard by which I would be judged by every one who may read this narrative.

"I had been at Beirut no long time when the Patriarch's brother, Priest Nicolas, arrived, and requested me to grant him an interview, which I hastened to do. Priest Nicolas then began to converse with me in the way of reproof for having any connection with Protestants. I replied that as we ought not to deny the unity of God because Moslems believe it, so we ought not to hate the Gospel because Protestants love it. He then began to tell me of the Patriarch's wish that I should come out to him to the convent of Alma, and of his great love to me. He said that the Patriarch had heard that I had received thirty or forty purses of money from the Protestants, and he assured me of his readiness not to suffer this to be any hindrance to my coming out from them. Now if my object were money, as some have seemed to think, I had then a fair opportunity to tell him a falsehood, and say, ' I have indeed received that sum from the Protestants, and cannot leave them unless I restore the whole.' In this way I might have contrived to take what I wished. But I did not so answer him, but told him truly how much wages I had received, which was no extraordinary amount.

" He then gave me a paper from His Holiness, in which he says, ' We request that when we come to Alma you will come up and see us. We expect your presence, and, if God please, we will provide you with some proper situation, and with an income that shall be sufficient for your support. Delay not your coming, lest the present happy opportunity should pass by.' Knowing as I did that many people supposed that my object in continuing with the Protestants was worldly gain, I did not delay to fulfil his request, hoping thus to remove this impression, and to enjoy an opportunity of speaking the truth without the suspicion of being hired to do it. On the 6th of January, therefore, I left Beirut with Priest Nicolas, and reached Deir Alma the same night. His Holiness was not there, but the next day as he came I met him, and saluted him in the road. In the evening he called me to his chamber and began to ask me questions, that he might discover what I was; and I told him the whole truth, although this course was against my own advantage. At this he seemed surprised, for he must have perceived that it was contrary to what he had been accustomed to see in me. Afterwards, when I declared to him that I had never before been a believer with true living faith, he was probably more astonished still. He then asked me if I believed as the Romish Church believed. I told him that I did not. He asked me then what

my faith was, and I answered, 'True and living
faith must be divine, and connected with hope, love,
and repentance, and all these virtues are the gift of
God. I believe the truth as God has inspired it,
and it would be but a lie if I should say that I
believe as the Romish Church does, while in fact I
cannot without fuller evidence of its truth.' After
some further conversation of this sort, he told me
that this doctrine of mine was heretical, and that if
after three days I did not give up this belief, I
must no more enter the church, and that for as
long as I remained of· that opinion he would suffer
no one to have intercourse with me in buying,
selling, etc. This prohibition reminded me of the
words in Revelation xiii. 16, 17 : 'And he causeth
all, both small and great, rich and poor, free and
bond, to receive a mark in their right hand, or in
their foreheads ; and that no man might buy or sell,
save he that had the mark, or the name of the
beast, or the number of his name.'

"At other times he pressed me to swear by the
Eucharist and by the Gospel that my faith was like
the faith of the Roman Catholic Church. He asked
me if I was a Bible-man. I replied, 'I do not take
the opinions of the Bible-men as my guide ; but
if you think me a Bible-man on account of the
opinions I have advanced, so be it.'

"Some time passed before the Patriarch again
asked me concerning my faith. I then explained
to him what I believed respecting the Unity and
Trinity of God, and that the Messiah was one person with two natures, and that the Holy Spirit
proceeds from the Father and the Son. Then arose
a dispute about who is the vicar whom Christ has
appointed to explain His law. I answered in substance, as I afterwards did in writing, that by
reason, and study, and prayer to God, with purity

of motive, we may know from the Holy Scriptures everything necessary to our salvation. My reply, perhaps, was not expressed with sufficient clearness, or perhaps I was not able to say it in the manner that was appropriate, for such a tumult and storm was excited in the company who were then present, that they seemed to me to be intent on overcoming me by dint of vociferation rather than by argument, and on drowning my voice rather than understanding my opinions.

"Some days after, Bishop Abdallah Blabil and Padre Bernardus of Ghazeer, came to the Patriarch, who one day called me to them into his chamber, and asked me what I wished, whether money or office, promising to gratify me, whatever it was; at the same time speaking of his love to me, and of his deep interest in my welfare. These professions I believed to be sincere, but they were according to the world, and not according to the Gospel. I assured him that I wanted none of the things he had mentioned; that I was submissive and obedient to him, and that if he thought I had taken money of the Protestants, he was welcome to shut me up in my chamber as in a prison, and take from me everything I possessed; that I wished from my superiors nothing but my necessary food and clothing, and that I was ready to give them a written assurance to this effect. The bishop and priest then begged me in presence of the Patriarch to say that my faith was like that of the Romish Church. I replied that I feared to tell a falsehood, by saying I believed a thing which I did not. 'But,' said they, 'the Patriarch here will absolve you from the sin of falsehood.' I then turned to the Patriarch, and put the question whether he would so absolve me. He answered that he would. I said, 'What the law of nature itself condemns, it is out of the power of any man to make lawful.' He then again asked me what I wished to do. I said I wished to go and see the Armenian Patriarch, Gregory, and inquire of him what I ought to do. He gave his consent, and requested me, when I had done this, to return to him, to which I also agreed.

"I was accompanied by a priest from the Patriarch to the college of Ain Waraka, where I found Priest Yoosef of Shaheen, with whom I conversed for a considerable time with great pleasure, because I found that he did not believe that the Pope was infallible in matters of faith, unless he was acting in concert with the Church assembled in council. I then began to confess to him. But soon I saw that he steadfastly held some opinions for no other reason than that the Church believed them, and this without bringing any proper evidence from councils or from the Fathers with regard to their truth. On my asking for evidence he burst out upon me with exceedingly bitter words, saying, 'Know that the Church neither deceives nor is deceived, and be quiet.' I wished him to instruct me according to the Word of God, and with the simple object of glorifying God and fulfilling His will, for I saw that he was not disposed to support any opinion because it was according to the Word of God, but because the Church thought so. I saw him also ready to maintain these opinions, although I should adduce the strongest evidence against them from the Holy Scriptures. He told me it was impossible for him to teach anything contrary to the Council of Trent. So I found I could not receive his system, because, even if it were shown him that it was wrong, he would not give it up, lest he should be obliged to give up his office. I therefore told him, 'You are bound, and shut up between walls, by the doctrines of the Pope and the Council of Trent.'

"About this time I heard that a certain Armenian priest, who was accustomed to come on Sabbath days to Ain Waraka to learn Arabic grammar, wished to converse with me about religion. I was much rejoiced to hear it and was impatient for an interview. When he came we had a short talk together about works unlawful on the Sabbath day, and on some other subjects, but he excused himself from further conversation at that time for want of leisure. I continued at Ain Waraka the whole week, reading with the rest at prayers, and confessing to Priest Yoosef. When the Armenian priest came again, he said that he wished the discussion carried on in writing, and to have an assistant with him, besides other conditions. On the whole I was more inclined than before to receive the doctrines of the Romish Church, since the priest had promised to bring his evidence on all points from the Word of God, and had assured me that they were walking in the light and not in the darkness.

"At this time word was brought me that Bishop Jacob, superior of the convent of B'zummár, wished to see me. Priest Yoosef had told me that this state into which I had fallen was a temptation of Satan, and that it was usual for persons when they came to manhood to be tempted on the subject of their religion. At another time he assured me that it was a state of delirium, and because I had heard that Bishop Jacob had himself been delirious, and that he was a man of good information, I wished very much to see him. On the same day I went to Priest Yoosef and disclosed to him my intention of going to the convent of B'zummár, where were the Patriarch Gregory, Bishop Jacob, and the Armenian priest before spoken of.

"I set off the same day, and on my arrival saluted

the Patriarch, and the same night we reasoned together on the subjects of faith, hope, and charity. In the course of our conversation it appeared to me that he was not a true believer, and from that time forward I could not confide in him as I would confide in a real Christian, but I was willing to hear his arguments. On the following day I asked him how it could be said that the Pope was infallible if there were no proofs to be brought to show it. After a good deal of conversation on what is the real Church of Christ, on pardonable ignorance, etc., he tried to prove that if the Pope is not infallible, then there is no religion, and even no God. To me all his proofs seemed so weak that I could not be convinced, and I fell into deep perplexity as to what I should do, for sometimes I greatly endeavoured to submit my judgment to his rules and opinions, and I made these efforts until my very head would ache.

"From this time I was with Bishop Jacob every day for three or four hours, and his best advice to me was, to pray to St. Antony of Padua, together with one repetition of the Lord's prayer, and one of Hail Mary, every day for three days. While I was thus in doubt on account of the weakness of their reasons, one of the monks said to me, 'The Patriarch knows well what is good tobacco,' and intimated that he knew little else.

"I hoped that the priest would explain to me those doctrines of the Romish Church which I could not believe, so I went into his chamber, and questioned him very particularly on all points. He expressed his wish that we might discuss together all the points, one by one, but only on condition that the Maronite Patriarch Joseph Habeish should appoint him to do so. He told me he had in his possession a book refuting the opinions of Luther and Calvin. I begged permission to read it, but he refused, telling me, however, that the doctrines of the Church all remained unrefuted. He wished me to go down to the Patriarch Joseph on this business. So after a stay of four days I departed for Ain Waraka, as I had promised to return to Priest Yoosef of Shaheen.

"Here I found one of my friends of whom I had heard that he had been very much astonished at my connection with the Bible-men. When we met and had conversed a little on some points, he would no longer hear me, fearing, among other things, lest he too should be crazed. I then finished my confession to Priest Yoosef, and about sunset the same day went down to the Patriarch to the convent of Alma. His Holiness once more urged me to declare in writing that my faith was according to the faith of the Romish Church. From this I excused myself, begging that such a thing might not be required of me, for the Council of Trent had added nothing to the creed which was established by that of Nice, which begins, 'I believe in one God,' etc. A short while after this I offered him my thoughts, with modest arguments and mild suggestions, on his duty of causing the Gospel to be preached in the Maronite churches, intimating that it might be done by the priests in the language of the people for one or two hours every Sabbath day ; and if this should seem to the people too much of a burden, then let them be relieved of some of the feast days.

"After this I remained silent in my chamber, which was near his own, and as there came to me a few of the Patriarch's deacons and some others, I read to them, at their request, from the New Testament printed in Rome. A short time afterwards, I entered my room and found in it none of the books that had been there, neither New Testament nor any other. I knew that the Patriarch had given the order for their removal, for he reproved me for reading the Gospel to those persons, but he could accuse me of no false or erroneous explanations, or of teaching them anything heretical.

"One day after this the Patriarch called me to his presence and began to threaten me in a most unusual manner. I said, 'What do you wish from me, your reverence? What have I done, and what would you have me do? What is my sin except that I conversed with some individuals, and showed them the errors of the Church of Rome?' Then again he requested me to say that I believed as that Church did, and added in an exceedingly loud and threatening voice, as he grasped his own beard firmly in his hand, 'See how I will take you if you do not repent.' I begged him to appoint some one to show me the truth, and he would not, but continued to express his own sentiment that we are bound to hold fast to the Church even to such a length, that if she should reject the Gospel, we should reject it too. Soon after this I rose to depart, but on reaching the door I turned and said to him, 'I will hold fast the religion of Jesus Christ, and I am ready, for the sake of it, to shed my blood. Though you all become infidels, yet will not I.' And so I left the room.

"One of my friends told me he had suggested to the Patriarch that the grand reason why I did not believe in the Pope was, that among other doctrines he taught that he could not commit an error. The Patriarch wondered how I could pretend that I held the Christian religion, and converse in such abusive terms against it. And I also wondered after he saw this, that he should not be willing so much as to ask me, in mildness and forbearance, for what reasons I was unwilling to receive the teaching of the Pope. But so far from this, he would not suffer the Armenian priest to discuss the subject with me, and he laid every person, even his own brother, under excommunication if they should presume to dispute or converse with me on the subject of religion. Under an entire bereavement of books, and shut out from all persons that might instruct me, from what quarter could I get the evidence necessary to persuade me to accept the Patriarch's opinions?

"Another cause of wonder which I had was, that no one of all with whom I conversed, after he saw me to be heretical and declining from the truth, thought proper to advise me to use the only means of becoming strong in the faith, namely, prayer to God alone, and searching His Holy Word, which even a child may understand. I wondered, too, that they should ridicule me abroad as one mad, and after all be so fearful of engaging in a dispute with the madman lest he should vanquish them in argument, and turn them away from the truth.

"After some time, there came to our convent the Bishop of Beirut. I gave him the usual salutation, and was greatly rejoiced to see him. I knew the excellency of his understanding, and his quickness of apprehension, and I hoped that, after some discussion between us, he would explain the truth, and that he would bring forward clear proofs in support of his views. Once more I was disappointed, for one day I asked him a question, and, during the whole of the short conversation which followed, whenever I began to bring evidence against him he grew angry, and he finally drove me from the chamber in a fury, for no other cause, as he pretended, than that he did not wish to converse with a heretic.

"By and by Priest Yoosef of Shaheen came down to us from Ain Waraka, and I endeavoured to get him to unite with me in persuading the Patriarch to send out some evangelists to preach the Gospel among the people, or that there should be preaching in the churches by the local priests. But he would not co-operate with me in this, and so I again failed of my purpose.

"When the Patriarch and the Bishop of Beirut wished to dispute with me, I expressed the hope that the discussion might be without anger. It was concluded that it should be in writing, that no one should afterwards be able to alter what he had once said. They then began to ask me questions. The first was, 'Has the Messiah given us a new law?' When I found that by a new law they meant the Gospel, I answered, 'Yes.' They then asked me if there were not to be found in this new law some obscurities, and again I answered, 'Yes.' They said, 'Suppose any difference of sentiment should arise between the teachers of Christianity, how are we to distinguish the truth from error?' I answered, 'We have no other means of arriving at the truth than by searching the Word of God, and inquiring of spiritual teachers, with purity of motive and with disinterestedness of inclination. If the obscurities of the Word of God cannot be understood by these means, our ignorance is excusable, and will not prevent our salvation. But if the obscurity respects our practice, so that any practice seems to us doubtful, desist from it; but if it is not forbidden, do it; and blessed is he that condemneth not himself in that thing which he alloweth.' When I had given them this answer they brought no evidence to prove any error in it.

"One evening as I was walking with the Bishop of Beirut, he began to tell me how much they all felt for me, and how unwilling they were to put me in chains, and that, if it were not for their sympathy and love to me, there were men who were ready to take my life. After some time I said, 'But how can we believe in the Pope's infallibility?' He quoted for proof, 'Thou art Peter, and upon this rock will I build My church, and the gates of hell shall not prevail against it.' He then resorted to another mode of proof, saying, 'It is desirable that the Pope should be infallible.' I answered, 'But your reasoning with regard to the Pope may be applied to all the bishops of the Church, for it is desirable that all should be infallible.' He said, 'No, for the bishops in that case feeling less their need of the Pope, would not look to him, nor submit to him as their head, and thus there would be divisions and contentions in the Church.' 'But why,' I said, 'did not divisions and contentions arise among the apostles? Were they not all infallible as well as Peter?' And when he would not admit that they were infallible, I told him it was a thing incredible that the Pope was infallible and the apostles were not. We conversed further, when the bishop concluded by saying, 'You have a devil and should be killed.' I asked the bishop his reason for wishing to kill me, and what evil I had done? Then was he filled with high and bitter wrath, saying, 'What! shall we let you go about to corrupt the people?' Then I said to him, 'God is with me,' and went away.

"One day the bishop reproached me with having blasphemed against the Eucharist, the Virgin Mary, and the pictures, because he pretended I had said before one of the deacons, that were it not for fear of the Patriarch I would tear all the pictures in pieces and burn them. I told him that the pictures were not gods, and that I wished to tell all the common people so, that they might understand it. To this, however, he would not consent. Then he talked to me further about the Eucharist, and not being able to substantiate his accusations against me, he again fell into a rage.

"Their treatment of me grew worse, and being so much troubled by them, I resolved to leave the convent at midnight and commit myself to the protection of God."

But while Assad then succeeded in escaping to the missionaries, he did not long enjoy his liberty. The priestly despot used every means to get him again under his cruel clutches, and was successful. He took him first to Alma, and from there he brought him to the convent of Kanobin, where poor Assad was beaten by the fanatics every day, and smitten by their hands upon his face. Yet as often as they struck him on one cheek, he turned to them the other. They then threw him on the ground, and smote him with sticks. The Patriarch ordered also that he should be bastinadoed for several days, in order to effect his recantation. Through all this Assad stood steadfast as a rock, which exasperated the clerical tyrant, so that he was more cruelly tortured than before, laid in heavy chains, and cast into a dark prison. As he was brought out several times a day to be bastinadoed, he often sank senseless to the ground, but when he came to his senses again, he began to pray for his persecutors. Finally the Patriarch determined to wall the poor martyr entirely up, with only a little loophole at the top, through which he was to be fed. This dungeon was only four feet square, and scarcely high enough for the prisoner to stand. In this fearful condition he often cried aloud, and said, "Oh, think of me, ye that pass by! Have pity upon me, and deliver me from these sufferings!"

His mother, his brother, and other compassionate people did their utmost to entreat the Patriarch to grant Assad his liberty, or at least to ameliorate his sufferings. The heartless monster did not comply, but left the poor martyr as he was, loaded with heavy iron chains, and walled up in that dark dungeon until he breathed his last, when his earthly remains were whirled over a precipice, and covered by a heap of stones, while his noble spirit was set free in the glory of the kingdom of God. This took place at Kanobîn, the residence of the Maronite Patriarch, Joseph Habeish, in October, 1830.

Since that year a number of Maronites have become Protestants, and some of them were eminent and learned men ; but, on the whole, the Maronites, and especially their clergy, remain obstinate and fanatical opposers to the Gospel of Christ.

MOSLEM CALL TO PRAYER.

CHAPTER XXI.

AS there are few Mohammedans in the district of Brummana, and their religion is already well known, it is not needful for me to describe it. But in the northern part of Lebanon we still meet with two religious sects which have sprung out of Mohammedanism. The first are called the Ismailiyehs, and the second the Nusariehs. Both sects are quite opposed to the Koran and Islamism, as well as to each other and the Druses. The Ismailiyehs originated in Alamout in Dilem, and Mazenderan in Persia; where they were influenced by the religious principles of Persia and India. Their originator, who was called Hassan, lived at the end of the eleventh century at Alamout. He regarded himself as a descendant of Fatimah, the daughter of the prophet Mohammed, and tried to trace his descent to Ishmael, the son of Abraham. As a descendant of Fatimah, he was related to the Egyptian king, El Hakem, whom the Druses regard as God. But in spite of this relationship, the Ismailiyehs are opposed to the Druses on account of some religious differences. At first the Ismailiyehs increased rapidly. Hassan was himself regarded as their Grand Master, to whom unconditional obedience was due. His religious system was and is still kept severely secret, but, from what can be learned, it appears to be nothing but a secret ignorance and superstition.

Like the Druses the Ismailiyehs believe in the transmigration of souls.   They consider Ali, the son-in-law of Mohammed, as an incarnation of God, and all the important good men of their sect as incarnations of the spirits who were connected with him.   They reject Mohammed as a prophet, and say with the Druses that he was a devil.   They consequently reject the Koran and all that pertains to Mohammedanism : in fact, their religion is mainly one of negation and opposition to all other religious principles, and to all laws both human and Divine.   In this they seem to possess the same spirit as the Commune of Paris, the Nihilists of Russia, or other social Democrats.   They reject heaven and hell, and believe in the eternity of the world.

Abulfetah, a relative of Hassan, transplanted the Ismailiyehs from Persia to the north of Mount Lebanon, where the fortification of Massiyad became the centre of their operations in that district. Their number was at that time very large and powerful.   The most terrible thing on earth is man in his folly, and to this the Ismailiyehs formed no exception.   They were the worst of all human creatures, and fearful enemies to peace and order. In the time of the Crusades, when Baldwin I. occupied Jerusalem, the Ismailiyehs, who were already well known throughout the East as robbers and murderers, became notorious to the Europeans also under the title of assassins.   In the East they had gained the name of *Hashshashin*,* from their habit of eating cakes of Oriental hemp, or *hashshash*, which excited them to bloodthirstiness and massacres. When passing recently through Egypt I was astonished still to see these *hashshash* dens in which the people smoke opium and eat cakes of *hashshash*, and

---

* The Crusaders could not pronounce the word "Hashshashin," but said "Assassin," which is the origin of the word in our language.

I was frightened to look at their distorted faces. In consequence of the fearful readiness of these Ismailiyehs for murder, they were often used by usurpers and other unscrupulous men to kill persons in high position who stood in the way of their ambitious or revengeful intrigues. They were engaged in warfare against the Abassides or Orthodox Mohammedans of Bagdad, as well as against the Crusaders and other religious denominations. In the year 1148 they murdered Raymond of Tripoli, in the church of Antartus; and they afterwards killed the Marquis Conrad of Monserrat. They tried repeatedly to kill the noble Saladin, and also Prince Edward, the son of Henry III. of England, but could not succeed. Sultan Bibar conquered the Ismailiyehs and took possession of all their fortified strongholds in 1269, but the greatest judgment against them was carried out by the destructive and powerful Tamerlane, in the year 1391.

At present we find only a few thousand Ismailiyehs in the north of Lebanon, and their political influence has died out, though they are still regarded as an obnoxious and dangerous people. They dwell in eighteen villages, and are mostly occupied in the cultivation of their land.

The Nusariehs are much more numerous than the Ismailiyehs and Druses. They number about 200,000 souls, and dwell on the mountains between the Orontes and the Mediterranean, and from Gebal to Alexandretta. This sect sprang from Kufa on the Euphrates, in the year 890 A.D., and were called after the birthplace of their leader, who came from the city of Nasrana. Being persecuted in that neighbourhood they took refuge in Syria, and settled down on the northern part of Mount Lebanon.

Though they hate the Ismailiyehs there is great similarity between their religious principles. They differ greatly from the Orthodox Mohammedans, and acknowledge the divinity of Ali Ibn Aby Taleb, son-in-law of Mohammed. They reject the Koran and curse Mohammed, Aby Baker, Omar, and Othman. They practise circumcision, generally when the children are eight years of age. Their prayer consists in the glorification of Ali, and they say, "There is no God but Ali, and Mohammed el Hamed is the prophet and beloved of God." They, too, believe in Metempsychosis or the transmigration of souls, and say that the good men among them become stars, but others must wander from body to body until they are purified for transformance into stars also. The souls of very bad men, they say, become Jews, Christians, and Mohammedans, while some enter into swine and other unclean animals. They call Jesus Christ a great prophet or Spirit of God. Like the Mohammedans they like the Old Testament and the Gospels, and when asked why they do not become Christians, they reply, "We are Christians, we like Jesus Christ, and celebrate the Christmas feast."

They are divided into two sections, the Shemsich, or sun-worshippers, and the Kamarich, or worshippers of the moon. These practices they must have adopted from the ancient Arabs, who worshipped the heavenly luminaries. The places of worship of the Nusariehs are generally upon the top of high mountains in solitary wildernesses. They keep their religion severely secret, and if one of them reveals the least of it to others, he endangers his life. Solomon of Adana, a Nusarich who became a Christian some years ago, wrote a little book containing a full description of their religion, but they did not rest till they had killed him.

They practice Polygamy. Each man is allowed to have four wives whom they treat as slaves, and regard as animals, saying women have no souls and consequently for them there is no such thing as Metempsychosis. If a Nusarieh wants to have a wife, he makes the bargain with her father, and pays him for her a hundred piastres, or about £5 10s. If he has no money the bridegroom presents his future father-in-law instead with a cow, donkey, camel, or horse, in exchange for the bride. When this has taken place, the friends of the bridegroom go up to the top of the bride's house with sticks in their hands, while the friends of the bride likewise arm themselves with sticks to protect her. The bridegroom fights his way through with a stick or sword until he reaches her. Then he beats her so hard that she howls and weeps aloud so that the people on the roof can easily hear her melancholy lamentation. This is the signal of their engagement, after which all the people retire, and the bridegroom takes his bride home with him.

The Nusariehs indulge in intoxicating drink, but do not smoke tobacco. They observe the law of Moses in regard to clean and unclean animal food. Their dress consists simply of a white cotton shirt and a white turban on their heads. They never button their shirts, as they say that it is a sin to cover the heart, because God must always look into it. They are ruled by their respective Sheikhs, who are also their religious leaders under the name of Mukaddin. They are tributary to the Turkish Government, which treats them often with cruelty and injustice. The result of this is that the Nusariehs often kill the Turkish officers, for which they are punished by strangling. To them this is the most fearful punishment which the Turks can ever inflict, because they believe that usually the

soul goes out of the mouth, but that when people
are hung or strangled it is obliged to depart from
below, which makes it unfit to enter into a superior
body or to become a star in heaven.

The Nusariehs have never become so warlike or
so notoriously bad people as the Ismailiyehs. For
the most part they peacefully work the land in
their wild regions, but when exasperated or excited
to warfare by their neighbours the Ismailiyehs,
they bravely defend their country. The Ismailiyehs
and the Nusariehs, as well as the Druses, are an
outgrowth of the Batenites or Gnostical Shiites,
who went astray through their speculative interpretation of their old religious teaching.

The American Presbyterian Mission have opened
some schools among the Nusariehs in the neighbourhood of Latakiah. They are doing a good work,
but it is very needful that it should be extended,
or that some other Protestant society should
take up the Ismailiyehs as the object of their
Christian interest and sympathy, and organize an
evangelical mission among them. The Ismaili-
yeh and Nusarieh converts to Christianity are not
exposed to the penalty of death by the Turkish
Government like the Mohammedan converts. These
two sects never had a good example in the
Oriental Christian Churches, which themselves had
lost their first love, and without love everyone was
against them, and they were against everyone. If
some Protestant Mission, like those carried on by
the Moravians, could be established among them,
they would soon learn to appreciate and love the
true principles of Christianity, and become Christians themselves; but hitherto, except the few
schools already referred to, nothing has been done
for these poor deluded sects, which are so truly
heathen.

BRUMMANA, MOUNT LEBANON, WITH FRIENDS' MISSION BUILDINGS.

CHAPTER XXII.

OUR REMOVAL TO BRUMMANA.

THE summer holidays fell during the few months between my resignation and the conclusion of my service in the British Syrian Schools. At that time people generally go to the mountains, in order to escape the burning and relaxing heat of Beirut. On the 3rd of July, 1873, my luggage was packed, and two horses and one donkey were ready to convey us to the mountains of Lebanon. Before starting I took my dear wife and four children into one of the emptied rooms of the house we had occupied in the past, and there we knelt before the Lord God, our Saviour and Father in heaven, and poured out our hearts before His mercy seat in thanksgiving and prayer for His protecting care and Divine guidance. While many tears flowed from our eyes we seemed to hear the Lord's voice saying, " Go forth with joy ; fear not, for My grace is sufficient for you." We left Rosa in the school at Beirut, and the three smaller children, one of whom was a baby, we took with us. The journey was rather hard for my poor wife, because the road along the precipices was very bad. The servant, who went with us, could not ride the donkey, and fell off with one child. Both began to cry aloud. My wife was frightened and the other children too, and they joined in the chorus of lamentation. I could not move, as I was on horseback with the baby in my arms, but just at this moment a man came down from the mountain, who helped us along until we were right again. In the evening at eight o'clock we reached Brummana safely, but no kind friends were waiting there for us, and no refreshing cup of tea or other food was presented. Our arrival was gloomy and melancholy, but we slept soundly and sweetly on the floor of the empty and humble house. A few. days after we were in a better condition, for our furniture and kitchen utensils were brought up. We had many visitors from the Druses, Greeks, and Maronites, whose wild looks seemed to indicate some truth in the reports which had been told us of them in Beirut. Our first and best friend was Semaan el Koury, who helped us in many difficulties. He was a native of Brummana who had been educated at the American Mission School at Abeih, in the southern part of Lebanon, under the venerable Dr. Calhoon.

Among the people who came to visit us were some nice looking old men, who said, "The American missionaries, Mr. Bird, author of 'Bible Works in Bible Lands,' and Dr. Thomson, author of 'The Land and the Book,' once came here and distributed many Bibles and Testaments, but the *Emirs* (princes) and the priests expelled the Bible-men, and diligently searched for the Holy Scriptures, and burnt them in the public place at Brummana." This was done by order of the Maronite Patriarch, Joseph Habeish, who killed Assad Shidiak, the first Protestant and martyr of Lebanon. The princes, Emir Besheer and Emir Mansour of Brummana, worked hand in hand with the fanatical clergy, and opposed every good work.

I went to work and explained the simple Gospel truth to the people. We had many visitors from

all classes and denominations, and returning their
calls gave me plenty of opportunity to teach these
benighted people the pure Gospel. For this work
I used nearly day and night. But though we
read that those that preach the Gospel should also
live of the Gospel, I saw nobody coming forward
with something substantial for our daily need. My
little money was coming to an end. What was to
be done? My wife and four children needed daily
bread. I came to Brummana in connection with
no missionary society, and with no promise from
anyone to bear my temporal support, but I came up
with faith, well knowing that our heavenly Father
will care for those who put their full trust in Him.
I was also aware that faith has often been tried
whether it is a real faith or an empty imagination.
I laid my pressing condition in fervent prayer before
the Lord, and prayed on, and believed on, and
worked on, that the mission might grow and be
blessed. I asked some of the American missionaries at Beirut whether they would take up this
new mission field, but they refused. Then I brought
my work and my own circumstances before Bishop
Gobat at Jerusalem, but he said that he was too
old to undertake new mission work, and thought I
had made a mistake in leaving the British Syrian
Schools. After this I wrote to Inspector Rappard
of the St. Chrischona Mission, and explained to him
my work on Mount Lebanon, as well as my own
condition. He replied that he sympathised very
much with me, but was too short of funds to take
upon himself the responsibility of a new mission
station. Then, just when my funds were exhausted,
I received offers from two other missionary societies
to leave Mount Lebanon and join them in other
countries, but I felt I must refuse them.

The people at Brummana and other villages asked

me for schools, and I thought it good to comply
with their wishes.   I therefore wrote to my friends
at Berne in Switzerland on the subject, and they
sent me at once the means for opening a Girls'
School at Brummana, which was done in the summer of 1873.   The first teacher was Hanni Ferah,
a native girl, who was a friend of Sybil and Eli
Jones.   Before the year closed means were sent from
Canton de Vaud and from Lausanne, in Switzerland, by Madame Clara Monneron, for opening
Boys' Schools at Brummana and Beit Mary.   But
for the maintenance of my family nothing was yet
done.   So I wrote to Hannah Stafford Allen in
London, and to Eli Jones in America, about the
Brummana Mission, and they sent me some pecuniary assistance in order to support my family; but
there was nothing fixed, and no society was yet
organized to support this Mission.   I looked very
sharply and prayerfully for the guidance of our
Divine Master, in whose hands people and circumstances are the instruments and means by which
He manifests His holy will to His children; and as
I was very much afraid in my greatest need to be
tempted by dependence on men, I was the more on
the look-out to keep my eye single, and my faith
pure from any dust of this world.   I did not yet
know what Church or Society would be ready to
take up this Mission, but I was at ease through
knowing that our Father in heaven always cares
for us and shows us the way, and I had only to
follow Him.

About this time Hannah Stafford Allen wrote:
"Most heartily do I thank our Father in heaven if
in any way He has permitted us to be instrumental
in helping and cheering you in the rough and thorny
paths of the pioneer Christian's life.   I assure
you we embrace every opportunity for interesting

Friends in the Lord's work at Brummana." Eli Jones, too, wrote from America : "I am glad to be able to say that our Friends in New, as well as Old England, seem much interested in thy work on Mount Lebanon. I think that thyself and dear wife and your helpers may be encouraged to give yourselves to the work of the Lord there with full trust that your temporal wants will be supplied. I am highly gratified that thou art able to give so good an account of Hanni Ferah." All these messages of love and Christian sympathy I hailed with intense interest, as proofs of the good will of our heavenly Father, and I desired to follow them as signs of the Lord's will.

In the autumn of 1873 H. S. Allen again wrote :—

" My dear Theophilus,—I am very wishful to reply to thy last letter without delay, for I feel sure thou hast need of sympathy amidst the many difficulties just now pressing upon thee. It cheers me to feel thou art in our Father's hand, and art looking unto Him for direction. He will not leave thee nor forsake thee. Hope on. Trust on. Rest on His gracious promises. Thine eyes shall see thy Teacher, and thine ears shall hear the voice behind thee, saying, when thou turnest to the right hand or to the left, ' This is the way, walk thou in it,' and in so doing thou wilt have peace. Day by day you will be led along, and though the paths may be chequered, and the way seem long and often dark and gloomy, yet may the weary heart find composure in the simple yet grandest source of it, ' The Lord reigneth.' It is not for us to dictate whether the paths shall be smooth or rough by which He leads His children unto the city of habitation. It seems to me, that if so permitted, thy talents, abilities, and experience, and thy knowledge of the Arabic language can be best turned to account on Mount Lebanon.   Affectionately thine,

"HANNAH STAFFORD ALLEN."*

I had to begin the Mission in Brummana under many trials and perplexities, but such encouraging letters from England, America, and Switzerland were the means in the Lord's hand to uphold me and my dear wife in the time of sorrow.   In the autumn of 1873 George Hessenauer, a young German, with whom I had Christian fellowship while at Beirut, came to Brummana for the purpose of studying Arabic, and preparing himself for mission work.   About this time I began to open a meeting for worship on Sunday, which caused no little excitement among the priests, but we went on in the name of our Divine Master, preaching to old and young the simple Gospel of the love of God in Christ Jesus.   The winter began to set in, strong tropical rains poured down, and fearful thunder-storms and hurricanes discharged themselves with hailstones and falls of snow.   The house in which we lived was not good enough to shelter its inmates against such fearful weather.   The rain not only poured into our room through the flat roof, but it forced its way through the badly made shutters.   I can never forget one night when the water stood four inches deep upon the earthen floor of our room.   I put all the children into their mother's bed and covered them all with an Abyssinian cow skin, while I cried out to the neighbours for help, and the whole night I was engaged with other people in carrying the water from our room.   In spite of all these uncomfortable circumstances, however, we all continued in good health.   The

---

* And it was H. S. Allen who sent me the first pecuniary assistance for my family.

HANNAH STAFFORD ALLEN.

winter passed away and the warm spring began to set in. I took another house for my family, but it did not prove a good one, and most of my family suffered much in it because it was damp. We could not get another at that time because the people were threatened with excommunication if they let their houses to Protestants.

Winter on Mount Lebanon begins at the end of October, and lasts to the end of March or middle of April. The rainfall reaches an average of 30 to 35 inches. In the mountains, 3,000 feet above the level of the sea, we have often heavy snowfalls with rain, while below 2,000 feet we have only strong tropical rain. We often see the sea along the Syrian coast of a yellowish brown colour because the mountain streams from the heights of Lebanon carry with them the fertile brown and yellow soil which tints the water. It is so especially with the Adonis, Damur, and Lycus rivers, which have for thousands of years been carrying on this process. With the cutting down of the forests the soil has been still further exposed to the action of the weather, till sterile rocks stretch their bare heads towards heaven and give to the mountains a melancholy appearance. The strip of land between the mountains and the sea is extremely fertile. Many of the people are employed in rearing silkworms.

In ancient times the silk manufacture was not yet introduced into Syria. The population of Lebanon was then not so great as it is now, and most of the people were employed in cultivating the fertile plain and parts of the mountain, while others were engaged in ship building and merchandise along the Syrian coast. As the pine and oak wood was so near at hand the people of Gebal were noted, in early times, for their skill in ship building, and this we find mentioned in Joshua xiii. 5; 1 Kings v. 18; Ezek. xxvii. 9. Though silk was known to the Greeks, Persians, and Romans, it was a long time before it was introduced into Syria.

Aristotle mentions silk in 330 B.C., as an article imported from China through Persia. Pausanius of Cæsarea in Cappadocia, in the second century A.D., gave a full description of the rearing of the silk-worm. In the middle of the sixth century we find that Beirut, Sidon, and Tyre in Phœnicia, provided the Greeks and Romans with silk which they had previously obtained from China through Persia. But the Phœnicians were also clever enough to procure the means of rearing the silk-worm themselves in their own country. About the beginning and middle of the sixth century the persecuted Nestorians settled down in the Western District of Shansi in China. There the mulberry tree (Morus alba) was at home, and the silk manufacture was in a flourishing condition. The Nestorians, therefore, engaged in the silk business, and it is generally reported that two Nestorian monks from Shansi brought the eggs of the silk-worm in hollow walking sticks to Constantinople, where they were hatched by the heat of a dunghill, and fed on mulberry leaves. These leaves did not belong to the Morus alba, because this tree was not yet introduced into Syria or Europe, but to the Morus nigra, which bears the black eatable berries so well known by Persians, Greeks, and Romans. The leaves of a certain mallow may also be used as a substitute for mulberry leaves. In the time of the Greek Emperor Justinian, the manufacture of silk was introduced into Beirut, Sidon, Tyre, and Byblus, but it needed a good deal of time before it took hold of the people.

CARRYING CORN IN PALESTINE.

In the time of the Crusades Jacob de Vitriaco informs us that the silk manufacture was a considerable business at Beirut and other places along the Syrian coast. It is also related by Makrizi and Brocardus that no less than 4,000 looms for silk weaving were found in the year 1283 at Tripoli in Phœnicia. At this time the white mulberry tree (Morus alba) with its white berries and large lustrous leaves was already introduced into Syria, as it gives the best leaves for feeding the silk-worms, but no one is able to say exactly from whence this tree was brought to Syria and Europe, though it is thought that it must have come from China or Kashmir. From Beirut the mulberry tree and the rearing of silk-worms was introduced on Mount Lebanon, where it became a perfect success. The silk business caused a great change for the better in the agriculture on Mount Lebanon, as the mountains became rapidly terraced, and every fertile spot was converted into a mulberry garden. The quality of the silk was very good, and consequently paid well, on which account the manufacture of silk is still the principal business of the people of Mount Lebanon.

The bombyx mori, which is the real silk-worm, belongs to the family of Lepidoptera or moths. The seed, or egg, of the silk-worm is as small as mustard seed, and its colour is darkish grey. It was produced plentifully in Syria, but when it got corrupted the people of Lebanon got their seed from France, Italy, Corsica, and China. The seed from Corsica is the very best, and gives the most beautiful silk.

During the winter the eggs of the silk-worm are kept in airy and cool rooms. Most of the people hang them in small bags made of unbleached calico inside the arched roof of their churches. In the

spring, when the mulberry trees are beginning to
spread out their leaves, the eggs of the silk-worm
are removed, and placed in a room full of smoke in
a temperature of 17° (Reaumur). In about a fort-
night's time out of every egg comes forth a little
worm. The natives of Lebanon make large round
trays, about two feet in diameter, from reeds, and
plaster them well with cow dung, but before use
they must be well dried. Then the leaves of the
white mulberry tree are brought, well minced, and
spread on these trays, after which the little worms
are strewn over the fine and tender leaves. In the
mountains the silk-worm has to be fed in the
houses, while on the plain the whole process is
carried on out of doors, under little reed huts in
the mulberry garden.

The little silk-worms are eating away day and
night, and after five days they begin to lift up their
heads above the leaves and cease eating for twenty-
four hours, which is called by the natives the first
fasting. After this the worm begins to eat again
for six days and nights, during which time they
must be supplied with fresh leaves continually.
After these six days the silk-worms lift up their
heads again off the leaves and fast for another
twenty-four hours, which is the second fasting.
Then they eat again for seven days and nights, after
which time they have another fast of twenty-four
hours, and eat again for eight days and nights.
Then they fast for the fourth and last time for
twenty-four hours, after which they eat nine days
and nine nights. By this time the worms have
grown to a length of two inches, and are as thick
as a thick lead pencil. During these last nine days
they consume an enormous quantity of mulberry
leaves, and men and women, boys and girls, are
engaged day and night in feeding them. Then each

A LEBANON SHEPHERD.

worm begins to spin his own silky shroud, which takes him two days to accomplish. During this process the silk-worm decreases in length. It becomes quite torpid, and soon changes its skin and becomes a chrysalis, the whole cocoon being about as large as a pigeon's egg. It remains in this state for fifteen days. By means of a fluid which comes out of its mouth it then penetrates the cocoon, and emerges as a kind of moth. The male then unites with the female, which lays about three hundred eggs, and these become the seed for the coming year. The cocoons which are to be spun for good silk must have the chrysalis suffocated in hot air, so as to preserve the whole length of the silk thread on the cocoons. The length of the silk thread of one cocoon is 400 yards.

On Mount Lebanon the people make shelves of reeds and straw along and around the inside of their houses from top to botton. These shelves are about two feet wide and look just like the berths in steamers. The silk-worms after the second fasting are taken off the trays and placed on shelves where they are fed until their spinning time, when the people put little bushy shrubs, such as heather, everywhere about them, into which the silk-worm creeps and spins his cocoon. This is generally at the end of May. At this time all the mulberry gardens look very bare as they have been stripped of all their leaves, but during the next two months they put forth new branches with another crop of leaves, not for the feeding of silk-worms this time, but for the feeding of sheep. This is likewise the business of the women. By stuffing the sheep night and day with mulberry leaves they become so fat that they are hardly able to walk. In September they kill these sheep and preserve their meat for the winter time. The new branches of the mulberry trees are not cut off, but are left for the next year's crop of leaves for the silk-worms.

The following average account will show how profitable the silk business is. One drachm of silk-worm eggs will produce 768 drachms of cocoons, which will produce 70 drachms of pure silk, the value of which will be 60 piastres, or 9 shillings. One drachm of silk-worm eggs requires 160 pounds weight of mulberry leaves, and ten middle-sized mulberry trees are needed to produce this quantity. These ten trees require 230 square feet of earth. Here we see that each 230 square feet of land will bring an income of nine shillings. The land must of course be well manured and ploughed from time to time, and as all mulberry trees raised from seed are wild, they must be grafted by good ones, which must be done in the beginning of July. It is calculated that this part of Syria produces 180,000 lbs. of finished silk, which is mostly conveyed to the silk-weaving factories of Lyons in France. From twelve pounds of cocoons the silk factors obtain one pound of finished silk.

CHAPTER XXIII.

A FTER earnest and prayerful consideration, it was thought best that I should go to England and plead the cause of the Lebanon Mission personally. On the 21st of April, 1874, I left my dear family and George Hessenauer at Brummana, and travelled by Trieste to Switzerland. I had several meetings in Switzerland with my friends in Berne and the Canton de Vaud, who supported the schools at Brummana and Beit Mary. I then went on to England where a cordial welcome was awaiting me at my English home with Stafford and Hannah Allen in Upper Clapton.

I consulted several friends prayerfully about the condition of the Mount Lebanon Mission, and I brought specially before them the building of a mission house and training school for boys at Brummana. Though I was not yet a member of the Society of Friends outwardly, I was in my heart, and I was allowed to attend all the sittings of their London Yearly Meeting, which strengthened my religious convictions as a Friend, as well as my faith and confidence in Jesus Christ. It refreshed my soul and kindled my zeal for more devotion to the Lord's work. I soon felt that it was the will of our Father in heaven that the Society of Friends should take up the Mission on Mount Lebanon, and on the 21st of May I pleaded its cause at their Foreign Mission Meeting in London, before a large auditory, and left it in the hands of the Lord.

Then having received an urgent invitation from the Swedish Missionary Society to be present at their Annual Meeting, and give them information with regard to Abyssinia, I felt it my duty to go to Stockholm, where I arrived on the evening of the 8th of June. Next day I went to the Johannaloun Mission Meeting where several thousand people were gathered together. I addressed the meeting in German which was translated into Swedish, and the next day I had another large meeting in another part of the city, when more than two thousand persons listened with interest.

As the Swedish Missionary Society was just at that time going to take up Abyssinia as one of their Mission fields I was asked to explain the circumstances of the country and give my advice and opinion about various matters connected with the new Mission. This I did to the best of my ability in accordance with the experience gained in my ten years of mission work, suffering, and captivity in that land. In the various meetings I had in Sweden I also pleaded for the Mission on Mount Lebanon.

Having much work in England, I left Stockholm on the 16th, with the young missionary, John Aspling, who was going to Stepney College. On the 24th, in company with Stafford and Hannah Allen, I was present at the Ackworth School examination, which greatly interested me, and gave me the opportunity of addressing those 300 boys and girls. I then went to Manchester and to many other places up and down the country, trying to interest Friends in the mission work on Mount Lebanon. It was a hard task for me, especially before Friends who were unknown to me, and I to them. I was often trembling while first breaking the ice, and I had to hold fast my heavenly Father's hand which I was able to recognise even in my greatest perplexity. It was not only very hard, but sometimes discouraging also, through feeling the want of interest and sympathy in this Foreign Mission work; but I was often made ashamed, for our Father in heaven blessed my weak endeavours and gave me many friends. This was a sign to me that the Mission at Brummana should in future be taken up by the Society of Friends in England and America, though Friends generally hesitate long before they take upon themselves any responsibility in supporting new mission work. During my visit a central and local committees were organized. William C. Allen of London, Edward Pearson of Manchester, and George Howland of the United States, were appointed treasurers; and Hannah Stafford Allen of London, and Alfred Lloyd Fox of Falmouth, in England, and Eli Jones of South China, Maine, U.S.A., were appointed secretaries. After my long journeys and meetings I had a sweet and blessed resting time at my English home, where the dear mother, Hannah Stafford Allen, took much care of the young Mission, and worked hard in it. She had a clear head, a good heart, a strong mind, and a sound judgment for the organization of plans, and much practical power to bring them into execution.

Some time before this I applied for membership with Friends, to Devonshire House Monthly Meeting of Friends in London; and on the 14th of July, 1874, I was received a member of that society.

As I saw the way clearly, I presented the following petition for a Boys' Training Home before the friends of the Mount Lebanon Mission:

"Dear Friends,—Having been engaged for several years in mission work in Syria, I have had much opportunity for seeing and learning the general degradation and misery of the people. I was surprised to find that the very nation which was the means in the hands of God for conveying the glorious Christian religion to the European continent, is now so deeply debased that the people are unable to help themselves, because they have lost those spiritual faculties by which a nation is elevated from its low estate. The repeated civil warfare, the miserable Turkish Government, the multitude of priests, and the large number of monasteries and convents, have ruined both country and people. The land is barren, and it is only with great difficulty and trouble that the people can build terraces on the steep mountain slopes for the mulberry trees, which are their principal means of subsistence. When these fail, as not unfrequently happens, the people are exposed to starvation. Brummana, on Mount Lebanon, where I have already commenced a new mission work, is most in want of help. I found the Maronites, Greeks, and Druses there all very ignorant. The Christians have the name of Christ but deny Him by their deeds. In their numerous churches we do not find Gospel truth but a Christian mythology and idolatry, which surprises the most careless observer. Under these circumstances generation after generation of the people, with their blind leaders, are going down to misery.

"I especially pity the children, who are under such poisonous influence. Even their own parents are not able to bring them up properly, either for the present or future world. They are early going astray, like sheep without a shepherd, and often they find an early grave. Some day-schools already established on Mount Lebanon, and supported by Christian friends in England, America, and Switzerland, are doing good work, but they do not exercise full power over the children, and often the impressions we give at school are banished by the evil

example and conversation of their families at home.
I therefore propose to build a Training Home for
Lebanon children, where we can have them under our
entire control, and where there will not be so many
hindering influences to interfere with our teaching.
The expense for such an undertaking would be
moderate, as most of the materials are to be found
on the spot.   The cost of the land and the erection
of such an Institution with the necessary accommodation for thirty or forty children would not much
exceed £500.   The premises for the Mission family
and the annual support of such an Institution,
including teachers, would be about the same
amount.   We might commence with a smaller
number at a cost of about £200, and the number
might gradually be increased as funds are received.
The pupils ought to be brought up, as much as it is
in man's power, in the way that will best promote
their temporal and eternal welfare.   Besides good
elementary knowledge, they ought to learn some
trade if possible, which would enable them to earn
an honest living in the future.   This is not the
place to enter into details of this proposed work,
which I leave for another time.   I simply say, with
many others who have a thorough knowledge of the
wants of the Syrian Mission fields, that such a
refuge would be a great blessing to the country,
and the surest and most powerful agency for enlightening the benighted regions of Mount Lebanon
with a sound Christian education.   But where will
the needed help arise?   Who will take an interest
in the cause?   Those who are interested in Foreign
Mission work have already so much to do, that I
am rather unwilling to bring new claims before
them.   I have brought, and still intend to bring,
the cause before my heavenly Father, to whom
belongeth all the silver and gold.   Before Him I

am pleading for the little ones upon those goodly mountains, and I believe that He will move some of His people's hearts to help us with their prayers and substance. Therefore I feel it is not needful further to press this matter, but will leave it all for our Father's hands.—THEOPHILUS WALDMEIER.

"August, 1874."

News from Mount Lebanon caused my return to Syria sooner than I expected. Enemies rose against the Mission, and when I arrived at Brummana in the middle of September, I found my dear family, George Hessenauer and Ibrahim Tasso, the teacher of the boys' school, all in deep sorrow. They all greeted me with streams of tears, so that I exclaimed, "What is the cause of this sorrow, when we should be glad and thankful for meeting each other once more?" Then my wife said, "Since you left we have all been ill, and yesterday we buried my dear sister's child, Dora Saalmüller, who was with us during the summer. Theophilus is still ill in bed; and besides all this, we have suffered much on account of the enemies of the Gospel." I said, "Be of good cheer now, and all will be right, because the Lord has done great things for us and for His work on Mount Lebanon." Then I told them all my experiences, and how the Lord had led me step by step among His people, and how Friends had become interested in the Lebanon Mission, and a good amount of funds had been collected for the Mission House and Training Home.

While I was in London I was on the look out for a place where George Hessenauer could qualify himself for missionary work. Mr. H. Gratton Guinness promised to take him into his College, so after my return to Mount Lebanon he studied English very hard, and finally left Brummana for London in February, 1875.

CHAPTER XXIV.

THE PURCHASE OF AIN SALAAM.

ON the 17th of October, 1874, I bought a plot of land at Brummana, which was called *Berkat Ghanem* (the pool of the conqueror), but is now known as *Ain Salaam* (the fountain of peace), for £72, for the purpose of building the Training Home upon it. I settled the title deeds legally at the local and central courts, and also consulted the Consul at Beirut, and showed him the title deeds, which he said were all legally right according to the law of the country. I told the Committee in England what I had done, and at the end of the year they wrote :

"We have heard with much pleasure of the purchase of a suitable site for the proposed Training Home at Brummana, and we hereby officially authorise thee to commence the building. We have been deeply interested in thy letter, and heartily wish the divine blessing on thy labours, and that the Lord's presence may go with thee to direct and strengthen thee for every good work.

"ALFRED LLOYD FOX,
"HANNAH STAFFORD ALLEN,
"ELLEN CLARE PEARSON,
"Secretaries of Friends' Syrian Mission."

Before the year closed I was enabled to open a fourth school at Dar Bsaleem. At the end of 1874 I wrote my first report of the Brummana

Mission to the Committee of the Friends' Syrian Mission :

"It is now one year and a half since the Lord first used me as an instrument in opening a mission station at this place. The outset was very hard, not on account of the privations we had to contend with, but more especially on account of the opposition of the clergy. I felt quite sure, however, that it was the Lord who brought me here. I did not come before asking His will, and believing His guiding hand directed us. This assurance gave me strength to meet the counteracting influences from every direction, and though I am well aware that difficulties, persecutions, and sorrows are not entirely overcome, I feel glad in my heart that we have taken possession of this part of Mount Lebanon. In the first place it is the most needy mission field in Lebanon, except the district of Kessrawan, where no Protestant missionary has been able to abide on account of the power and fanaticism of the Maronite Church. In the second place this station, eighteen months ago, was unoccupied mission ground, so that we do not come in collision with any other missionary agency. The Lord is leading His people, and enabling them to do the right work in the right time. My many years' residence in Abyssinia gave me an experience in mission work which is very useful to me now. My dear wife and myself had to learn many lessons of patience in the hardships and trials of that time. Those who feel the value of a saved soul, and what a blessed work it is to be instrumental in the hand of God to lead souls to Jesus, will not be cast down when they meet with trouble; neither will they look nor seek for their pleasure so much in outward circumstances, because their highest aim and joy is to proclaim to poor sinners the heavenly message in Christ Jesus.

There are thousands of souls here like sheep without a shepherd, and others who are being led away by false shepherds, who feed themselves, but not the flock (Ezekiel xxxiv). These we must strive to lead to the good Shepherd who shed His precious blood for them.

"In looking back upon the past year, I very thankfully remember my visits to England, Stockholm, and Switzerland. Especially did the Lord bless me in England amongst the Society of Friends. Led step by step by His gracious loving hand, He brought me through many years of trouble, and taught and prepared me to join this section of His Church. Attending the Yearly Meeting of Friends in London was a great blessing to me, for on several points I was informed and strengthened, and I felt the overshadowing power of the Holy Spirit in some of those assembles more than I have ever felt it in my whole life, or in any other religious meeting before. Surely there were many sighing and pleading for the inspiration and teaching of the Lord's Holy Spirit, and His power is the secret strength of the Society of Friends. Just as the Lord had led me to Mount Lebanon, so has He led me and helped me to become a Friend. I can be no other, for I feel it was the Lord's own doing, and if, even yet, much trial and affliction should come upon me on this account, I cannot help it, for the Lord put it into my heart and conscience, and His will be done!

"During my visit to England I was privileged to make acquaintance with many dear Friends, the remembrance of whose words is still a comfort and blessing to me. The fellowship of the children of God will ever be helpful and strengthening. It gives power to know and feel that we are not standing isolated and desolated, but are marching along through our pilgrimage hand in hand, united in the love of Jesus, our King, Priest, Prophet, Commander, and Leader, who will, in His own time, bring us safely to our eternal home.

"I am thankful to tell you respecting the Training Home at Brummana, that the Lord has thus far greatly blessed our weak efforts for this special cause and labour of Christian love. The land has been bought and measures about 20,000 square yards. There are a number of fir or pine trees, mulberry and fig trees, with two fountains of water. The foundation ground for the proposed building is not entirely level. The western front towards Beirut will have three stories, while the eastern front towards Brummana will only have two. The kitchen will be placed under the dining-room, whilst the store-rooms, wash-rooms, and workshops will be under the class-rooms and sleeping rooms. I have endeavoured to make the plan as best adapted to the convenience and climate of the mountain. The length of the house will be eighty feet, and the breadth forty-three feet. Pecuniary encouragement we hope, may justify our commencing the building before long. It will be an altar upon which many spiritual sacrifices may be offered up for the glory of our God, and I feel sure that even this proceeding will bring a blessing upon the Society of Friends, and more especially upon those who have taken closest interest in it. Such an Institution which is built upon our own ground will much strengthen our missionary efforts in these Bible lands. 'It shall be to the Lord for a name, and for an everlasting sign that shall not be cut off' (Isaiah lv. 13).

"The four day-schools of our Mission are partly at the central station, Brummana, and partly in villages in its neighbourhood. They are getting on, though under much opposition and difficulty from the Maronite clergy. In these four schools there are about 110 boys and girls, from five to fifteen years of age. They belong to the Druses and to the Greek Orthodox, Maronite, and Greek Catholic Churches. All these children get instructed from the Holy Scriptures, as well as in elementary knowledge, and we try as far as it is in our power to lead them to their Saviour, the Lord Jesus Christ. The schools are free, being supported by my friends in Switzerland. It would lead me too far to enter much into detail, but it is only right to give you a general knowledge and account of all the business, and expenses, etc. A Bible woman came to us lately as an additional help to our Mission. She was recommended by the American missionaries, and seems a good and zealous labourer. Her work is of great importance, for the native women need especial care and attention here, because they are so deplorably degraded and ignorant. My friends at Neuchatel promised to pay all her expenses. The mission field, which we directly occupy, comprises seven villages, of which Brummana is the centre. Three of these villages are located on the north-western side of Brummana, and in one hour-and-half I can reach the furthest of them. It is much better to have the work thus concentrated than to be scattered more widely, and thus lessen the immediate influence.

"About a year after I began to occupy the western part of the district of Meten, it came to pass that Mr. Rae, the clerical superintendent of the schools of the Scotch Mission on Mount Lebanon, began to occupy the eastern part of this district, and I am very glad that I am not working alone in this field, for it needs many labourers.

"For our own edification and strengthening in

spiritual things, we have a weekly meeting every Friday at my house, where all our teachers, and others who may incline, gather together in order to wait upon the Lord and to seek for fresh strength and wisdom, of which we feel our need very much. We know that without a close walk with our heavenly Father, through Christ Jesus, we are unfit to work aright in the kingdom of God, and until self is brought low, the Lord will not entirely use us as His servants for the welfare of our fellow-men. May the Lord bless us individually and unitedly throughout the Society, and enable us, each in our several allotments, to bring forth fruit unto His glory.—THEOPHILUS WALDMEIER."

CHAPTER XXV.

EARLY in the spring of 1875, I was much engaged upon the newly-acquired land. I
planted fruit trees, digged for a larger quantity of water with great success, and began to ex-
cavate the foundation of the new building according
to the plan, and all was going on very briskly and
satisfactorily. I had always a large number of
visitors at the place, among whom were many priests,
who went away muttering curses and perdition to
the Protestants, for having taken the nicest spot
on Mount Lebanon for their own building from the
hands of one of their adherents, in order to under-
mine the good old Maronite religion, by planting
the new Protestant heresy. Bishops and priests
sat together consulting about ways and means to
expel us from Mount Lebanon. The ecclesiastics
instigated a process against me, by means of some
of the relatives of the seller of the ground, who
made claims upon the plot of land which was sold
to me lawfully, and on the 3rd of February, 1875,
I received an official order from the local governor,
Emir Joseph (by whom the title-deed had been
legally completed, sealed, and signed) to stop all
operations upon the land, as a law-suit had been
raised. This was like lightning from a cloudless
heaven, and great perplexity took hold of my heart,
while I reluctantly ordered a temporary cessation of

the work. I had to appear at the law-courts of
Mount Lebanon, where unjust claims were made
upon Friends' property by the mother and sisters
of Daibes Safrawy, who sold me the land, and to
whom I paid the price before many witnesses.
This was one side of the difficulty; but the other
side was much more stinging and provoking, because Daibes Safrawy accused me also at the same
time of not having paid the price of the said land.
I was told that the Maronite bishop induced Daibes
Safrawy to accuse me thus, and that he had said to
the bishop, "But is this not a sin?" when the
bishop replied, "The sin shall be upon my head!"

One day Daibes Safrawy and I stood before the
Lebanon central law-court, and I shivered with
awe as I heard him swear an awful oath before
the tribunal, saying, "I have not received the
price of the land." The judges knew that I paid
him, and that Daibes Safrawy was guilty of a
false oath, but nothing could be done; and this
dreadful law-suit, with the other in regard to the
unjust claims upon the land, encamped like dark
and heavy clouds around me; but these were not
all, for more trials were still in store for me.

> " Ye fearful saints, fresh courage take,
> 　The clouds ye so much dread
> Are big with mercy, and shall break
> 　In blessings on your head."

Meanwhile I went on with my mission work,
teaching the young in the schools, and preaching
the Gospel to the old, in season and out of season,
publicly and privately. I also opened a school at
Roomy and another at Neby, so that we had now six
schools in operation; and one Bible-woman and one
Scripture-reader were engaged. While in great
perplexity on account of these dreadful law-suits,
I received many encouraging and comforting letters

from England and America, which cheered me not a little in my many trials.

About this time I succeeded in hiring the house of Emir Ameen, before which the Holy Scriptures had been burnt, and which was now converted into the residence of a Protestant missionary. The Maronite priest Boutrus, of Brummana, said, " I have seen many bad things in this world, but I have never before seen the palace of a Lebanon prince converted into the lodging of a heretical imposter."

Muallim Semaan el Koury, the Scripture-reader, was one of the first true Protestants in Brummana. He was educated at Dr. Calhoon's School at Abeih, and there began to love the Lord Jesus sincerely. He was afterwards engaged as teacher by Elijah Saleeby, and was already advanced in age when he returned to his native village of Brummana, where he desired to do something in the Lord's service. In 1874 I engaged him as teacher of our Boys' School at Brummana, where he worked faithfully for the first year; but he afterwards desired to go among the people to preach the Gospel, to which I gladly agreed. He taught the people the salvation which is in Christ Jesus alone, by conversation as well as by preaching, and proved himself, both in words and conduct, a faithful, humble, and sincere Protestant Christian. He was hated by all his relations because he had left the Greek Church. He was known as a Protestant in the whole district, and persecuted as such. In June, 1875, he fell sick, and in spite of medicine his sickness daily became more serious, so that I had but little hope for his earthly life. On the 17th of September he sent for me to pray with him, after which he made his last will, in which he desired to die as an Evangelical Protestant Christian, and to be buried accordingly

in our new burial ground, by the side of his two
children, who had been buried there within the
previous twelve months. This caused a great commotion, for the fanatical priests and superstitious
inhabitants of Brummana did not like to have a
Protestant burial ground there, but were obliged
to yield.

Muallim Semaan also intrusted to me his infant
son Naseem with all that he possessed of earthly
things, which, however, was little indeed. All this
was written down, sealed with his own signet ring,
and witnessed by seven witnesses, who signed their
names at the end of the writing. Muallim Semaan
said further, "Now my soul is going to Jesus. I
am ready to depart from this wicked world, to be
with my Saviour. Please pray with me." After
we had prayed he asked us to sing to him in Arabic,

> " Joyfully, joyfully, onward we move,
>   Onward to meet the dear Saviour we love."

I watched dear Muallim Semaam closely from that
time, and prayed often with him. He grew gradually weaker, but had his full reason to the last.
On the 20th September he called for me, and I
soon saw that his life was drawing to its close. He
said, "Be glad, for there is great joy and great
glory! Oh, how delightful it is to go to heaven!
how wonderful it is there! be glad with me!" His
countenance was like an angel's, and beamed with
the heavenly peace which rested upon him. The
people were solemnly affected. I said to them,
"You see now how beautiful it is to behold the
departure of a faithful servant, who rests fully in
Jesus."

But what followed? Muallim Semaan's fanatical
brother Kaleel, who had no idea of the religion
which made his brother so happy, brought the

Greek priest Tanius to perform a prayer over him. When Muallim Semaan saw the Greek priest he said to me, "They have brought me this Greek priest against my will. I do not like such things; take him away. I do not wish to see the Greek priest here, because I am now a Protestant Christian! Let all the people know I am a true Christian! Jesus is my priest alone."

Georgius Aid asked Muallim Semaan, "Into whose hands will you commend your body? into Mr. Waldmeier's hands, or into those of the Greek priest Tanius?"

Muallim Semaan replied, "I commend my body to Mr. Waldmeier, but my soul I give to Jesus." He was asked the question twice, and twice he returned the same answer, which all the people present heard distinctly. The fanatical brother took his place near Muallim Semaan, who, when he saw him, looked very sharply upon him and said, "Kaleel, you belong to the Greek Church, but I belong to the true Protestant Church of Christ."

After this, Kaleel became excited, and troubled his dying brother greatly by saying, "You are not a Protestant, you are a Greek, and the priest shall bury you, not Mr. Waldmeier."

When Muallim Semaan heard this, his soul was fearfully grieved, and gathering up his remaining strength, he said, "I am not a Greek, but a Protestant Christian. I do not wish to be buried by the Greek priest."

His brother replied in anger, "I do not allow you to die as a Protestant; you must die as a Greek."

Poor Muallim Semaan could no longer endure this cruel treatment. A few tears fell from his eyes, and shortly after he breathed his last. Then Kaleel said to the priest, "Please to pray over my brother and anoint him." The Greek priest then commenced his performances, threw our Bible away, and began to scold us in a most dreadful manner.

After being assured that his spirit had really passed away, I read the will of Muallim Semaan, which referred also to the burial of his body, when Kaleel exclaimed in the wildest manner, "Let all the Protestants go out of the room. If they remain here we shall beat and kill them on the spot." In order to prevent any commotion we went out for a time. After about two hours John Effendy Abcarius, Secretary of the English Consul-General at Beirut; the Rev. John Rae, Superintendent of the Scotch Lebanon Schools; William Staiger, Director of the Scotch School at Beirut; Rev. William Torell from Sweden, M. Knobel from Switzerland, and all the native Protestants went with me to the house where Muallim Semaan had died. When all the people were gathered together we declared in a friendly way that he had died as a Protestant, before which he made his will and had expressed his desire distinctly and repeatedly that Theophilus Waldmeier should bury his body.

His brothers and some of his fanatical relations, together with the Greek and Maronite priests, replied, saying, "We cannot allow Theophilus Waldmeier to bury Muallim Semaan because he died as a Greek Christian, in consequence of which we shall bury him in our own churchyard."

In order to prevent any further confusion we bade them good-night and went away. We tried to carry out the will of the deceased, and wrote a letter to the Governor of Meten, who sent word that the body of Muallim Semaan should not be buried until a thorough examination had been made. One man from each side was, therefore, sent to the Governor to explain the full truth as witnessed by many witnesses. Before the Governor had decided about the matter the Greek and Maronite priests took the body by force and carried it openly through the village into the Greek church, and then into their adjoining churchyard where they buried it amid fearful tumult and disorder. It can easily be imagined what terror this act of force and injustice produced upon the other members of our little Church, not on account of the handful of dust, for it does not matter very much where that is buried, and I did not come to this dark fanatical place to gather the dead bodies of the people, but to be used in my heavenly Father's hand in saving immortal souls; but on account of the violation of that order by which the will of a dying man should be carried out faithfully. The Protestants became much afraid, for they thought and said, "If we die it may be thus with us and ours. The Greek and Maronite priests may come and pray over us by force, and bury our dead in their churchyards, which it is against our will even to think of. Whatever any liar may choose to say against us is accepted by the Government which is under priestly influence. Our opposers can easily engage all sorts of evil against us, however cruel and unjust it may be, while we, as true and simple Christians, cannot employ anything but the truth. We cannot swear as they do, for they will swear at any instant with all readiness, whether it is true or false, just or unjust, if they only see silver or gold before them."

During the summer of 1875 water was very scarce at Brummana. More than fifty women were one day impatiently waiting at the fountain until each one's turn came. Our servant was there, but instead of allowing her to stay they sent her back saying, "The priest told us that Protestants have no right to drink from the water of Brummana."

All the ecclesiastical craftiness was now systematically opposed against me, for the clergy said, "If we trouble the Protestant heretics as much as we can, they will leave the place, and go away." The Maronite clergy paid all the expenses my opposers incurred in raising and carrying on the law suits against me, over the land I bought from Daibes Safrawy. For a whole year I was bitterly tried by the maliciousness and injustice of litigation in this country. It seemed as if I was bombarded in all directions, by excommunication, by their preaching against Protestants in the Maronite churches, by their working against me in the Government, and by their trying to unite members of the Greek Orthodox Church, Greek Catholics, and even Druses, with the Maronites to expel me from the country. One morning all the Brummana roads were overstrewn with thousands of little and large papers upon which was written in Arabic, "Waldmeier is a devil; run away from him. He is not sent from God, but from hell. He is a devil; flee from him." My dear wife often said, " I thought we had suffered enough in Abyssinia, but it seems that we are made for trials." When my friends in Beirut heard all this, they said to me, "Did we not tell you before that the inhabitants of Brummana are the worst people in the world?" But I said, "I have not regretted coming here because I see daily more clearly, by the very wickedness of the people, and chiefly of the clergy, that it is the Lord's will I should be at Brummana."

> "The path of sorrow, and that path alone,
> Leads to the land where sorrow is unknown;
> No traveller ever reached that blest abode
> Who found not thorns and briers on his road."

CHAPTER XXVI.

WELCOME VISITORS.

EARLY in 1876 we had the great pleasure of welcoming our dear friends Eli Jones from America, and Alfred Lloyd Fox and Henry Newman, from England, who remained with us for three months and strengthened our hands and hearts. Alfred Lloyd Fox wrote about his journey to Brummana as follows : " We left Beirut December 1st, 1875, under the guidance of Theophilus Waldmeier, with each a good horse under us. As we slowly rode out of the town we saw the camels and mules, and the women with faces quite concealed as at Damascus with green and flowered handkerchiefs ; and the weavers of silk, each sitting on the floor of his room ; and the blacksmiths at their forges, with a woman between two bellows alternately pushing them outwards and pulling them inwards ; and the *kibaub* sellers with their long skewers of meat grilling over little charcoal fires. Then there were the handsome faces of the Syrian women who walk erect without veils ; and the crippled dwarf carried on the back of a stout fellow that he might keep pace with us and beg ; and the fat middle-aged beggar who had made himself an arbour to shade him from the hot sun. These, with the thousand picturesque sights of the East, all interested us. At last we got rid of the suburb, and our way lay through cultivated fields ; but the path being bounded by tall reeds we could see hardly anything of the agriculture. Then we took to the shore and rode along the edge of the waves where the sand was rather harder, until we turned inland up the dry bed of a torrent. Presently our clever little nags scrambled out of the river way and began to climb the rocky sides of Lebanon, up steep stony rocks, or over smooth surfaces of stone where even a Syrian horse could hardly keep his footing. You must fancy us led by Theophilus Wald-meier on a slight grey mare, and Eli Jones following on a brown cob. There is no possibility of going faster than a walk, up, up, up always. We stopped at Dar Bsaleem and were glad to relinquish our horses and stand on our feet. Here is a mixed school for boys and girls with an attendance of about forty. They rose to greet us and then sat down again cross-legged on the mats, with their backs to the wall, against which hung good English maps. This school is supported by Neuchatel in Switzerland, and is called after that town. The reading was fluent. The oldest in the school was fifteen, the youngest six. A register of attendance and progress is kept, and the former appeared creditably regular.

"This was our first glimpse at the work of the Brummana Mission. Another hour up the mountain brought us near our journey's end, and we could see a crowd of villagers and a long line of children standing on a terrace to greet us. The children waved branches of evergreen, and shouted 'Welcome, dear friends!' The suggestion of discretion that we should leave our terrified steeds and enter humbly on foot was promptly acted on. The villagers greeted us with the graceful courtesy of the East, which we clumsily returned by shaking hands. I also spoke to and shook the hand of everyone who could say a word of English. Then we slowly wound up amongst the houses accompanied by a somewhat excited but perfectly well-behaved crowd. Mrs. Waldmeier met us in the courtyard of their house which she and her husband begged us to consider our home. The house is situated at the edge of the mountain range on which the village stands, so that we look out into the deep valley on one side, and across to the higher range of rocks beyond. They say it would take one hour and more to reach the bottom of the ravine, which looks just below and quite near. We also, by a slight change of position, look up to the snow-clad summit of Jebel Sanneen, and by another change see over the Great Sea with the port of Beirut on its jutting headland. Truly the Lebanon is glorious. They tell frightful tales of the savage inhabitants of the district. Close by this house is a small ruin where the Emir formerly invited forty people whom he did not like and then blew them up by gunpowder, so that all horribly perished. Red stones are abundant in our path everywhere as we walk through the village ; each is a token of the devastation by fire of the houses of the Christians at the time of the Lebanon massacres, for fire turns this stone red."

On the 4th of December a meeting was held in my house, when Eli Jones, Alfred Lloyd Fox, Henry Newman, and some native brethren were present. Eli Jones read an epistle from the Foreign Mission Committee appointed by New England Yearly Meeting of Friends held in Newport, Rhode Island, expressing the belief that it was now time that we should become an organized Meeting of the Society of Friends. After serious deliberation and prayerful consideration, such a congregation was organized according to the Evangelical principles and the customs of Friends, with its special meetings for the transaction of Church affairs every month. Six members from the native Christians, with ourselves, at first constituted the little Church.

The Lord made our friends a great blessing to the whole work. While they were staying at Brummana we bought the beautiful hill of Rooisee for the purpose of building our Mission House there if our opposers succeeded in depriving us of the first piece of land.

On the 1st of January, 1876, we opened the Training Home for Boys in the house of Emir Ali, until we succeeded in building our own premises for this purpose. After having examined the branch schools, Eli Jones, Alfred Lloyd Fox, and Henry Newman left Syria for England on the 4th of March. It was very hard for us to say "farewell," because we had received from them great comfort, encouraging sympathy, and very present help in need ; and a dark cloud still troubled all of us in the unfortunate law-suit about the land, which was not yet settled at our friends' departure.

Late one evening, soon after their departure, somebody knocked at my door. I opened it, and, to my astonishment, my bitterest enemy, Daibes Safrawy, came in and said, "My conscience has troubled me all the time since I denied the payment of the land. Please forgive me."

I said, "That I will gladly ! But as you denied my payment before the Government, you must also confess before them that you told a lie."

He said, "I will do so."

Next day my other adversaries who had made unjust claims upon the land, came and confessed that they had done wrong and proposed peace. I said, "I am ready for an amicable arrangement of the long law-suit, but as the matter is at the law

court you must go with me to the tribunal, and
there we will arrange the matter." To this they
agreed.

On the 15th of March, 1876, the whole party,
including Daibes Safrawy and myself, went to
Ghazeer, the seat of the Government for Mount
Lebanon at that time, and there the whole law-suit
was brought to an amicable conclusion, which was
cause for great thankfulness. After we had returned to Brummana as friends, Daibes Safrawy and
our other opponents made a feast of reconciliation
on the piece of land about which they had made
the law-suit, and invited me and my fellow-workers.
They killed a sheep and roasted it, and we sat down
as brothers on the ground together, in the open air,
and feasted on the lamb of reconciliation. It was
at this time that I changed the name of the place
from *Berkat Ghanem* (the pool of the conqueror) to
Ain Salaam (the fountain of peace). About this
time also we had the pleasure of welcoming at
Brummana Mr. and Mrs. Richard Allen, of Dublin,
who became much interested in Mount Lebanon,
and assisted the Mission a great deal by their
prayers as well as by their substances. It was
therefore a cause of great sorrow when the Mission
last year (1885) lost in dear Richard Allen one of
its faithful supporters by death.

During the spring and summer I was busy in
preparing for the building, and on the 4th of
August, 1876, we were enabled to lay the founda-
tion stone of Friends' Training Home for Boys at
Ain Salaam. Many people from different denomi-
nations were present, and friends and enemies min-
gled with each other on the occasion. Emir Ali,
John Effendy Abcarius, Joseph Abdelnour, William
Staiger, Sister Louisa Kaiser, and other friends from
Beirut were with us. The three former took an

active part on the occasion, and the speeches they delivered were most interesting. A small tin box was prepared, into which I put the holy Bible, a description of the history of the Mission, with the names of the Committees in Old and New England, and some current coins of the present time. The box was then hermetically closed and placed under the north-western corner-stone.

BEIRUT MERCHANT.

CHAPTER XXVII.

WITH the laying of the foundation stone of Friends' Mission House and Training Home at Ain Salaam, the period of founding the Mission came to its close. From that time the work entered upon a state of steady progress through the opposition and trials which always accompanied it.

While I was energetically proceeding with the building during the summer and autumn of 1876, I saw one day some priests standing near it, and soon heard their curses against the harmless building, and the workmen who were engaged on it. Next day a number of workmen failed to come, and when I asked about the cause, I found that some of them had run away for fear of excommunication. The Training Home for Boys on Emir Ali's premises went on very satisfactorily, and we had thirteen boys in the Home and sixty day-scholars besides.

In the spring of this year I opened a girls' school at Mansourieh, and in the autumn a school for boys at the same place. Scander Kattar, the son of the mayor at Mansourieh, was studying theology at the schools of the Greek Orthodox bishop at Beirut. He had nearly completed his studies, and was going to become a priest, for which purpose he was already clothed in dark priestly robes, with a long ecclesiastical cap on his head; and to their mind nothing was wanting but his consecration. By means of the girls' school at Mansourieh, he came in contact with our religious principles. I invited him to Ain Salaam, and in a long conversation with him told him plainly that he was on the wrong way. His heart was touched by the Spirit of God, and after earnest consideration he laid down his priestly clothes and dressed himself like other men. He then wrote to the bishop to say that he had given up the idea of becoming a priest, which enraged the bishop fearfully. Scander Kattar afterwards became the schoolmaster of the boys' school at Mansourieh, and was subsequently engaged as a Scripture reader, chiefly for Mansourieh and the plain.

Near the Training Home was an old silk factory, which was purchased about this time, and converted into a School of Industry, where the boys could learn carpentry and other useful handicrafts.

At the close of 1876, the Christian population of Syria was in great uneasiness on account of the Russo-Turkish war, especially in the interior of the country, and at Jerusalem, Damascus, and Aleppo, where the Mohammedans threatened the Christians with a massacre.

During 1877 all the branches of the Mission were carried on with energy and enjoyed the Divine blessing. All the religious meetings were regularly held and well attended. The branch schools conveyed Evangelical light and instruction into the dark villages of Mount Lebanon. The Maronite and Greek priests saw the progress of the Mission, and the very Mission House which they cursed brought under a nice tiled roof, with no accident or misfortune, in spite of their curses and excommunications. I often had meetings in the open air at the side of the new building, where many fanatical priests and monks went by, as the road passed near our new building. A Maronite priest once said to the workmen, " It is a punishment from God that the English are able to build here. It is a sign of the end of the world. Waldmeier, who is the Antichrist, takes away our most holy religion, and the English engineers down at the Dog river (Lycus) take away our water." The head of the convent said, " Since the English Mission was established at Brummana, we have lost a great deal of our income, for people do not like to pay us any more."

When the building was nearly completed I began to look out for someone to take charge of the Training Home. I went to Beirut and searched diligently and prayerfully. I saw a number of young men, but my heart felt that the Lord had not chosen them for His work at Ain Salaam. When engaged in the British Syrian Schools, I met a young man, Beshara Manasseh, whom I recommended to Rev. Mr. Frankel of the Jewish Mission at Damascus, as a teacher for his school. After taking charge of the Jewish mission school for some time to Mr. Frankel's satisfaction, Beshara Manasseh returned to the Syrian Protestant College at Beirut to study medicine, and took his diploma as M.D. in the summer of 1877. I met him at Joseph Abdelnour's house and asked him whether he would like to take charge of our new Training Home for Boys at Ain Salaam, until we should be in condition to open a regular medical mission. He said that he would think about the matter and let me know or come himself to Ain Salaam.

During the summer we had a nice visit from George Hessenauer, who was engaged in temporary Christian work in Bulgaria after the desolating

Russo-Turkish war, in connection with Mr. Mackenzie, the Scotch philanthropist. George Hessenauer remained for some weeks with us at Brummana, and I then encouraged him to pursue the study of medicine if possible in order to become a medical missionary ; and he soon after went to England for this purpose.

During the summer and autumn of 1877 I was still much occupied with the new building, as I had no architect, and was obliged to carry out my plans by the help of stupid workmen and simple masons. In spite, however, of all disadvantages the new premises were completed in September, and on the 12th of November I and my family left the old house of Emir Ameen to lodge in the upper story of the new Training Home. At the beginning of December Dr. Beshara Manasseh, who had accepted the post of teacher in the new Training Home, came up to Ain Salaam to help to prepare the new Institution, and on the 1st of January, 1878, the new Home was opened and dedicated to the Lord's work.

The length of the house is twenty-seven, and its breadth is fifteen English yards, externally. The walls are two feet six inches thick. The building contains nineteen spacious rooms, besides one large meeting room, and a stable. Towards the west front is the basement floor, before which a large plateau is levelled for a play ground for the children. Then come the first floor and the upper story. Towards the east we have only the first floor and the upper story, because the building is on a declivity from east to west. The situation is a most healthy one, and subsequent experience has proved that in all sanitary matters connected with the building everything has been well calculated and arranged. The view which it commands is one of

THE BOYS' TRAINING HOME, AIN SALAAM, BRUMMANA.

the finest on Mount Lebanon. It is 2,600 feet above the Mediterranean Sea, and three hours distant from it. On the slope of the mountain, between the sea-shore and Ain Salaam, are the different villages in which our branch schools for boys and girls are doing a great work. Down in the plain is the city of Beirut, with its 100,000 inhabitants, to which we have daily to send down our donkey to bring us the needful things for our Mission. From Ain Salaam we see the steamers coming in and going out from the harbour of Beirut. The adjoining wood-cut will give an idea of Friends' Mission House and Training Homes.

At the opening of the new Training Home we took ten new pupils, in addition to ten who had already been under training for the previous two years, and Dr. Beshara had much to do because he also opened a Dispensary in one of the rooms of the new building. Many poor patients from near and far came to us for help, because our Dispensary was the only one on Mount Lebanon. The open place in front of the Training Home was crowded daily by sick people, and Dr. Beshara had to work too hard to take charge both of the Home and Dispensary. I saw that we must make better arrangements, and soon found another teacher in the person of Lotfallah Rizkallah. From this time Dr. Beshara gave only one lesson daily, for the Medical work increased so much that he could no more take part in the teaching of the Home. As it was undesirable to have the patients hanging round the Boys' Training Home, we were forced to make special accommodation for the Medical work. The upper story of the old silk factory, or School of Industry, was therefore raised, and before the year closed four nice rooms could be made use of there for the purpose of the Medical Mission, while

Lotfallah Rizkallah and Ibrahim Tasso took charge of the Training Home. All seemed to work well together, though we had always many trials and discouragements, for it could not be otherwise in such a Mission station. Our little Church was blessed of the Lord, and several young men and women asked for admission to membership in it, but after prayerful consideration we found it better to tell them to wait still longer until their conviction had become surer and stronger, and their conduct more improved. The people in this country are often able to comprehend the truth by their minds, but their hearts remain unchanged, and what we prayerfully desire is true conversion.

This year we lost Abu Joseph, a member of our Church, by death. He was about sixty years of age when he was summoned from his earthly pilgrimage. He belonged formerly to the Greek Church, but when I came to Brummana and preached the Gospel, his heart was opened to the influence of the Holy Spirit, and he received the Gospel with pleasure, even under many trials, while his life bore witness from that time that he was really converted. He was a bright, good, and simple follower of Jesus Christ, and the Gospel showed its renewing and enlightening powers upon his heart and mind. A short time before his death, his son, who was an enemy to the Gospel, said to his dying father, " I shall not let you die as a Protestant, and you shall not be buried in the Protestant burial ground. I shall not only bring the priest but the Greek bishop to make you recant and return to the Greek Church."

Poor Abu Joseph said : " I do not know any priest or bishop. I know only Jesus. In Him I will die ; and my body shall be buried in the Friends' burial ground at Ain Salaam."

Abu Joseph wrote a paper concerning his burial, but his son Georgius snatched it from the trembling hands of his dying father, and said, " I shall do with you as I like.   Let the Protestants go out from my house, or else I shall fire upon them."   Abu Joseph wept.   All this passed in the night.   When I saw that it was not Georgius alone who opposed us, but that there were with him a large number of opposing Greeks and Maronites, who do not like each other but unite to oppose our Mission, I wrote letters to the local Governor, Emir Joseph, and to the Governor-General of Mount Lebanon, Rustem Pasha, asking them to help me against the unjustifiable interference of Abu Joseph's son with our carrying out his father's wishes.   I sent the letters off in the middle of the night.   Next day before noon came the first delegates from the local Governor, Emir Joseph.   A crowd of people gathered at Abu Joseph's house while the delegates went in and inquired as to his intention and religion.   The crowd expected that Abu Joseph would return to the Greek Church, but he said to the delegates, " I am a Protestant Christian.   I do not recognise any priest.   I look only to Jesus who is the Saviour of my soul.   I want to die in the arms of Jesus like a true Evangelical Christian ; and I want to be buried in the Friends' burial ground at Ain Salaam."

Many questions were put to him by the delegates. They asked him : " How old are you ?   What was your profession ?   What is your religion ?   When did you enter the Protestant Church at Ain Salaam ? Did you become a Protestant from your own free will, or did anyone force you ?   What is your will in the event of your death ?   Where do you want to be buried ?"

Abu Joseph answered : " I am sixty years of age.   My trade was a dyer.   My religion is Evangelical. I have been a member of the Protestant Church of Brummana for two years. I became a Protestant from my own conviction and free will, and no one forced me ; and I want to die as a Protestant Christian, and be buried as such in the Friends' burial ground at Ain Salaam."

All this was written down by the delegates and sealed by the local authorities. When the crowd knew that their expectations were disappointed they began to break out in fearful alarm, especially those who belonged to Georgius' party, but the authorities rebuked them and made them silent.

In the afternoon some more delegates arrived from the Governor-General of Mount Lebanon, and Emir Haider came himself and rebuked those who caused opposition to the will of Abu Joseph. A second paper was written, signed and sealed by the Sheikh of Brummana and the Emir himself, and sent to the central Government. The delegates of the Governor-General said to the people that nobody was to interfere with other people's religious convictions, because there is liberty of religion and of conscience ; and he who causes opposition, like Georgius, to the will of a dying man, shall be punished by imprisonment. This caused great silence at once, and all were astonished, saying, "We never thought that the Protestants had so much power, or that Abu Joseph would remain so faithful to his new religion." Then Abu Joseph rejoiced, and said, " Now I am at rest, for which I am glad. Thanks to God, the matter has been settled very well indeed. Let me depart in peace."

On the 18th of November he entered into his heavenly rest. His end was glorious indeed. Before he closed his pilgrimage he said : " I feel myself as a stranger who has been a long time in a far-off country and is going home to his native land.

I am so glad that my soul will now be delivered from this bodily prison. It is wonderful how my heavenly Father deals with me. He never deals with His children according to their transgressions but according to His great mercies in Christ Jesus. Oh, how sweet it is to feel His presence at the hour of death. Some people are afraid to die, but I rejoice in Him who conquered death for me. I do not need a priest or any other mediators or ceremonies, because Christ has completed His work in me and for me."

He then asked me to pray; after which he asked Hanni Ferah to read from the nice tract, "Come to Jesus." He then wished us to sing a hymn; and after this he fell asleep in Jesus. While he was sleeping Georgius came and asked his blessing and pardon, but Abu Joseph could no more hear or answer. I made arrangements for his funeral, which we were enabled to perform in all devotion, silence, and peace. More than seven hundred persons attended the funeral, and we had a very good opportunity to witness for the truth and preach the glorious Gospel of Jesus both in the house of Abu Joseph and at the Friends' burial ground at Ain Salaam.

After the death of dear Abu Joseph, my own son, Theophilus, fell ill with malarial fever, which brought him nearly to the shore of death, but it pleased our Father in heaven to give him back to us anew. Soon after his recovery, our youngest child, Lily, fourteen months of age, was taken ill, and after ten days suffering, she died on the 19th of December, which caused us deep sorrow, and it was, indeed, hard for us to say, "Thy will, O God, Thy will be done." Despite many a tear and sigh, however, we could but thank our Divine Master, at the close of 1878, for all His blessings, and, not least, for the growing interest in our Mission work, which had led to the establishment of another station at Ramallah, in Palestine. When the Lord blesses, He blesses abundantly, and to Him alone is due all the glory for ever and ever.

While these Mission stations in Bible lands were welcomed by the people, they were looked upon with contempt by the priests of the Oriental Churches. Some of the ecclesiastics said to me one day, " Though we do not like your way of preaching the Gospel, we respect your great zeal for teaching the world, but we cannot understand why you endeavour to preach the Gospel among our Christian people. Go and teach the heathen and the Druses, and leave our people alone. They used to be at perfect ease, but since you came we have found their minds disturbed." I told them, " Christ said He was sent to the lost sheep of the house of Israel, otherwise He would have gone straightway to the heathen ; and in like manner we have to look for lost sheep among nominal Oriental Christians. If I were not perfectly sure of my work here being appointed by the Lord, I should prefer to leave this place and omit the difficulties, opposition, and trials which I have had and still have to endure ; but as I am sure that my mission to these mountain people is not my own, but the Lord's, I must stand faithfully in my place until the end." So the priests said nothing more then, but were always working against me secretly.

Another important point which gladdened my heart was that our Divine Master showed me also very clearly, step by step, the spirituality of the Gospel ministry. As the people of Israel failed through looking too much upon outward ordinances, so the Oriental Churches lost their spiritual life by outward show, religious ceremonies, and useless forms. The more I learned to know the corruption of the Eastern Churches, the more I was glad and thankful in my heart that our heavenly Father prepared me in the school of the Holy Spirit for this needy Mission field, which does not need the introduction of other ecclesiastical forms, however few and improved they may be, but the simple preaching of Gospel truth, and I could say with the Apostle Paul (1 Cor. i. 17), " Christ sent me not to baptize but to preach the Gospel." I will not judge others, but as for me, coming out from the worst of the ritualistic Churches, I do not like religious ceremonies, and hold that God must be worshipped in Spirit and in truth (John iv. 23).

CHAPTER XXVIII.

ON the 12th of April, 1879, we had the joy of welcoming Henry Newman and George Satterthwaite from England, who had been visiting the Mission station at Ramallah as a deputation from the English Committee. They remained only twelve days with us, but during that time they were present at all the examinations of the branch schools in the different villages, besides that at the Boys' Training Home, and they saw all that was being done at the dispensary, and attended all our religious meetings, in which George Satterthwaite's ministry was greatly blessed by the Lord. Thus, though their stay was so short, it was a precious time, which never will be forgotten. They were much pleased with the progress of the Mission, both with regard to its outward extension and spiritual growth. They became acquainted also with all the great difficulties and opposition to which a Mission like this is exposed in the midst of a superstitious population and fanatical priesthood. The Committee thought that I should have a change of air and accompany the deputation to England, to which I agreed with pleasure. We left on the 24th of April, and arrived in London a few days before Friends' Yearly Meeting. It was an indescribable joy to go to my English home and meet Hannah Stafford Allen, the mother

of the Mount Lebanon Mission, once more. The
Yearly Meeting also was a time of refreshing and
blessings for my thirsty soul. I afterwards visited
Reading, Plymouth, Brighton, Bristol, Birmingham,
Manchester, Sheffield, Leeds, York, Bradford, Ken-
dal, Liverpool, Sunderland, Darlington, and many
other places, and was thankful to see how the
interest in the Friends' Mission in Syria and
Palestine had spread and increased. I then returned to London, and took leave of dear Hannah
Stafford Allen. " Farewell dear Theophilus," she
said, " thou wilt see my face no more in this world,
but in the better land we shall meet again." Then
we committed each other in fervent prayer to the
loving care of our heavenly Father, and with deep
and holy emotion I left the dear mother, but
through the small opening of the door I looked
back once more upon her bright angelic countenance. This was my last glance upon one who
was a true mother in Israel, for the following year
she passed through death unto eternal life, and her
labours follow her.

'Twas well that she did live.
Thank God ! Praise God alway
That He such good did give !
He gives ; He takes away ;
And bids us yield the treasure that He keeps
In perfect peace, for she in Jesus sleeps.

I should have liked to have paid a visit to our
dear Friends in America, but circumstances pressed
me to go back to Mount Lebanon. On my way I
went to Germany and Switzerland, where I had
meetings at Stuttgart, Bâle, Lörrach, St. Chrischona,
Berne, and Lausanne; and my dear friends in
Switzerland promised me anew to support four
schools in our Mission field. At the end of August
I arrived at Ain Salaam.

During the autumn I purchased, for a reasonable price, a good house in the middle of Brummana, to be used for the day schools for boys and girls and the residence of the teachers; and also for the mothers' meetings, and as a place of worship. On the 21st of December, 1879, we had our first meeting there, when the whole house was dedicated to the Lord's service. More than 200 people of different denominations were present in the large room, and all listened with great attention to the various speakers who explained the texts, that God does not dwell only in temples made by men's hands, but with him also who is of a contrite and humble spirit (Acts vii. 48; Is. lvii. 15).

This year we had a Christmas tree at Ain Salaam, as our dear English friends had sent enough woollen clothing and other presents to supply all the poor children under our instruction, about 300 in number. All these, with their parents, were present, and also the Governor with his whole court. The children repeated the texts which they had learned, prayers were offered, and addresses delivered. For the time all the differences between Greeks, Maronites, Druses, and Protestants were forgotten, and lost in the love of God through Christ Jesus. The Governor made a speech, in which he said, "I am exceedingly pleased to see all the good which is done for our country by this Mission. May God richly bless this house and its inhabitants. I feel it my duty not only to protect this most interesting Mission, but also to help by a subscription."

In order to complete the agencies which compose a well-furnished Mission-station, I felt that a Girls' Training Home was greatly needed. I therefore addressed the following appeal to our American friends :—

"No nation can be civilized, no country can be elevated, unless good and educated women take a share in it. I am sure you love the Bible lands, and you have already done much for their welfare; but I want to direct your attention to that which is still lacking in this Mission field. We have a Training Home for Boys, a Medical Mission, an Industrial School, nine Branch Day Schools, and four Sabbath Schools. Much has been accomplished by our Divine Master's blessing, but there is one thing still left out, which has long rested on my heart, and I cannot but bring it before you, so that my conscience may be at rest. We need a Training Home for Girls for this part of Mount Lebanon. In day schools only we cannot have sufficient control over the girls to enable us to mould and form their young hearts and minds according to our desire. It is really very sad to see them go every evening to their dark miserable dwellings, where they get influenced by bad example, and often the impressions of school are quite lost at home. Besides this there is another evil, which is, that girls of nine or ten years of age get married before they are able to learn or become useful. If these children were taken away from their relations, and trained in a Boarding School, where we could keep them till fifteen or eighteen years old, they might become, by Christ's blessing and our efforts, well educated, good, and pious women. We must sympathise with the poor women of Mount Lebanon, for they are despised, ill-treated, and regarded as having only so much understanding as a hen. We need a Training Home in which we can have about twenty girls to train in such a way that the people on Mount Lebanon may have good mothers, who will bring up their children in the fear of God, and take an active part in the elevation of

the social and religious life of their people. When
there shall be good mothers here then we can say
that our victory over degradation and superstition
is won, and the day-break of better times will be
at hand. Some young girls were taken up by one
of the very first American missionaries, Dr. Eli
Smith, and trained in his house. These have all,
without exception, become good mothers, and are
good examples to those around them. This shows
the power of training. It will be a great blessing
if our American friends will take up this matter
and look upon it as their own.

"The land is already in our possession, and we
only need the building, which will cost, when completed, £600, and the current expenses of twenty
girls, which will cost £350 a-year. Now this is a
large sum I know, but remember, dear friends, that
one good woman and pious mother is a thousand
times more precious in this and the other world
than this sum of money, and we trust by our
heavenly Father's help not only one pious woman,
but many will come forth out of a Training Home
like this. I ask you earnestly to look upon this
matter with prayerful consideration, and please
let me know your conclusion.

"THEOPHILUS WALDMEIER.

"April 14, 1880."

Not long after this appeal arrived in America I
received the following information from Eli Jones:
"At the Yearly Meeting of Friends in New England thy appeal for a Girls' Training Home was
read, and elicited a ready and remarkable response.
Soon after the close of the meeting we found that
the subscription had reached eleven hundred dollars. The women Friends of New York Yearly
Meeting also raised two hundred dollars, thus making thirteen hundred dollars in the hands of the

WOMEN GRINDING CORN ON MOUNT LEBANON.

Treasurer, George Howland, for the purpose of erecting a Home for girls on Mount Lebanon."

The Western Yearly Meeting of Friends in America in their Epistle to the Brummana Monthly Meeting, expressed themselves in the following words : " The appeal forwarded to this meeting by Eli Jones has been read by men and women Friends. We have been touched with a deep feeling of sympathy in the desire to have a Girls' Training Home on Mount Lebanon. Woman's elevation to her proper place in society is an object that should never be overlooked in any system of Mission work, or of Christian civilization. We cordially appreciate your earnest appeal in her behalf, and desire to extend to you our warm and earnest encouragement, and our united contributions.—Signed by AMOS DOAN, Clerk.

" September 23, 1880."

Our Father in heaven blessed this part of the work so much, and funds were so rapidly collected, that Eli Jones could authorize me in the name of the Committee to begin the building of the Girls' Training Home on the 4th of February, 1881. In this we see again how the Lord blesses all that is undertaken in His name for the welfare of His poor.

During the spring of 1880, Dr. Beshara Manasseh went to England to visit hospitals and increase his theoretical and practical knowledge of medicine and surgery. He also attended the Yearly Meeting of Friends in London, and tried to increase the interest in the Mission. Meanwhile, we had had the privilege of a short visit from Anna Maria Fox of Falmouth, and Caroline Tangye of Birmingham. In November, 1880, we had the great pleasure of welcoming Maria Feltham of Hitchin, and Ellen Clayton of Chelmsford, who came to visit us in the love of the Gospel. They were with us for three months, and helped in the Mission with their hearts and hands.

After Dr. Beshara Manasseh came back from England, the old silk factory which had been used for the School of Industry was converted into a Hospital, and on New Year's day, 1881, it was opened, and dedicated to the Lord's sick and suffering people. The upper story of this building was occupied by the dispensary and out-patients, while the ground-floor was converted into a hospital with fifteen beds. At the end of February the foundation-stone of the Girls' Training Home was laid, in the presence of a large number of people.

During the summer of 1881 we had an extra-ordinarily great and depressing heat, and the labour of superintending the building of the Girls' Training Home, in addition to the ordinary work of the Mission, was often too much for me. The building, however, was safely roofed before the first rain set in, which in this country is at the end of October. During the year 1882 the Girls' Training Home was completed and furnished, and on the 27th of October it was opened with fifteen promising girls. It was a day to be remembered always. Dear Eli Jones, in spite of his old age, came from America to be present, and to assist us in the various branches of the Mission. Three hundred persons, among whom were Princes and Princesses and the members of the Tribunal, were waiting in the large arched room on the ground-floor by ten o'clock, when the opening ceremony began. Eli Jones read Proverbs xxxi., and spoke for one hour and fifteen minutes on the subject of female education, his address being translated into Arabic. Dr. Beshara and I also spoke, and the Judge of the Tribunal expressed his hearty thankfulness to the Society of

Friends in England and America for their help, and much earnest prayer was offered. The fifteen girls sat in a semi-circle on chairs before Eli Jones, and stood up and sang a hymn at conclusion of the meeting. After a little refreshment the people dispersed, rejoicing. Miriam Abu Nasser, who was educated at Miss Lucy Hicks's school at Shemlan, in connection with the Society for Promoting Female Education in the East, was appointed teacher of the Girls' Home, under the superintendence of Maria Feltham, who came back from England, leaving her comfortable home and friends, in order to help us in the mission work.

In the spring of 1883, Eli Jones paid a visit to Ramallah, Friends' Mission station in Palestine, three hours north of Jerusalem, and tried to encourage and improve the work there. Meanwhile, I finished the preparation of the transference of the whole Mission estate into the names of three English and three American trustees.

In April it was found needful for Friends' Medical Mission that Dr. Beshara Manasseh should go to Constantinople to pass his official medical examination, in order to obtain his doctor's diploma from the Imperial Government at Constantinople. Having passed his examination successfully and got his diploma he came back at the end of July, and resumed his medical duties at Ain Salaam. We also had the pleasure of welcoming Ellen Clayton, who lived at first with Maria Feltham at the Girls' Training Home until the alterations of the building were completed, when she took her position as lady superintendent in the Friends' Hospital at Ain Salaam, where her faithful service is being blessed by the Lord.

Dr. George Hessenauer and his young wife also paid us a visit on their way to Ramallah. After

George Hessenauer had obtained his needful diploma in medicine and surgery in London, he desired to work as a medical missionary in connection with the Society of Friends, of which he is a member. Their Syrian Mission Committee received him with gladness, and sent him out as medical missionary to the Mission station at Ramallah. It is very interesting to see how our heavenly Father leads His children and qualifies them for His service.

Towards the end of 1883 we had the gladness of welcoming Joseph Bevan Braithwaite, who comforted and encouraged us all by his knowledge, humility, and brotherly love. I regard his presence and prayerful interest at the solemnization of the marriage of Dr. Beshara Manasseh with my daughter, Rosa Waldmeier, which took place on the 23rd of November, 1883, as an especial blessing and privilege for us. J. B. Braithwaite was accompanied by Rev. R. Weakly, and Rev. C. E. B. Reed of the British and Foreign Bible Society, and by Charles E. Gillett and William C. Braithwaite. The brief visit of Rev. Charles E. B. Reed, Secretary of the British and Foreign Bible Society, son of the late Sir Charles Reed, M.P., has left a lasting memory of sunshine in the hearts of the mission circle on Mount Lebanon. He subsequently made a tour through Palestine in company with J. B. Braithwaite and party, and returned to England early in 1884. In the spring of that year an affection of the throat caused him almost entirely to lose his voice, and he was ordered by his physician to the bracing air of Switzerland, where he lost his life by an accident. In the spring of 1884 we enjoyed a long expected visit from the Treasurer of the Mission, William C. Allen.

In the autumn Sheikh Akel, who had been a Scripture-reader for many years in our Mission,

MISSION HOUSE, RAMALLAH.

was taken seriously ill, and lost his mental powers. At that very time his fanatical brother Georgius, in connection with some other superstitious people, called the Greek priest Ibrahim, who forced the Elements of the Communion, with which he had come prepared, into Sheikh Akel's mouth, and declared him to have returned to the Greek Church. We sent to the Pasha for justice in this affair. He delegated Emir Haider to investigate the case, but as Sheikh Akel was not in his senses, the investigation was unsatisfactory, and the fanatical priests and fiercely excited mob turned the matter to their side. After greatly disturbing the poor man's mind during his last days, they buried Sheikh Akel in the Greek graveyard, as they did with Muallim Semaan years before. Sheikh Akel was a good advocate of Christ's cause. He grew in grace, and his words at our meetings were blessed to many, while his Christian conduct was an example to all.

During the year 1885 the Mission lost one of their Secretaries, Alfred Lloyd Fox of Falmouth. He was indeed a man of God in whose heart self had no longer place. His delight was to work for Jesus, and to do good to his fellow-men at home and abroad. His presence was like that of an angel, and his correspondence was an uninterrupted stream of blessing and love.

> Living epistle of God's love, was he ;
> On all mankind his clear blue eyes, like heaven,
> Beamed charity.
> In him God's love reflected, shone most clearly,
> Love, sunny, human, never waxing dim ;
> God must be love, who to His blessed likeness
> So fashioned him.

It only remains to say a few words with regard to the present condition and future prospects of our work on Mount Lebanon.

The various agencies of Friends' Mission on Mount Lebanon all show steady progress. The accompanying sketch shows the different Mission buildings. On the left, stretching westward, are the blue waters of the Mediterranean. In the background are some of the higher ranges of Mount Lebanon. High up on the right stands the Mission House, comprising the Boys' Training Home. Below it, in the centre of the picture, is the wind-motor from America, which forces up the water from Ain Salaam to the reservoirs which supply the Mission Houses. Further to the left, on the spur of the hill which descends so rapidly towards the sea, is the Girls' Training Home. In the foreground is the Hospital and Dispensary.

In the village day schools, as well as in the Training Homes and in the Medical Mission, we now have Druses, Greek Catholics, Maronites, and members of the Greek Orthodox Church under our influence, and we preach Jesus Christ freely to every one of them. Many, both old and young, rich and poor, have learned to know the truth, and have received salvation as it is in Jesus Christ alone. We cannot put down here a statistical account of all the converts of our Mission, but that account is correctly kept in our heavenly Father's hand. We have to sow the seed in faith and patience, and often with sorrow. The Lord gives the increase, and He will finally gather His sheaves. We can truly and thankfully say with all those who know Mount Lebanon, and who have seen Friends' Mission station at Ain Salaam, that the Lord has done in a short time great and wonderful things. More than 700 children have learned to read and write in our branch schools, and, what is more than that, they have learned to know the Holy Scriptures, which are able to make them wise

Hospital and Dispensary.   Training Home for Girls.   Training Home for Boys.

AIN SALAAM, BRUMMANA, LOOKING NORTHWARD.

unto salvation. In our Training Homes we are training boys and girls by a thorough Christian and practical education, to be good Christians, faithful citizens, and leaders of others. Some of the boys who have gone forth from our Training Home are already occupying most useful positions.

More than 500 poor sufferers have been healed from their bodily diseases in the Friends' Hospital, and we trust that many were cured of their superstitions also. More than 30,000 out-door patients have been treated in the Dispensary, to whom the Gospel has been preached. Two Scripture-readers and two Bible-women are engaged to carry the good message of the Gospel into the dark houses of Mount Lebanon. Mothers' meetings are held to lift the poor degraded women to a higher standard in Jesus Christ, and through the preaching of the Gospel we try to build up a spiritual temple of God in opposition to the lifeless Eastern Churches. Surely the Lord is to be praised for all His goodness, and for His wonderful work among the children of men. Though we have to struggle with many unfavourable circumstances and oppositions we will yet rejoice in the Lord who giveth us the victory. We cannot, of course, expect that all the people of this country will come out at once from their respective churches and declare themselves Protestants. But if we compare the condition of the country fifty years ago, when the American Presbyterian Mission began their work in Syria, in the midst of horrible darkness and superstition, and unlimited fanaticism, with its state now, we find a conspicious and wonderful change for good among the Syrian people, which is due mainly to the Protestant Missions. To guage results only by the handful of Protestants who have come out from the Oriental Churches would be a mistake. We must look rather to the general regenerating and elevating influence of Protestant Mission work among the Syrian nation. It has given them good examples and strong impulses for higher life, and they are imitating the good work of the missionaries, by opening high and common schools, by organizing benevolent societies for the poor and needy, by opening hospitals and dispensaries for the sick, and by taking more care in general for the welfare of the people. Many of these Oriental Christians express themselves very freely on religious matters. I have heard them say, "We know very well that there is no salvation but through faith in Jesus Christ. The Virgin Mary and all the saints and priests cannot save us. If we die without Jesus all the many outward ceremonies in our churches are a mere farce." I know a good number of people of sound Evangelical principles, whose names are as yet in the list of their Oriental Churches, while many more have already left this world whose faith was completely resting on Jesus Christ and His atoning blood, and on Him alone. The power of priestcraft is no more that which it was before, fanaticism is greatly weakened, and superstition and ignorance are giving way to the light of the Gospel, and to spiritual liberty. A member of the Greek Church at Brummana thus expressed his opinion in their church before the people, on the text: "Behold the veil of the temple was rent in twain from the top to the bottom; and the earth did quake and the rocks were rent" (Matt. xxvii. 51). "Why should our churches be separated into two places, one for the people, and the other, the sacred and secret place, for the priests, while we see that the veil of the temple was rent from the top to the bottom, so that everyone could look into the most holy place which was no more a secret! Through

Christ the way is ever open to the throne of God for penitent sinners. Another mistake of our church is that the walls thereof are full of pictures, which is forbidden by God."

Such voices in the Greek Orthodox Churches are not a little thing. We see by them how the lever of Gospel truth is working among people who are under the blessed influence of Protestant Missions in this country. I am sure that the time of a great revival in this interesting Bible land is not far off, when our heavenly Father will gather in a great harvest for His glory; and until that time comes, we must run the race which is set before us with power and patience, and not get weary in well-doing.

In the spring of 1886 I visited Switzerland and England in order to increase the interest in the Mission on Mount Lebanon. I attended many meetings in different towns, and greatly enjoyed the Christian fellowship of God's people in England. At the Yearly Meeting in London, I missed a number of dearly beloved friends who have entered their eternal home. Faithful supporters of the Mission are being called one after another to rest from their labours, and we ourselves will have soon to lay down our pilgrim's staff, and go to the better land. Others will go forth and work in the vineyard, and may they with us remember the words, "Be thou faithful unto death, and I will give thee a crown of life" (Rev. ii. 10).

INDEX.

THE END.